PENGUIN BOOKS

ADMIRING SILENCE

Abdulrazak Gurnah was born in 1948 in Zanzibar, Tanzania. He is the author of the highly acclaimed novels *Memory of Departure*, *Pilgrims Way*, *Dottie* and *Paradise*, which was shortlisted for the 1994 Booker Prize and is also published by Penguin. He teaches literature at the University of Kent.

ADMIRING SILENCE

Abdulrazak Gurnah

PENGUIN BOOKS

PENGUIN BOOKS

Published by the Penguin Group
Penguin Books Ltd, 27 Wrights Lane, London W8 5TZ, England
Penguin Books USA Inc., 375 Hudson Street, New York, New York 10014, USA
Penguin Books Australia Ltd, Ringwood, Victoria, Australia
Penguin Books Canada Ltd, 10 Alcorn Avenue, Toronto, Ontario, Canada M4V 3B2
Penguin Books (NZ) Ltd, 182–190 Wairau Road, Auckland 10, New Zealand

Penguin Books Ltd, Registered Offices: Harmondsworth, Middlesex, England

First published by Hamish Hamilton 1996
Published in Penguin Books 1997
1 3 5 7 9 10 8 6 4 2

Copyright © Abdulrazak Gurnah, 1996
All rights reserved

The moral right of the author has been asserted

Printed in England by Clays Ltd, St Ives plc

Except in the United States of America, this book is sold subject
to the condition that it shall not, by way of trade or otherwise, be lent,
re-sold, hired out, or otherwise circulated without the publisher's
prior consent in any form of binding or cover other than that in
which it is published and without a similar condition including this
condition being imposed on the subsequent purchaser

For Sarah and Leila

PART ONE

'he is an admirer of silence in the island; broods over it like a great ear; has spies who report daily; and had rather his subjects sang than talked.'

R. L. Stevenson, 'The King of Apemama', *In the South Seas* (1890)

I have found myself leaning heavily on this pain. At first I tried to silence it, thinking it would go and leave me to my agitated content. That it would linger for a season, a firm reminder of the disquiet that lurks and coils below the surface of the stubbornly self-gratifying vision of our lives. Far from going, it became more clear, more precisely located, concrete, an object that occupied space within me, cockroachy, dark and intimate, emitting thick, stinking fumes that reeked of loneliness and terror. When I woke up in the morning, I groped for it, then sighed with plunging recognition as I felt it stirring inside me, alive and well. Emma said it was indigestion or something similar, but I could see from the surprised anxiety in her eyes that she did not believe that. For a few weeks she persuaded me to try a variety of powders and tablets, and she began to read about special diets, and acidity and roughage and vitamins. Emma was like that with problems. She gave them her careful attention, at least for a while. We never got to try the special diets, some of which sounded fine, because every morning I could feel the beast in there getting stronger.

So I went to see my doctor in the end. I became afraid for my pitiful life and went to see my doctor. You can say that in England. My doctor. Here everyone has a doctor all to themselves. Who sits on a swivel chair behind a big desk, flanked by medical books and a neat tray of tools. Whose surgery, including the curtained corner concealing the examining table, is lit by lamps thoughtfully angled to avoid straining the patients' eyes. I explain this for the benefit of my less fortunate brethren and their females, their sisters and mothers and aunts who have to mute their voices and blather platitudes to appear normal and solicitous of family honour. I mean the poor sods who live in the darker corners of the world and who have to camp in the sun and rain for days, buffeted by tornados and dust-storms, waiting to have a gangrenous limb amputated, or receive an antidote jab for snake-bite, or even some anti-bacterial cream for their festering wounds or just to treat a touch of sunburn. The idea of having your own doctor might sound like an impossible fantasy to them.

Here it's different. Health care from the first to the last day of life, delivered with courtesy and consideration in spacious clinics set out for the patient's comfort and convenience, and all of it free. And if it's not really free, then it feels like that. It's a small comfort which was not won without a struggle but which England now allows herself after the ages of toil and the centuries of hardship it took to build her beautiful ruins. Just stand on the banks of the Thames anywhere between Blackfriars Bridge and Westminster Bridge and look north, and see if your heart is not filled with awe at the labour that has gone into constructing that: the huge spires and great offices and colonnaded vaults and sprawling cloisters and rich pavilions and prim mansions and gilded bridges festooned with lights. Then let your eye wander farther afield, and there are the factories and warehouses and mechanized farms and model towns and chapels, and museums bursting with booty from other people's broken histories and libraries sprawling with books congregated over centuries. If you compare that to any one of the seething cesspits that pass for cities in the dark places of the world, and take into account the dedicated exertion that made it possible, then as small a comfort as your own doctor does not seem over-indulgent.

The ruins are one of the many things which make England a nation, along with a certain over-confident, hedonist cynicism which passes for sophistication and street-wisdom. Because the England of those ruins does not exist any more. Not that one, ask

4

anybody. Not the England which was luminous in the dark, and which gave the world the steam railway and the Greenwich Meridian and penicillin, all invented by Scots in exile. Not the England whose stories of the world brought us into being. It's Britain and the United Kingdom now, and the looming Holy European Empire, despite the loud protests of some in England's ancient colonial provinces, who see this apparent transformation as a fluid ruse to keep them in the same historical bondage which has lasted for generations. People even flinch guiltily when they say England, afraid that others will think them ranting, nationalist, racist fascists. And when her murky, free-booting history comes up for observation, Scots and Irish voices quietly forgive themselves for their part in those rousing adventures, and remind anyone interested of their own deprivations under England's colonial heel. The only parts of England that can be spoken about with a free, liberal conscience are her countryside or one of her many struggling sports teams, which are a constant source of joyful loathing and contempt – although this is liable to turn to demented cockiness and euphonious hyperbole when an unexpected triumph comes to pass.

Anyway, after all those austere ages of exertion and strife, just when the fatigued people were about ready to sit back and watch the play of light on the shrubs and the water, to unnotch the sword-belt, attend to the sweetly singing zephyrs and relish the fecund fruit of their endeavours, all at once a crowd, a host of strange people set up a clamour outside the walls. Every age and every town and hamlet has its madmen, its lepers, its outcasts, its itinerant tinkers and reclusive sages, but how did such a crowd get to be here? How did they all end up here? Yes, of course we know how. But why could they not be satisfied with the knowledge their voyage to Europe would inevitably have brought them, however monstrous the events that might have made the journey necessary? Knowledge as an end in itself!

5

Why could they not marvel and delight in the ideal? And what's wrong with a little detachment and a certain dignity in bearing in the face of adversity? What's wrong with being like Pocahontas?

This is what was said of her. She was an Algonquian princess, daughter of their King Powhatan. The events of her story concern the planting – sweet word – of the English colony in Virginia, in the days of Good Queen Bess and her successor Jimbo Stuart. John Smith, the English hetman of the operation, was captured while out on reconnaissance – checking out the odds on a small ethnic-cleansing project he had in mind – and was handed over to Powhatan. After being feasted and fed for several days (guess what for), he was invited to place his head on a rock, while around him stood various noble Algonquian specimens with clubs in their hands. Pocahontas threw herself on the Englishman, placing her head on top of his and therefore preventing his death. It was a moment to be repeated again and again in stories of imperial adventure: the beautiful native princess is smitten senseless by the European knight and recklessly risks everything for love. But Pocahontas was there first. It comes as a shock to discover that Pocahontas was only eleven years old when she did this, precocious little devil. In due course, she crossed over to the English Colony (she was taken captive when she was eighteen years old), and obligingly revealed the daily daring treacherous plans of the Algonquians to attack the English. Soon after that she was baptized Rebecca and was married to an Englishman. Rebecca: be thou the mother of thousands of millions, and let thy seed possess the gate of those that hate them. But an even more hazardous journey lay ahead of her than this first passage into civilization. Her husband took her to England, where she was fêted as a noble native curiosity, then died soon after in Gravesend in Kent, a clammy, swampy cloaca on England's nether end and a long way from Virginia. Perhaps she would have done better to stay at home instead of inserting herself into stories of Empire. Yet nobody reported her complaining about it.

But not so this strange crowd, who seem unable to sustain their calm or dignity, or even just to act with an uncomplicated, restrained exoticism. They wave their flimsy contracts and spit out their sad stories, yelling and bellowing with rage. They want more space in newspapers, they grumble when no one reads their endless books, and they demand time on TV. The stories they tell, so many accusations! The claims they make, for Heaven's sake! Nothing seems to subdue them and it is impossible to know what they mean. History turns out to be a bundle of lies that covers up centuries of murderous rampage around the globe – and guess who the barbarians are supposed to be. The most gentle of stories are interpreted as cunning metaphors that turn them into beasts and sub-humans, miserable creatures and slaves. Even their evident brutalities against each other can always be blamed on something else: slavery, colonialism, Christianity, a European education, anything but their own unmasterable greed, or their unregulated violence, or their artful dodges to escape the burden of having to do anything about anything. The law's against them, employers spurn them, banks discriminate against them. Such rantings!

And they barge in on the doctors as well, baring their grotesque lumps and their gaping sores. The doctors do not even wince as they palpate these ancient wounds, some swelling under diseased skins, some running and dribbling potent whey. I think of doctors like that: impossibly empirical and programmatic, handling flesh which exhales grievance and then writing a little chit to banish the pain away.

My doctor smiled, a young man in a bright white shirt, with fairish brown hair and deep blue eyes, the kind of man you would find running the world from whichever angle you squinted at it. I

7

imagined him getting wearily into his Range Rover after work to go to his pretty wife in their comfortable house in a pleasant suburb. The moment he turns the engine off in his gravelled drive, he is swamped by the adoration of his bouncing progeny (eleven-year-old girl and nine-year-old boy, I guessed) and perhaps an affectionate blonde collie. Maybe the wife is expecting another child, a belated third to regenerate the youthful love that their first two so completely symbolize.

Anyway, he smiled and then sighed contentedly, stretching out his six-foot frame in the comfortable swivel chair. 'Now then, how can I help you?' He drummed and poked my chest, and listened to it with a far-away, quizzical look in his eyes, and then could not help squeezing the small tyre that had recently wrapped itself round my midriff. Though what he expected that to emit I don't know. A squeak, a forbidden curse, a dribble of homogenized pus, an involuntary thrashing of atrophied muscle, what? I stood silently while he kneaded my smouldering flesh, pinching and squeezing, and cracking his knuckles on my bony plates. Then, frowning, he told me that my heart was buggered. I could have told him that, truly. It was what I was here to tell him, but I sat in respectful silence while he went through his lines.

Something about my manner or appearance must have made him think I had been to a public school. It wasn't just because of the brusque male bonhomie of that *buggered*. He asked me about what kind of *grub* I was prone to and whether I had any particularly unusual *whims*. The only people I could imagine calling food grub and speaking of trangressions as whims were readers of comics and men who had been to public schools – though this is only a guess and the experience of life from which it is drawn is inevitably circumscribed and limited. I told him I liked green bananas and smoked monkey for breakfast. He seemed taken aback by this for a moment, no doubt surprised that I had no problems with supplies, but then he nodded in recognition. He

8

was getting to me. I considered saying that, as a whim, I often wanked the monkeys off before I chucked them into the gas barbecue – for some reason this improved the texture of the flesh – but I was afraid he might slap me on the wrong shoulder and put me in the hands of the jinn with a stop-watch in his left hand and a sword in his right, the huge, bearded fellow who says, *You've got one more year to live and then your life belongs to me.* I needed his goodwill. I didn't want him provoked into malign prophecies. The doctor gave me a soundless grin, perhaps to let me know that he was on to me, and with a frown and a stare he set off again. The more he talked the worse he made me feel, as if I was a slow child or a palsied ancient who had lost hearing and speech, as if I was an uncomprehending native.

'Afro-Caribbean people have dickey hearts,' he said, smiling to give me courage at such a distressing time, 'and they are prone to high blood pressure, hypertension, sickle-cell anaemia, dementia, dengue fever, sleeping sickness, diabetes, amnesia, choler, phlegm, melancholy and hysteria. You really should not be surprised at this state you find yourself in. These are all diseases for which no known cure exists, of course, but there's no need to panic whatsoever. No need to throw your wicket away, if I may use an apt metaphor. Now let's see. When was it you first had problems with your heart? Is there a history of broken hearts in your family? You really mustn't worry. You only have a mild problem, I think, something not entirely unexpected of someone of your age and race, but I'll send you to a specialist who will run tests to confirm my diagnosis. If you find yourself distressed by this, remember that there are very good counselling services available at the health centre which will help you adjust to this current situation. Do you pay for yourself or are you on private insurance? We could've arranged the tests much more quickly if you were on private insurance. There's no need for panic though, do you understand?'

Of course, after all this drama I did not have the heart to tell

9

him that I was not Afro-Caribbean, or any kind of Caribbean, not even anything to do with the Atlantic – strictly an Indian Ocean lad, Muslim, orthodox Sunni by upbringing, Wahhabi by association and still unable to escape the consequences of those early constructions. I swallowed all those incurable diseases with a stoical gulp and an inward sneer at his smug ignorance. He didn't mention Aids, for example, which has its headquarters in our part of the world, probably because we seem unable to restrain ourselves from having relations with monkeys. I suppose I could have put him right, but just then I felt like showing solidarity with my brethren. They couldn't help their afflictions, so why mock? Anyway, if I had told him, he might have lost confidence in his diagnosis, and might have started his kneading and pounding all over again, and asked for blood tests and mercury cures or whatever it is they do nowadays to test out their theories on degenerating *races*. I did not think I could bear that. My body felt bruised and feverish enough already.

He didn't mean *Afro-Caribbean people* anyway. He meant darkies, hubshis, abids, bongo-bongos, say-it-loud-I'm-black-and-I'm-proud victims of starvation and tyranny and disease and unregulated lusts and history, etc. You know, my race. I could see he approved of my respectful silence, because he smilingly issued his prohibitions and instructions, wagging his finger now and then to warn me off naughty temptations.

I didn't know whether to tell Emma as soon as she came home or to wait until the specialist had done all his tests and put his imprimatur on my faltering heart. But the specialist might not have time to see me for months, or something might go wrong with the post when the hospital got round to fixing the appointment, or a machine might break down during the consultation, requiring a further visit. Anything could happen. Really, I knew I would have to tell her right away – I always told her everything. And anyway, how would I explain giving up my three rums and three cigarettes when I got in from work, as the doctor had demanded? It's usually the happiest hour of my life, faithfully repeated every day except for such rare catastrophic times as parents' evenings or holidays. Three rums and three fags, one after the other, until all of life seems to last only the few minutes behind and ahead of me, and everything else turns into impotent gurglings in a far ditch. Emma had had to learn to ignore me during my hour, because if she spoke to me I moved away . . . out on to the fire escape, on to the tiny and unsafe ornamental balcony, anywhere to escape her. Sometimes she was unable to contain herself and followed me regardless, bursting with stories of abuses she had suffered at work or on the Underground. After unburdening herself, her resentment at my evasions and what she called my spineless egotism then made her begin an assault on the author of all her misfortunes, which is how several of our conversations ended. Fair is fair, perhaps not without cause. I've received enough colonial education to be sporting on such matters.

What was there to tell anyway that would not already have been evident to her from those early descriptions of the pain lodged in my chest? But I knew she was going to put on her long face and look glum, and even weep – then cheer herself by plotting and planning the changes in our lives as if we were off on holiday somewhere and all the arrangements were in her hands, which they usually were and which was where I was happy to let them be. Of course that was not how I expected, hoped she would react. I imagined that she would be silent and devastated for a moment, and then envelop me with affection and warmth, take our clothes off and make gentle love to me for hours. She is capable of that. I know.

So there was no helping it. I would tell her as soon as she came in. I couldn't hide a thing like giving up three rums and three cigarettes. I considered not giving them up, of course – then she wouldn't know and I wouldn't have to explain anything – but that just seemed spinelessly egotistical and deceptive. I hate deception. Also, the sooner I told her the better for me, because she could then tell Amelia, our daughter, and we could get that over with as well. I have to tell you about my daughter. It's not that she's a disappointment to me, it's just that from about the time she reached fourteen I have been a disappointment to her. I could imagine how sad she'd look when she heard about my buggered heart, and how she would gaze at me with bewilderment at yet another failure to evade trouble. Then she'd ask me an utterly practical question about something it would never have occurred to me to do, demonstrating to me how weak my grip on the world was. 'Have you thought of seeing a specialist?' *Not really, dear, I never thought of that. What a clever idea! What a bright young darling you are! You really are indispensable around here. Let me do it straight away.* Then she'd walk away with a pained look, muttering snivelling impudence about me. That's why I talk to her in that sarcastic way. It's my only defence – feeble and futile, but it's all I have. What else can I do? Beat her? Talk lovingly to her? Ignore her? Two months before she had walked away from me like that and had thrown this over her shoulder: *You can bully me if you like, but it doesn't prevent you being a failure.* My first reaction was to chase after her – if I had been calmer I wouldn't have bothered – but in any case she was too quick for me.

'I'm not a failure,' I shouted at the closed door. 'I'm a tragedy. This dead-pan world is full of chaos and I am one of the lost.' Through the door I heard a choking noise and hoped that she was hanging herself from the curtain rail. Adolescents do it all the time, disgusted by rampant materialism or demoralized by poor physique or sexual frustration. It was nothing remarkable.

It couldn't be helped that she was like that – it was just how she was. I had hoped otherwise – no special reason aside from the manic ambition we place on our conscripted progeny – but she has turned out no better than the rest of us, except that her line in pathetic egotism is set off by a sharp and squeaky insolence. All right, she has several other sides to her, probably, but for me she reserves a hurtful impudence to which I have no answer. Emma would glare at me during these outbursts as if I had fed Amelia gall when she was an infant, trained her and coached her through her endless childhood, and then torn her away from her home-work to give her the latest in sullen bad mouth.

Emma glaring at me! Demanding that I take the blame for my ineffectual love for a daughter willingly overwhelmed by the gloat-ing self-assurance of the culture that had nurtured her. It was like blaming the hole in the ozone layer or the disappearing rain for-ests or leaking nuclear reactors for all the troubles which beset our stumbling world. Well, it wasn't me who did all that, nor was it the North African migrants in France or Tadjik horsemen thundering across the plains of middle Asia or Winnie Mandela or a passing comet. How is the rottenness of Amelia and her generation to be passed on to me? Did I glut them with enriched vitamins and mushy love and fairy tales of the world and a self-importance beyond their means? Was it me who filled their heads with the beastly plebeian hubris which makes thought, art or principle equal to eating raw offal in public or indulging petty sensualities? What part did I play in persuading them that there is something witty in degradation and perversion?

Emma grinned mockingly when I said things like that, which I did now and then when Amelia's glares and charged looks over-came me. She didn't always use to mock, and sometimes she had led the charge herself, but that was in earlier days when we were young enough to flatter ourselves that our little world was chan-ging, and that in some indefinable way what we said and thought mattered to its direction.

'Here we are again, decadent England in the dock,' she would say after one of my outbursts. 'For our child-rearing failures this time, as well as everything else in the universe. Actually, I'm not even sure that the child is doing anything wrong. It can't possibly be your fault, oh all right, our faults. Well, it so happens that she's your daughter, and that's a responsibility you'll never be able to evade by haranguing me about how corrupt we are and all those other things. There's no need for you to repeat them! We're all quite familiar with them by now, and I may even agree with one or two of them. But since you're uninfected by all this pestilence, you save her. Teach her about nobility and principle and sacrifice and laughter and whatever else it is that our degraded culture is no longer capable of. Rescue her.' *Say, who else could return the memory of life to men with a torn hope?* I used to quote that line by Leopold Sedar Senghor to her when we first knew each other, and sometimes she remembered it and threw it into her England-in-the-dock routine. There were times when I quite enjoyed this scene. It allowed me to bellow against the historical and cultural oppression under which I found myself. To her it sounded like a rant, but that's how the savage's critique of Europe unavoidably ends up sounding. (I read that in a book.) The general drift of these conversations was that I usually finished up being called intolerant, ungrateful, a fundamentalist, a raging mujahedin, a pig and a bastard. Just think about that. After these exchanges and against all the odds, we sometimes ended up in passionate late-night orgies of forgiveness and affection. I swear that those moments made the rantings seem worthwhile.

I liked to dwell on differences – I still do – to reflect on how hubris and greed have eaten away the foundations without discrimination, and how the continent on which we live is now sliding on pools of slime and waste and sleaze, and how cynicism and exhaustion are condemning all of us to live on bullshit, and how the over-fed can sneer unreflectingly at the ones they have browbeaten and defeated. Emma called me narcissistic – or as an embellishment she decribed what I did as the narcissism of minor

14

difference. She always was good with phrases, although this one she picked up somewhere. When she found a little phrase, she polished it and rubbed it until it was hard and glinting. Then she kept it by her in case she needed to blind me with her cleverness. I don't think she did it to be cruel. It was just that she liked to win her arguments, and not always without charm.

Anyway, she thought I gave these differences too much importance, especially since in the end I was only trying to say NO to stories that rose and swelled heedlessly around me despite my feeble refusal. My indignation and grievance were not going to change the way the story went: in it my maladies and inadequacies would be perpetually in the foreground, my churlish cruelties would not diminish in their pettiness, and when all was said and done I would still live in civil chaos given the slightest opportunity, would starve myself through sheer lack of foresight and would forever need the master's firm guiding hand if I was to be prevented from being a danger both to myself and to everyone else. She waited for me, her eyes bright with cleverness. 'Because, you see, you can't change the story while you are in it, and therefore it follows certainly, without question or doubt, that you can't achieve anything by saying NO to what happens in it. The story exists because it has to, and it needs you to be these things so we can know who we are. So your huffing and puffing is nothing more than a temper tantrum, and your indignant fictions are only corrosive fantasies. We need you too much, and we need you as you are.' This was where my narcissism lay, I suppose, in my desire to insert myself in a self-flattering discourse which required that England be guilty and decadent, instead playing my part as well and as silently as Pocahontas.

'What's the point of dwelling on these things, anyway?' she said. 'You only make yourself feel impotent and oppressed, as if in some way you are uniquely victimized by history. We keep talking of horrible events that have happened, but that doesn't seem to stop them happening again. It's just that we got there first with the steam engine and the cotton ginny or whatever. So it fell to us to do the dirty deeds.'

And our part of the deal was to be colonized, assimilated, educated, alienated, integrated, suffer clashes of culture, win a flag and a national anthem, become corrupt, starve and grumble about it all. It's a good deal, and we perform our parts to the utmost of our humble talents, but not adequately enough to satisfy over-sensitive patriots who feel put upon by hysterical strangers squatting dangerously inside the gates. They got the loot and we got the angst, but even that is not good enough for this lot. So they work up their beastly plebeians with rousing folk-tales of past glory and present squalor, provoke an incident or two, perhaps an unavoidable death here and there, and back to the library shelves for more tales of resolution in the face of stubborn circumstance and the declamation of the undiminishing coda: the Triumph of the West. And all the while the hubshi find it harder to resist the tempting and shameful suggestion that they inhabit a culture of grievance, that they have grown dependent on the corrupting smell of their wounds, that they dare not face the truth of their limitations, that they are not up to whatever it is that would release them from their bondage to historical inertia.

She grinned at this, acknowledging my overcharged ironies, and then continued, 'But just think of all the things we gave you, that you might not have got otherwise. At least admit that. We may have taken away the odd trinket to exhibit in the British Museum, but we didn't come empty-handed. We gave you individualism, the frigidaire, Holy Matrimony . . .'

'Holy!' This is what I used to like about her. When we first met, we cultivated an obnoxious hatred of everything that was part of the life we lived. Holy Matrimony was one of these things, and slums, and tomato ketchup and sausages and Irish stew and cottage pie. We thought we were hilarious and anarchic, putting noses out of joint. But that Holy Matrimony also touched on a problem which was always with me, although she did not know it. I knew I would have to find a way of telling her before long; it was all becoming a little ridiculous.

'If it wasn't for us, you'd have been marrying your third wife by now, a seventeen-year-old kid who should have been thinking of her homework instead of the tired penis that was coming to ruin her life,' she said. 'That's what you would've been up to by now. Admit it.'

Sooner or later I am going to have to go back to the beginning and tell this story properly. I can't quite fix on the beginning yet, where it is as such. When I think I've found a good position from which to start, I am tempted by the possibility that everything would seem clearer if I began with what led up to it. In my mind, I take up various starting positions – some before I was born, some after, some yesterday, others in the living present – but after a few minutes of reflection I am thoroughly sick of each of them. They all seem calculated and transparent. I stumble about in this sullen thicket, hoping that I will bump into the moment of release.

So, back to Holy Matrimony. The joke about that was that Emma and I were not married but had been living in increasingly fractious sin for the last donkey's years. I mean, it wasn't all fractious, but the peevish quota could sometimes be significant, and I am not quite sure how it got to be like that. As for Holy Matrimony, we did not just drift into this state of detachment from it, but chose to take it on glare for glare, brazenly outstare middle-class respectability and turn our faces to the freedom of the seas. It was mainly Emma's idea. She had many ideas about middle-class respectability, by which she meant her parents, I'm afraid. Her blows against *class* were inbred in this way, intimate resentments against family Christmas celebrations, for example, or a loathing for the faintest glimmer of interest in opera, which her parents *adored*, or sneering contempt for matrimony. She loved music, and had played the piano with real seriousness throughout her years at university, and even now was still at her most intense when listening to a variant performance of a favourite piece. But the briefest snatch of opera made her reach for the power button, making disgusted faces and uttering strong words against the fascist Establishment as she did so. It was something like that with matrimony. I took my lead, as I did in so many things, from Emma. She wanted to be the anti-bourgeoisie rebel and that was fine with me. Everything about her was fine with me.

She abhorred neatness and order, so she said, especially if her mother was around, which meant I got to do all the cleaning and clearing up. When she was irritated with me, she noticed that my obsession with order was a reflection of my authoritarian nature, an undeniable confirmation that I was a natural bourgeois. But for a few accidents of time and place, I could have been standing on Liverpool dock seeing off my slave ship as it set off for the Guinea coast, or could have been one of those cheering the troops as they murdered the strikers in Peterloo, or might have been observed tucking contentedly into a roast shoulder of mutton while concentration-camp chimneys smoked downwind. She only said that when she was really pissed off, or irritated with some stubborn defence I was putting up against what to her seemed manifestly indisputable, or if she was drunk, or most likely all three, but it gives some idea of what she thought of middle-class respectability.

It was always roast shoulder of mutton I was tucking into contentedly while some horror took place under my nose. To Emma, this was the archetypal bourgeois dish; somewhere between the soup, the smoked mackerel, the boiled beef, the ham and the damson pie, there sat the shoulder of mutton, as greasy a lump of shame and reprehension as could be found anywhere, the very emblem of smug, coercive egotism. When someone monstrous

18

appeared on the TV news, I sometimes thought – there goes another eater of roast shoulder of mutton. And if I thought Emma looked a bit fed up, I would shout it out to make her smile. I don't think she has ever seen a shoulder of mutton – I'll have to ask her – but I would not be surprised if this turned out to be the image which flashed through her mind when she accused me of harassing Amelia with capricious displays of authority.

In any case, we did not marry, and Emma's mother behaved with gratifying predictability on the issue, raising the subject in a voice of checked anguish at least once a month. It used to be more frequent than that, and battle would be joined, and mayhem and slaughter would ensue. Well, hard words and long silences anyway. But age, or exhaustion, or familiarity dimmed the spark of these clashes, and soon they were undertaken with only a hint of polite malice on the part of Emma's mother, and quite casual insolence on the part of her daughter. They then became mere rites of being, mindless like the courtship dances of terns, whereas before they had been bitter encounters awash with bile and poison.

I don't think Emma was always like that with her parents. When I first met them – have I bumped into my beginning? *When I first met them* has the authentic sound of leather on willow. When I first met Mr and Mrs Willoughby, Emma and I were both students. Mr Willoughby had recently retired from a quiet life as a solicitor in the City, specializing in dealing with companies that traded in the dark corners of the world. Mrs Willoughby was, as I guessed she had been for many years, in active charge of his life. I could not help laughing as I was introduced to them, because of all the stories Emma had already told me. Perhaps I was nervous, in case they said or did something embarrassingly opinionated, something that would diminish me and which I would be unable to handle with the right degree of courteous indifference. My first view of them was coloured in this way. Their first view of me was coloured differently, and I think theirs was the bigger surprise. It appeared that they had had no idea . . . So I stood giggling in front of them while they took me in. Mrs Willoughby was the first to recover, as usual. She was a tall woman, in her late forties at the time, stiff and matronly, but in a pleasing way – although I wouldn't have thought so then. Later I saw something of that look in Emma and I found it attractive.

'Hasn't it been lovely these last few days?' Mrs Willoughby said. 'I hope it lasts, though I don't expect it will. Have you been in England long?'

Long enough to know how to respond to intimate small talk of that kind. Murmur audibly, smile brightly, say nothing. In general that did not seem to me at the time to be a contemptible philosophy, and there were many occasions when I rebuked myself for failing to live by it more consistently. I felt Emma watching me, waiting for me to take offence about something. I had been well primed for this, to expect to be offended by something her parents were bound to say, or imply, or disguise in an apparently innocent commonplace. Mr Willoughby came up with the goods at once, casually, almost kindly, staring at me with bristly intensity, curious to hear my opinion. 'I expect there are thousands of darkies in universities these days. It wasn't like that in my day. Perhaps the odd maharaja's son, or a young chief. The rest were too backward, I suppose. Now you see them everywhere.'

I heard Emma heaving a triumphant sigh. Good old Daddy, trust him to come up with his predictable filth. Mr Willoughby was moderately constructed: of medium height, neither thin nor fat, slightly balding but not strikingly so. He was dressed in woollen trousers, cardigan and tie, and in this habit managed to look as if he was briefly taking time off from more public duties. He wore thick-framed glasses, behind which his eyes stared at their subject with little sign of humour or self-consciousness. Murmur audibly, smile brightly, say nothing! My mumbling made Mr Willoughby's eyes brighten even more, as if I had said something witty. Or perhaps he was only responding to my smile. I could tell from Emma's fallen jaw that she did not see anything to smile about. After such deliberate provocation could I do nothing more than twitter and smirk? But these were early days between us, and she expressed her horror at my spineless and unglamorous behaviour with long disbelieving stares rather than with a few choice and well-polished phrases. You have to remember that at that time it seemed that the black revolution was just round the corner, when everyone would get a chance to be a victim at last. Emma had already enlisted and was a bit of a Young Turk about it all, a zealot. She was quite ready to sacrifice her parents to the cause.

I saw what I would now recognize as a punitive look appear in her eyes, and she twitched her eyebrows slightly in a gesture of incomprehension. Then, though she smiled a little before she did so, she abandoned me to Mr Willoughby and turned her full attention on her mother. *If you like him so much you can have him.* After a while she appeared to forget about me, or at least to forget about her disappointment with me, and I watched with envy as she chatted with her mother. Laughing, touching, rebuking each other's mild misdemeanours, making vague plans about shopping for a silver cruet, exchanging promises to go to Portobello market one Sunday. I was filled with nostalgia and longing.

Mr Willoughby mulled me over for a few minutes, throwing in a question or a remark between silent appraisal while I muttered and smiled heroically. 'What are you studying? Will you be able to do anything with it afterwards? Is the British government paying for you? I suppose we've given your country independence. Do you think it's too soon? What's the political situation like?' In the end I told him that the government had legalized cannibalism. He must have thought I said cannabis, because he asked me if I thought that should happen here too. Everyone seemed to think so, as if there didn't seem to be enough abandoned behaviour already. I told him that the President had syphilis, and was reliably reputed to be schizophrenic; he was practically blind and was drunk by about three in the afternoon every day. Everybody knew this and avoided calling on him after that hour because his behaviour could be dangerously erratic when under the influence. I said that in my father's house all the beds were made of gold, and until I was sixteen, servants bathed me in milk and then rinsed me in coconut water every morning.

He smiled suddenly and told me about the year he had spent in France when he was younger. It had done his French no end of good. He had lived in the country, staying with a farming family and working for an estate agent who was a friend of his father. It had been warm most of the time, but the winter was quiet and long. We kicked this around for a while before he returned to the attack, giving me a long glinting stare before he spoke. 'There was a chap at school, a darkie like you. Splendid runner. He was Mohammedan, though. I can't remember where he came from, somewhere in darkest Africa. Black as the ace of spades, he was, but splendid runner. Natural athlete, and one of nature's gentlemen.' So I told him that I used to wake up at four in the morning, milk the cows, weed the fields, help with the harvest and then run six miles to school on an empty stomach every day. Then one afternoon a European official from the Education Department visited our school, an Inspector of Schools. He stood in front of our class and chatted for a few minutes, then suddenly he asked me a question, but I was too feeble with hunger to answer.

'What was the question?' Mr Willoughby wanted to know, leaning forward with interest, his face alight, eyes burning with attention.

'He wanted to know who was the first European to eat a banana,' I told him.

Mr Willoughby nodded slightly, approvingly. 'Good question. Then?'

Well, normally I knew the answer to this question all right, –

and at this point I gave Mr Willoughby an interested glance: did he know the answer to this historically vital question? Wasn't his nod just a little too casual? – but on that afternoon I just did not have the strength to say it aloud. Somehow the European official seemed to know this, to understand the state I was in, and brought his ear close to catch my whispered reply. *Alexander the Great*, I croaked. After that he adopted me and gave me huge meals to eat every day and a second-hand bicycle so I didn't have to run six miles every morning and paid my fees through school, which at that time were thirty-two shillings a term. Mr Willoughby pondered on this, and when he spoke his eyes were muddy with feeling. 'That was that made it all worthwhile. Was it fair to abandon the Empire? Was it fair to them?' he asked. I knew who he meant by them. And in all this time I could see out of the corner of my eye how Emma and her mother were laughing and telling stories, while I had to sit in bright attention in case Mr Willoughby began a flanking attack or a slithery guerrilla raid.

I don't imagine the effortless affection I saw between them that first time, because I saw it again on other occasions. But Mrs Willoughby was not happy about me. It was not *me* as such, but that she wanted better for her daughter, a more normal friendship, an untroubled future. Later, when Emma told her we had decided to live together, she looked at her hands in silence for a moment and then said, 'I'll go and make some tea.' She returned after a few minutes with tea and biscuits, settled herself down carefully, and with the measured gaze and voice of someone doing everything to be reasonable, she asked Emma: 'Aren't you too young?' I saw the effort it took her not to bluster or shout, not to get up and hurl the steaming teapot at me and then bundle me out of her house with imprecations and insults and accusations. 'Have you had news from your family recently?' she asked as she handed me a cup of tea. As was her habit with me, she did not wait for my answer but carried on talking. 'I hope everyone is well. Will you be

23

taking her away with you? I hope not. You must make sure that all this does not interfere with your studies. After all, that's what you're here for.'

Her tight dissembling smile never wavered; if anything, it grew more assured as she worked herself into the part. Not a word about what was really making her unhappy with the new (informal) addition to the family. And because she was dissembling, Emma took up her challenge and confronted her on all her objections, even the ones she did not raise. *No, I'm not too young. You were already a mother when you were my age. Of course it won't interfere with our studies. Why are you making such a fuss? Is it because he's black?* On that last question, Mrs Willoughby looked pained; she refused to stoop to that level of discussion. Look who's coming to dinner. The damage was already done by then, and I am not sure that I played the principal part in causing it. In any case, mother and daughter had by this time settled into a routine of attrition and ambush which would sometimes break out into open war. When Emma became pregnant (unplanned), Mrs Willoughby launched an all-out assault, enlisting Mr Willoughby, middle-class respectability, the future, the welfare of the unborn child . . . in short, Holy Matrimony, adoption or abortion. And Emma on her part resisted with relish and zest, repelling attack after attack with contemptuous assurance.

'But think of the child,' Mrs Willoughby demanded. 'What will it think of itself? It'll be neither one thing nor the other. And think of what it will be like to be born to an unmarried couple.'

'I am thinking of the child! That's exactly what I'm doing,' Emma declared. 'I don't want her oppressed by all your obsessions with class and neighbours and foreigners.'

It was gruesome stuff. Mr Willoughby watched with his eyes sparkling, glancing at me now and then with surprise when an atrocity took place. His look said: are you really responsible for all this? When he was called upon to intervene he took so long to think of something wise and mollifying that the women soon ignored him and returned to work. I think he preferred it that way. I was only rarely called upon to say anything in the open battlefield, although at times Emma looked accusingly at me and made me feel that I might have offered more support had I been of a less spineless constitution. Mr Willoughby and I were required to be present as a kind of strategic reserve, to be deployed if matters became desperate. In the end, Mr Willoughby was brought into action as it became clear that Emma was immovable. He invited me to the pub.

'Dreadful,' he said after sipping at his beer, so I tried mine and was forced to agree. I was quite used to Mr Willoughby by now. We had been seeing a lot of each other since we met the year before. 'Would you like some faggots?' he asked, glaring at the handwritten menu on the blackboard. The other items were mixed grill, sausages, baked beans, or macaroni cheese. That's what pub food was like in those days, even in Blackheath. 'Used to have faggots at school. In Kent. Everyone but Lawson used to ask for seconds. Kitty Lawson.' I nodded and Mr Willoughby nodded back and briefly shut his eyes. Yes, we knew Lawson. Awkward customer, too big for his boots. The memory of Kitty Lawson made Mr Willoughby's face glum, or perhaps it was the thought of the faggots all those years ago. So I began to tell him about the free milk they used to give us at school and his eyes lit up as usual at the prospect of an Empire story. As soon as we arrived at school we lined up under the shade of the huge mango tree which stood in the middle of our assembly yard, humming devotional songs while the milk was warming in the urns. The teachers walked among us uttering softly spoken greetings and a quiet word of approbation where it was deserved. The milk was flavoured with cardamon and cinnamon, and generously sugared. The first mouthful was like sipping nectar. Then we were offered a choice of the fruit in season: oranges, melons, mangoes, jackfruit, lychees and, of course, bananas. Then we strode to our well-lit class-rooms to break the chains of ignorance and disease which had kept us in darkness for so long, and which the Empire had come to bring us respite from. That was what school was like for us. Mr Willoughby shook his head at the beauty of it all, and sipped at his beer to disguise the emotion he felt. He sat with his eyes lowered, his hand clenched round his glass, shaking his head now and then as the scale of the tragedy returned to him. 'It wasn't right, to abandon them like that,' he said. 'Cruel. Think of all the terrible things they've been doing to each other since we left.'

'Shall we go back then?' I asked, and saw Mr Willoughby's eyes leap with amazed interest.

'Not possible,' he said after a moment, his mouth a thin bitter line, his eyes shifting into the middle distance. 'Everything's turned to shite. Let's have some faggots.'

They looked like shite when they arrived, too, generous lumps of dark, solid shite squatting in a shallow pool of brown gravy. After we had contemplated our faggots for several pregnant sec-onds, Mr Willoughby said, 'My face is inclined to be round, but not oval.' I waited, but when there was no more I nodded sympa-thetically. Must have been something Kitty Lawson said. What-ever mission Mr Willoughby was sent on in the war of Holy Matrimony he never performed, or if he did then he was too subtle for me. There was a moment when I thought we had got to it. 'Sambo,' he said as we rose to leave the pub. It looked like a dramatic change of tactics, to chase me away with racist abuse, but I wasn't sure if Mr Willoughby had the talent for that kind of rough stuff. His eyes were blazing again. 'The darkie at school. We used to call him Sambo. I knew it would come back to me. Splen-did runner. Black as the ace of spades. I expect he's President-for-Life in his country now. What will your chaps out there say about all this? Complete mess.' But he did not seem interested in my reply and I mumbled audibly, smiled brightly and said nothing.

Good old Mr Willoughby. He probably thought of it himself. What will your chaps out there say about all this? Mrs seemed too caught up in the heat of battle to have given the matter any thought. Emma asked, of course, and I told her that they were bound to make a fuss, at first. She chose to be satisfied with that. I say chose because there was something reluctant in her eyes, but perhaps she thought we would go into it later.

Everything went into abeyance with Amelia's arrival as we all abandoned whatever else we were doing to cluster round the baby while it shitted and screamed. She screamed a lot, so much that I sometimes felt that the revulsion she felt for what she had been landed into was tragic. Everyone said it was normal, or she had colic or whatever, but I could not help feeling that she was raging with self-pity. It didn't do her any good, of course. She was here, she was wanted, she was loved, she didn't have a chance. Whenever she was given the opportunity, she clung to her mother's breast as if to freedom itself. Life's like that, clinging futilely to the very objects that imprison us.

The moment of her arrival was the climax of weeks of preparation and anxiety, desultory and spasmodic at first but growing into all-consuming absorption. There were new bits of furniture to acquire, bedding, a bucket for the nappies, baby lore to mug up on, names to play with, bulletins on the expectant mother's condition to keep abreast of, the approach of celibacy to reflect on, etc. Emma's alarming size, apart from anything else, gave her a veto on every decision, but in any case, to hear her speak you would not have thought this was happening to her for the first time. Years of education and training had prepared her for just this moment. She had known for years that she was going to have a baby girl called either Amelia or Beatrice (sometimes Beatrix). Her thesis was set aside, and instead of Lukács and Benjamin and Heidegger – this was before Foucault and Derrida dominated her discourse –

it was Dr Spock's text we attended to. So it was appropriate that when the critical moment arrived our lives were sharply focused on the baby's coming. Its undaunted completeness and surprising mobility – I had somehow expected it to lie still – provided miraculous closure to the narrative fragment. Mr and Mrs Willoughby, me, a friend of Emma's from the university called Judy, we all gathered round the bed at various times to share in the drama. I basked in the approval the nurses bestowed on me when I came visiting, and smilingly complied when they encouraged me to sit on Emma's bed and hold her hand, and was even happy enough to make the infantile noises that they seemed to think necessary for the baby's health and well-being. I have to confess that Amelia did seem to like the silly antics I used to perform, and would take time off from her combative engagement with existence to kick her feet in the air and make squeaky noises as she was supposed to.

Emma herself was surprisingly casual about everything, more interested in talking about the meals I was cooking for myself in her absence and in the friends she had made in the ward, than about the tribulations and agonies her body had recently suffered. That she had done all that made her seem even more heroic. I had been there, of course, starving and dying for a pee while Emma went red with her efforts and groaned for release, and the midwives bustled in and out with what seemed to me to be gloating callousness. You did this to yourself, so stop moaning, I imagined them saying.

So I joined in the fuss we made of the mother and child, and felt rewarded and proud of our joint efforts, but I must confess that when we got back to our flat I began to see a different aspect of our achievement. For a start, Emma did not seem quite so casual with only me around. The things I said appeared to irritate her. When I checked a crisis she was having with the baby in Dr Spock and read her what it said there, her eyebrows flew up in disbelief while she carried on as if I had not spoken. She only smiled at me if I rolled about on the floor making silly noises, like a puppy. Or when I lay beside her while the baby eventually slept and stroked the parts of her body she allowed.

Amelia seemed to like it in the flat. Her range of noises extended, and she even fell silent at times, though anguished screams still tore through her at frequent intervals.

Emma and her mother were absorbed with the baby, handling her with a breezy familiarity which seemed effortless. They watched her and stroked her, guessed at and debated the sources of her frowns and screams and mocking gurgles. Emma seemed to forget herself at these times, in a way she only rarely did when I was around – as when I rolled about and played the fool. Perhaps she was afraid I despised her pleasure, mocked her for descending effortlessly into instinct. It was one of her ideas, that women are crushed by their *finer feelings*, which they are socialized to consider essential to their nature. They are trained to sacrifice themselves, she would say, and only find fulfilment when they become servants to their children. Perhaps her mother's pleasure allowed her to shelve these concerns. Mr Willoughby, when he was invited to the feast, hovered prettily at the edges of the firelight, making wise and comforting noises, and baring his teeth at the baby.

Mr and Mrs brought gifts with them whenever they came (every day), from washing-up liquid to a kilo of beef. She washed the nappies in the bath while he took the baby for a little stroll round the dog-turd-littered pavements, so that Emma could have a snooze. Then Mrs made tea, fed the baby and cooked the beef (as it may be) they had brought with them. She even stayed the odd night, for some reason, sleeping on the floor in our bedroom – I had been evicted earlier for talking in my sleep and waking up the baby. 'What was I saying?' I asked her, but she said she could not understand the language. It was a distressing episode. At times

I felt invisible to them. My voice sounded strange when I spoke in their midst, as if I was speaking in an incomprehensible tongue. I found myself losing track, confusing words, and becoming tongue-tied. When they talked about me (or even to me), it felt that they were pitying me, that I was a victim of unavoidable natural forces, a cyclone or a cholera epidemic or an inherited deformity.

At times Emma gave me suspicious looks, wondering if I was making fun of them. 'Why don't you and Dad go and wet the baby's head?' she suggested.

We sat in the almost empty pub (it was just 6.30), holding on to our glasses and not speaking. When I glanced at Mr Willoughby, his eyes were dancing on me, which made me want to cry out and run screaming into the gloom. He was hungry for an Empire story, but my tongue felt leaden and discoloured, my head pounding with discontent. In the end I started to tell him about the English hospital sister who saved my life. I had gone to the hospital to say goodbye to an aunt who was just about to expire from a complex amalgam of bush yaws, leprosy, bilharzia and infectious boils, all of which are brought on by inherited effects of dissipation and lasciviousness. As I was descending the stairs on my way out, I was suddenly overcome by the onset of a tropical ague. I collapsed on the steps, where the sister found me and had me carried to a bed. She did not leave my side until I was fully recovered two weeks later, bathing my brow with watered wine, and placing her wetted handkerchief in my mouth so I could drink. It was a simple story of everyday imperial heroism, but the emphasis was wrong in my telling. Mr Willoughby did not seem too discontented, although I could tell he had not found the story as moving as some of the others, and the artist in me felt a twinge of disappointment at this failure.

'Getting on all right at work?' he asked after we had sat for another eternity, gripping our glasses in silence. I had just started my first job then, teaching in a school full of ignorant and deranged maniacs who seemed afraid of me, a strange but gratifying response. The school smelled of sweaty necks and burnt stew. I found my new job a daily persecution, and was constantly afraid that the schoolchildren were going to rise in rebellion and force humiliations on me. My constant vigilance, above any other consideration, was to pre-empt this fate, to survive each day, each hour, without falling victim to the savagery I could see barely checked in the children's faces and in their shouted exchanges. Some of the older boys stood taller than me, and the girls were well into child-bearing age, yet they seemed selflessly to devote their energy and passion to antics and abuse, to acting like the kindergarten age-group in a baboon homestead.

'You have to think of someone else now,' Mr Willoughby said as we walked back. 'Serious business.'

The flat smelled of scrambled eggs when we got back, and mother's milk and tinned food and wet nappies, etc. These implacable tokens of the predictable and crushing quotidian wore down the novelty of Amelia's arrival and eventually drove Mr and Mrs Willoughby back to Blackheath. They also drove Emma to decline and gloom, a depression which everyone from the district nurse to Dr Spock had warned her about and which she found impossible to resist. To my joy, I discovered that one of the few things which alleviated her misery was bracing and uninhibited abuse of my good self. I hurried home from school, knowing that I would soon be able to stretch my feet out while Emma exhibited my selfish thoughtlessness or analysed my intolerance. I did what I could to help, smiling in the wrong places, toying with the salad (instead of wolfing it hungrily down as I was supposed to), suggesting that I could cook if she wasn't feeling up to it, lighting a cigarette in the same hemisphere as the baby. After bearing as much of this provocation as she could, she did herself a favour and described my several shortcomings.

One day, sitting in this comfortable intimacy while Amelia guzzled at Emma's breast, making her wince now and then with her greedy sucking, I told her of my earlier discomfort with the ecstatic occupation of the flat by Mr and Mrs (but not about feeling a stranger in their midst). 'They can't help it if your parents happen to be so far away,' Emma said. She waited a long time before speaking, stretching out the silence to force me into a confession. I felt guilty about my silence, but I hung on. 'They weren't trying to deny them their share of the baby, if that's what you mean.'

Emma's long accusing looks said more, although she was sure to say it all fully later anyway. *The trouble with you is you only ever think of yourself. She's their grandchild. They have every right . . . Your parents have not even sent us a card or a present for the baby. I'm not trying to impose our customs on them or anything, but I'd have thought just a little token . . . I know their lives are hard and they have all those terrible things to deal with, so I'm not just being critical out of irritation and pique. But honestly! Not even a card!* Nothing was ever the same after Amelia came, and the subject of my parents and my home was no different.

When we first knew each other, Emma was full of questions about me and about my home. She was so beautiful and so full of life (even her hair seemed quickened) that I could not imagine that she really wanted to know about the calloused and stiffened memories that attached me to my past. But she swore she did. What did my father do? (That question often seems to come first in England.) How many of us were there? *Oh, so you are the eldest.* How many rooms did our house have? There was nothing she did not want to know: how big was my school, how many times had we won the inter-schools football cup, the names of my childhood friends, my mother's name. She listened with rapt attention as I poured out. At first it was sheer relief to be able to talk endlessly about things that were so far away and yet never seemed to stop causing me pains and guilts that were delicious despite the anguish

32

they left me with. I realized with small stabs of shame afterwards that I had embellished my story to make it less messy, and had fabricated details where these had escaped me. The shame was intense for a few minutes but it soon passed and I became used to my lies. It made me happy, and above all it made her happy. No, above all was that it could do no harm. She never seemed to tire of hearing about my home and my people, and I confess that my fabrications were generally to repay her interest, although some were obviously to make us appear less petty to each other, to make our lives seem noble and ordered.

Then after a while she stopped paying such intense attention. I am not sure exactly when this happened; I don't think I noticed at the time. It must have happened slowly as we got used to each other. I've wondered whether it was because she had seen through my fabrications and could no longer bear to hear them, but to be honest I would have expected her to see through them from the start. She was dead keen on the shape of narratives (and went on to take it up as her PhD project), so she was sure to know that my stories had been adjusted to reward and satisfy me in the telling. Perhaps the stories wearied her with their sameness. If they hadn't happened I could have invented them, and so could she. No, I think she must have seen and heard all she needed to complete the stories for herself, and then good-naturedly switched the lights off. After all, there were other things to attend to. When she referred to these places and people whom she had not seen or met, she did so with a familiarity I found pleasing. She talked of them as if they were predictable and ordinary, which was not how they felt to me. To me they were foreign, strange, different, as far away from where I was as night from day. So when she mentioned someone's name and then explained to whoever she was talking to that that was my uncle, it made my uncle seem present, acclimatized to England's curt self-regard, as fluent and comfortable in its chit-chat as any other person. It made my uncle seem normal and

33

unremarkable, not a stern, slightly irritable man who is always too busy making money, and who never fails to observe a single prayer every day.

2

I don't have an uncle. Or a father. I created those two figures for Emma out of my one stepfather, more or less. My Uncle Hashim was my mother's elder brother and had great influence over her. The difference in their ages was twelve years, for they were children of separate mothers. There was another brother in between, but he ran off to become a sailor, stowing away on a ship transporting coal from South Africa to Japan, and was never heard from again. There was a rumour that he had settled in Hamburg, and another rumour that he was a criminal in London, but at home we were discouraged from showing any interest in his whereabouts or his life, past or present. He was a same-mother brother to my mother, and his flight had caused great distress to his ma, who had cherished him with jealous pride. He was a mark of blessing on her marriage, which she sometimes suspected people scorned because of the difference in age between her and her husband. She had been married before to a younger man, but he had been impatient for children, and when she could not oblige to his schedule, he divorced her. May God rot his mean soul and plague him with boils in old age. If people despised her for the alacrity with which she had married a widower more than twice her age, the boy had come as a gift from the Almighty to scold their envious souls.

Their father was still alive when my mother's brother ran away, but because of the dishonour his son's disobedience brought on him, he did not mention his name again in the few months that remained to him. When people in the streets asked after his son Abbas, he shook his head and was silent, and sometimes tears came to his eyes. Everybody understood that Abbas's spurning of his father's authority was too profound a misdemeanour for them to attempt to make the customary pleas of mercy and forgiveness for the delinquent. The father's death so soon afterwards was naturally blamed by everyone on his son's departure, even though they all knew that the old man had been steadily shuffling off this mortal coil for a while. It would have been cruel to refuse the family this bit of drama and scandal. When their mother surprisingly died a few months after that, having shown no sign of illness until two days before she gave up the ghost, the Hand of God was clearly evident, and those who remembered Abbas with any fondness trembled at the fate which awaited him when he came to meet his Maker. Uncle Hashim and my mother had no choice but to continue the silence about their brother. My mother sometimes mentioned him, describing something he used to say or do, but on these occasions she kept her voice free of sensation or regret, as if she had no need either to lament or blame his flight.

Uncle Hashim liked to say that he had brought up my mother. She was thirteen when her parents died, and he was twenty-five, so (I can imagine) he ruled her life. When I knew him, he was a solemn man who liked to have his word taken seriously. By his appearance and demeanour alone, you could tell that he was a pillar of the community, a notable. There is no reason to suppose that he would have been any different when my mother was younger, at least *with her*, even if his manner outside had not yet become assured and grand. It was Uncle Hashim who, in due course, arranged my parents' marriage.

He didn't do it, of course, just to please himself and demonstrate his authority over my mother's puny life, although he could have done. He himself was still unmarried and preferred this uncomplicated arrangement. They lived on the first floor over a row of three shops near one of the main roads to the docks, a prime site which their father had bought years ago and which, along with the house he built on it, was their chief inheritance. The rent from the three shops – three rooms fronting on to the road, each with a smaller room at the back which was the store – provided enough for Uncle Hashim to conduct his business. Their accommodation upstairs was more than ample for two: a bedroom for each of them, a room for receiving visitors with shuttered windows in two walls, one of which faced the shore, a kitchen, a bathroom and a terrace where my mother hung out the washing every day and grew roses and lavender in rusting kerosene tins, and where at times she sat in the evening, listening to the noises of the street below and looking up at the crowded sky.

Uncle Hashim had come home earlier than usual one evening, suffering from biliousness brought on by drinking yeast which had obviously lost its freshness. He was a man who favoured routine and order, a proclivity all the easier to indulge in a small place with few diversions. Usually after isha prayers he went from the mosque to the eating-house operated by the Yemeni baker for a drink of yeast and a small round of bread, and then on to the café on the main road to listen to the news on the radio before coming home for supper. He found my mother sitting on a mat on the terrace, her form in silhouette from the light in the kitchen. 'Why are you sitting in the dark like this?' he asked her. 'We must have a light put out here.' 'No,' my mother said, 'I like it like this.' He asked her to bring him some coffee but no supper, and because it was a cool March evening just before the arrival of the rains, he asked her to bring it out to the terrace rather than to his bedroom. Then he sat on the mat from which she had just risen. As he did so he saw movement out of the corner of his eye, and when he turned to look he saw someone move away from the window of a house nearby. It was only a slit in the wall about nine or ten inches wide, neither shuttered nor glazed, an aperture to illuminate a turn in the stairs or ventilate a store. The house itself was obliquely angled from them, so the slit appeared even narrower from the terrace. The light in the room behind the window was dim and steady and golden, the light of a kerosene lamp. Yet Uncle Hashim was sure that the figure he had so fleetingly seen move away was a man, and he thought he knew who it was.

My father had recently come from the country to live with relatives in that house so he could go to the teacher-training college in the town. He had completed Standard Eight the previous year, aged eighteen, but had failed to get a place at secondary school on account of his age, and because the competition for secondary school places was intense, and the town schools always did better than the country ones. Not only because town schools were nearer for the students to get to, were better resourced with teachers, books, toilets and sporting equipment, but because students in country schools were required by their parents to take time off to help on the land, and sometimes had to repeat the year. Most of the students in town schools would have reached Standard Eight at the age of fourteen. It was because of his absences at inconvenient times in the school year that my father was so much older by the time he finished, although he was by no means the oldest even in his own school. In any case, the best he had managed was a place at the teaching college. Uncle Hashim had seen the new neighbour, a slim young man with a lithe athletic look, who had greeted him as they passed in the street. He had been struck by his gentle manner, which he had thought close to meekness.

Uncle Hashim sat on the half-lit terrace and realized with mild surprise that he could smell the perfume of the roses which my mother grew. He found that as he concentrated on the perfume, as he flared his nostrils and took a plunging breath, it evaded him, grew fainter. After a moment or two he gave up trying. None the less, he felt as if it had been a bit of cleverness on his part to have caught that subtle drifting scent so unexpectedly. When my mother came with the coffee, she would not stay, saying she would put some clothes to soak and then go to sleep. But she stayed long enough, and the light was clear enough, for Uncle Hashim to ascertain what he already knew with a disquiet which he firmly suppressed: that my mother had the body of a woman. It was not that he was unaware of that. She covered herself differently now in his presence to disguise her maturing shape, and there was a new secretiveness about the way she lived in their shared space. She became different when her visitors and friends called, all of them glowing with a kind of exuberance and playfulness which Uncle Hashim found distressingly shallow. Their perfumes and powders, their sandalwood and musk rising from hot flesh, made him heave for breath even though he sat in another room.

Her lingering on the terrace within sight of an admirer filled him with alarm and with a sense that havoc was about to engulf his life again. He sat in the gloom, and was struck once more by the perfume of the roses. Only this time the smell made him think of corruption and chaos.

After that evening, he kept an eye on the young man and asked some questions about him. He found little to recommend him apart from his good manners and his upright youthfulness. His father had a small piece of land near Bunge, a meagre holding that was enough to bring some bananas and mangoes to the market now and then, and feed a sizeable family for the rest of the time. He lived as a dependent with the relatives who were their neighbours. Uncle Hashim heard of his diligence, and his willing deference and subdued amiability, though he once heard him speak with surprising forthrightness at the café, on a matter he thought himself knowledgeable about. He seemed already the inevitable figure of a teacher, and Uncle Hashim thought that in time he would become respectably poor and increasingly pedantic, the way teachers did.

So it was not out of liking for him that Uncle Hashim began to proceed towards my parents' marriage. He just did not want to be encircled by shadowy intrigues and suppressed resentments which would one day erupt in reckless outbursts and a new shame. There was no female relative for him to turn to and suggest that she commence the subtle approaches that precede negotiation, and he could not speak to my mother for fear of seeming to encourage her in wanton behaviour. Who knew what might happen while he was out on business during the day if she thought he smiled on her affections? But Uncle Hashim was capable. He revelled in his capacity to deal with things. Abbas's flight, his father's shame, the funerals, my mother's upbringing, all dealt with without fuss or neglect. This other little task proved equally manageable. He showed unmistakable friendship to my father, asking for his assistance in small matters and therefore putting himself in his debt, inviting him to eat with them when they had guests, and finally bringing up the subject of his marriage twice, once in jocular male company and the second time when they were sitting on their own on a bench by the road outside the house, taking the breeze. Who could resist such encouragement? Within a few months, when it was in any case clear that my parents spent their evenings ogling each other in the gloom, my father's relatives made their first approaches. Uncle Hashim dealt with that as well, making the touchy matter of the meagre dowry for my mother seem a deliberate act of pious humility by everyone concerned. After all, he was a Wahhabi and such worldliness was distasteful to him. It was only the arrogant and the ill-bred who made a show of their wealth. Once the dowry was sorted out, there were no further obstacles to the arrangement.

After the wedding, which, as is usual with weddings, was taken firmly out of Uncle Hashim's hands by women who considered themselves better able to arrange such matters, my father moved into the rooms above the shop. In the evenings, my parents sat on the perfumed terrace and whispered, at least in the early days, while Uncle Hashim reflected on the return of equanimity. Their whisperings late into the night charged the air and disturbed him at first, but he learnt to suppress his irritation about that and about my father's relatives who took to visiting the house to greet their new sister and to size up Uncle Hashim's money bags.

Uncle Hashim had a reputation for wealth which he never bothered to confirm or deny. He dealt in anything which came his way, in life as well as in business – and after all the two were not that different – and somehow or the cther came out safe. He bought and hoarded in times of plenty and sold when there were shortages. When the British were ruling, they let everyone get on with it, unless *it* was something they wanted or thought they needed, or its scarcity (because hoarded by some conniving banya or ruthless Arab trader) made them seem incapable of keeping their colony in good order. But then they got tired of all that ruling and the ungrateful bad-mouthing of the sullen and no longer silent people they had come to work for, and so they went away and left the unruly hordes to their own havoc.

Later, much later, when times became harder under our own home-grown bullies, Uncle Hashim diversified. He changed money into foreign, knew how to satisfy shipping regulations and customs restrictions, could be relied on to smuggle in whatever was needful: an electric oven, a toilet bowl, a consignment of cement. He was able to do this because he procured these things for the mighty but impoverished officials too, the very ones who might have stopped him in his affairs. They had to live as well, and cook and flush toilets and build houses for themselves and for their mothers and sisters, even though they were the ones who made and upheld the idiot laws that created scarcity. But that was what they were there for, what they had put themselves there for: to make laws and issue decrees which would be seen to be obeyed by everyone – on pain of some barbarism or another – while they, the lawmakers and the bullshitters, squatted over everyone's faces and issued their wastes on them.

41

Uncle Hashim knew how to deal with them, too, and did so with a kind of style which made him seem unsoiled by his dealings. He gave and took with equal courtesy, so that those he dealt with felt slightly flattered by their exchanges. His restraint was finely modulated. His voice was never raised except in greeting, yet an edge in his eye and tone gave a glimpse of the inner metal. When a shoplifter was caught in the area, he was first brought to Uncle Hashim, who then advised if he should be taken to the police or given a little beating to put him straight. If people argued about money, or some other honourable matter, they were sure to ask Uncle Hashim to arbitrate in the end. On every notable date – the eve of Ramadhan, Idd, the maulid Nabi, the return of a long-absent traveller – he invited a few people to his house to eat with him. As time had passed, Uncle Hashim had grown in wisdom. To him now every created thing had allegorical meaning. God created it all, and Uncle Hashim submitted himself to Him every day and prayed for guidance and mercy.

Emma called him *your cut-throat uncle*. Uncle Hashim would have stared with amazement at her directness, and then smiled with pleasure. He liked to think himself practical and attentive to his limitations, and Emma's assessment would have appeared as a flattering form of the same thing, that he recognized the boundaries of his interest and pressed home every advantage.

At first, my parents were too preoccupied with themselves to notice anyone else. They were full of smiles and a new significance. My father's college was six miles out of town by the sea, and he left early in the morning to catch the special bus for students who lived in town. Most of the students were boarders, and the out-of-town site comprised their quarters and their playing fields as well as their class-rooms. Classes went on into the afternoon, so all the students ate lunch in the college dining-hall together. By the time my father came home, shiny and sweaty from the long day, my mother would have done the washing, cooked and cleared lunch for Uncle Hashim and for herself, and cooked the supper. So, free of all her chores, she was ready to be attentive to him. He bathed himself in the warm water she had ready in a bucket, scooping the water over himself and humming with an undertone of anticipation, and then he joined her in their room. Later he went for a stroll and sat in the café for a while, but he returned home soon after sunset, and did not go out again until the following morning.

Their life together was an idyll. They stayed up talking into the early hours, whispering with their heads inches away from each other, telling stories about what had befallen them. He told her how his father, a short, combative man who loved to demonstrate his strength, ruled the family like a dictator. He forced everyone to wake when he woke up, issuing orders for the day's tasks without consulting anyone's wishes or opinions. It was important, he said, that they should live and behave as a family. His rules about what was acceptable and what was not in this regard were detailed and mostly inflexible: they consisted of everyone doing what he said. He worked the hardest and longest of all of them, talking all the time at anyone within hearing – hectoring, blaming, advising – leaving not a chink of space for eccentric ideas to take root. If he sensed resistance, he glowered with his crushing smile and said, *So you think you know better than me.*

My father, the youngest of the family, had two brothers and one sister. The sister was the eldest, eight years older than my father. None of them had been allowed to go to school, even though they asked. At the brothers' request to join the school which had just been opened, his father had grinned with surprise, a special grin which he kept for such absurdities. *You can't be serious*, he said. *I need you on the land.* He berated the sister for days about her wanting to go to school so she could do filthy things with boys. It had been his practice never to hit his daughter. He left that to her mother, while he dealt with the boys when need arose, which it did regularly. But in his rantings about her desire to go to school, her disgusting betrayal of his care, her filthy plot to dishonour herself and her family, he came close to slapping her several times, only prevented from doing so because her mother never strayed far when he began his harangues, and threw herself at him with cries of warning and pleas for mercy.

When my father was seven years old, his eldest brother, who was thirteen, had taken him by the hand one morning and walked with him the one and a bit miles to the school on the main road to town. His father had said nothing as his mother fussed about his hair and his dirty feet, making these ugly noises to keep him from intervening. His mother often fussed over him, protecting him from his father's rages and saving him from the harshest of the chores decreed for him. When his father was defeated in this way, he called him *ayal mama*, mother's boy. After he started school, his father called him this all the time for the first few weeks, as if he had forgotten his name, but also to make it clear that it was only because his mother made such a fuss that he was allowing these insane goings-on. But whenever he thought it necessary, he told my father to stay behind and help with the work. Sometimes this staying-behind lasted for several weeks, until it was obvious that there was nothing for my father to do, when one of his brothers or his sister would say sharply to him, *What are you hanging around here for? Go back to school.* He missed so much school-time in this way that he had to repeat years because he was absent during examinations or was simply too unprepared to pass them. Then when he completed Standard Eight and was offered a place at the teaching college, his father refused to pay the fees, though these were only thirty-two shillings per term, a sum so small that it could only be a token of the student's goodwill and commitment, yet impossible for someone like my father to find for himself.

By this time my father's sister was already married. Her husband came from a family which was distantly related. He lived in the town and was apprenticed to a house-painter. It was this sister who went to see the relatives on her mother's side, and took with her a gold bracelet which her mother had given her to pawn for the fees. In this way my father came to live in town and go to college. His relatives fed him and gave him a place to stay. Times were hard then, just after the war, and there were food shortages of all kinds, so he was grateful to them for the way they had taken him in with such little fuss, and he tried not to be a burden. His sister would have had him, she said, but they rented one room in a poor quarter of the town, and struggled to feed themselves. He was better off with the relatives. She came to visit him now and then, and whenever she had been to the country to visit the family, she brought them all gifts of fruit.

He made friends at the college, and in the late afternoon after class he strolled on the sea-front with some of them while they gossiped and teased each other frenziedly. After the sunset prayer, they went to the café or went home to eat, while some of the older ones went for another stroll in search of more secret pleasures. My father had no money and felt very conscious of this when he sat in the café, empty-handed and on the edges of the crowd, listening to the exchanges. Every evening they came back to the subject of India's independence, marvelling at the collapse of British resolve. One evening, one of the big talkers at the café was making fun of Gandhi as the naked banya who had scared the British away with his lingam. My father found himself speaking heatedly about the power of the skinny old man who refused to be intimidated by the crushing force of the British Empire, and the disarming impact of his non-violence, and how his willingness to give his life for the liberation of India gave energy to hundreds of thousands. When he had finished he expected to be mocked, but everyone was polite, and he left gratefully soon after.

He stayed home in the evenings after that, feeling sure that everyone despised him for his poverty and for his high-handed intervention in their conversations. After supper he did whatever college work he had, which was never much, and then read through his text books: geography and history had the best stories. He had been given a tiny room which was previously a store – there were still two locked trunks one on top of the other at the foot of his bed – and the room had not been wired for electricity. So he worked by the light of a kerosene lamp which sat on the trunks while he balanced a board across his lap as a writing surface. He could only half open the door, and when he changed or dressed he had to stand in one place or lie down on his bed. But he was grateful for the security and the privacy of his little space. No one harangued him about anything, and he was free to withdraw whenever he wished.

He had caught glimpses of my mother on the terrace, coming and going between the lines of washing, and had looked away politely in case she should see him and take offence at his scrutiny. One Sunday morning, when he had lain late in bed, he was leaning on the wall by the little slit of his window, looking idly down at the terrace and wondering what he could do to fill the empty day. He saw her come out with a bucket full of washing and watched her as she hung it up. She stretched for the line, frowning in the mid-morning sun, and he saw that she was beautiful. He watched her for only a minute and then drew back, but after that as soon as he entered his cell he went to the window to see if she was on the terrace. Once she caught a glimpse of him and he retreated in confusion, but the next time he stood his ground, though he pretended to be looking in another direction. He found out that she sat on the terrace in the evening, and he took to standing by his window, looking towards her and falling in love with her, imagining the fragrance of roses and lavender swirling around her. Sometimes she sang, or she stretched out on the mat, gazing at the sky. She only stayed for half an hour or so, and did not always even glance in his direction, but he waited for the moment every day, woke up with anticipation of it, stumbled through the day towards it. Very occasionally she did not appear, when perhaps they had a guest in the house or she had gone to call on a bereaved family or to celebrate a wedding (he explained to himself), and then he felt abandoned and sore in his heart, as if she had died and left him for ever.

Whenever he saw Uncle Hashim in the streets he felt absurd about his secret love. He greeted him politely when they passed, as did everyone, even though Uncle Hashim was only in his late twenties. He was a tall man, with a firm assertive stride and an unambiguously assured manner. Whenever he saw him, my father felt as if he had been laughably naughty to have spent all those dark hours staring at this man's sister and making fantasies about her. Then one evening Uncle Hashim came on the terrace and turned and saw my father there at the window, prying dishonourably on women's lives. My father was sure he had been seen. The slit in the wall was the only window on that side of the house, and for some reason he thought that everyone knew he lived in the tiny store-room in his relatives' house. At the least he expected exposure and scorn, perhaps a beating. But Uncle Hashim did not even break his stride when they next passed in the street, while my father was already cringing in expectation of a blow or an insult. Even more surprisingly, he was shown marked favour, so much so that his relatives began to say among themselves that Uncle Hashim must want him for his sister, and so it unmistakably proved.

My father's sister worked out the strategy. She would speak to the relatives, and get their uncle to go and have a quiet chat with Uncle Hashim, just to see how matters stood. In the meantime, my father was to go home for a few days – he had only been once in the seven months he had been living in town – and explain what was going on to their father. Would she not come with him? She would come later, she said. In a few days.

So this is the kind of education you've been getting, his father said. *That's not what I sent you to school for.* One of his brothers farted at this point. It was done deliberately to provoke, for his father could not bear anyone farting within earshot of him, was driven into a frenzy by it, felt it as a deliberate insult to his person and his honour. He rose and chased after his son, down the front steps into the grove of breadfruit trees, shouting obscenities and curses, as far as the first open field of maize, where he stopped for a few minutes for a final round of malediction and a piss against the trunk of a coconut tree, and then strode back to the house. *So this is the kind of education I sent you to town for,* he said when he had finished describing the intimate shortcomings of his son. *I've no money for a dowry, and your two elder brothers are still not married.* My father had nothing to say except that he loved the girl and that he thought her elder brother wished for the marriage. It seemed as if his father could keep the conversation going for years, in between insisting that my father change into working clothes and come out on the land. After a few days of this, his sister turned up with the arrangements that had been agreed between their uncle and Uncle Hashim.

My mother was a willing party to these arrangements, and even before she was officially betrothed to my father, she uncovered her face and spoke to him when they met in the streets, marvelling at his clear smile and his laughing voice. People saw them like this and grinned as they saw how things were. When it came to signing the marriage certificate, she put her thumb on it and wrote an X. She had never been to school at all, she told my father, though Uncle Hashim had attended up to Standard Five. Her father had opposed the idea when her mother asked. Other mothers were beginning to insist that their daughters should be sent to school as well as their sons, which is what had emboldened her mother to raise the matter. But he had said no, and that was that. After her parents' passing away, she had gently asked Uncle Hashim, expecting a refusal or worse, if it was too late for her to go to school (she was then thirteen), and he said it was. In later years she would lament to him about that, accusing him of keeping her as ignorant as a beast when an opportunity had been there for her to educate herself a little, perhaps learn to read and write and do sums, so she would not have felt quite such a child when these things needed to be done. She told my father about that time during those first months, when the stories seemed endless, and the desire for them and for other intimacies seemed impossible to satisfy.

I remember the first time your sister visited me after the wedding, my mother said, lying as close as she could to his miraculous warmth, their heads close together. His sister had stared at my mother's gold bracelets, part of Uncle Hashim's wedding gift to her, with such calculation that my mother had laughed. It was as if she was weighing them with her eyes, which then travelled around the reception room looking at the rugs and the mirrors and the stoppered glass jars that their father had bought as decoration when he furnished his new house. Despite the crudeness of this appraisal, my mother was still inclined to like her sister-in-law because of the stories her husband had told her. They laughed over her antics, and he explained how poor she and her husband were. And anyway, all their lives they had been poor. Their house in the country was overcrowded and primitive, with only two rooms and a store. His parents slept in one room and the three brothers had slept on a mat in the other. His sister had slept in the hallway. There was no electricity, their water came from the well at the end of the yard and there was a pit-latrine at the other end of the backyard. Everything about that house reeked of paltriness and poverty.

So my mother did not at first mind the cold scrutiny she was subjected to by her sister-in-law. But when she began to come to the house just before lunch, not once or twice, but every other week or so, to ask Uncle Hashim for help with the rent, or to say that they had run out of cooking oil, or that her husband's last pair of sandals had broken and she had no idea when he could get another pair, my mother felt humiliated by her display. It brought disgrace to her husband, who did not know about these visits because no one told him, but who none the less was the one who had made them possible.

Uncle Hashim did not appear troubled by them. He greeted my father's sister politely whenever she came, and asked about her health and her family's health as he handed out whatever had been asked of him. He gave my mother the daily housekeeping as he had been doing for the last couple of years (and sometimes brought some nice fish to add to the one she bought daily), and every month gave her some money for herself and for my father. He just gave her the money, giving no explanation and requiring no account. *Here, take this.* And my mother took the notes with cupped hands and understood. People she had known for years as Auntie this and Bibi that called on her now entreatingly, recounting petty tales of woe for small alms. Uncle Hashim's money allowed her to act with dignity towards these old mothers. My father's fees also came out of this money, as did the new shirts and trousers he bought to wear to college, as well as the odd bit of material for a new blouse for her. Sometimes my mother suggested something my father should get: a new pair of sandals at Idd or another bag for his books, and once she gave him a belt which she had had the cobbler make for him. It was the same cobbler who had made the sandals for him, proper makbadhi in beautiful soft leather, and who had refused payment when he went to collect them, saying he would settle up with Uncle Hashim. When he exchanged casual greetings with people in the streets he heard them say after him that he was Uncle Hashim's brother-in-law –

mkwewe wake – and sometimes they asked that they should be remembered to him.

It came to him slowly, over a year or so, that he had grown to fear Uncle Hashim. He had always been intimidated by his assurance, but now he was afraid of his displeasure and was sure that Uncle Hashim felt only scorn for him. He did not feel this all the time, and not because of anything Uncle Hashim said, though he had a way of smiling at him which he found quelling. They even sat together at times, and exchanged their days' news or stories they had picked up in the streets, but it was always clear that Uncle Hashim preferred these exchanges to be brief. Sometimes my father would forget his fear and his dependence. It might be while he was at college, immersed in work or playing hard at games. Or when he was sitting alone in their room lost in one of the books he borrowed from his friends, or when my mother came to lie beside him in the dark at the end of the evening. But sooner or later every day, without drama or suddenness, these feelings of dread and misery rose from somewhere inside him and made him feel as if he was drowning. Then he felt his shoulders drop and his chest cave in and a strange soreness in his temples. He would throw his shoulders back and stride off in one direction or another, barking at himself and slapping his thigh (surreptitiously, so people should not think him mad as well as pitiful), trying to free himself from the sensation of choking. But after a few wild strides he would slow down and feel himself subsiding again. Whenever he thought of himself and how things were with him, he felt himself burning.

When he found out about his sister's begging missions, which he was bound to sooner or later, he was so ashamed that he could not return to the house for hours; he went charging towards his sister's house instead, but turned back without confronting her. The rivulets of slime which snaked through the alleys of the area she lived in and the middens beside which people sat in conversation and which chickens scratched at, made him calmer. Why could he not be like her? Why could he not make the most of the good fortune that had befallen him? What was it that made him feel so desolate? When he got back, he sulked at my mother, asking her how she could bear to touch a stinking pitiful beggar like him. She did not scold or soothe him, did not know how to. She sat in front of him with shining eyes and watched the man who had glowed for her in the dark turn bitter and afraid of the world. And her love for him diminished with every day of his misery and his loneliness.

That was how they were when I arrived. My father's sister came the day after the birth and spread her bedding on the floor of my parents' room, and stayed for weeks. My father was ejected to the reception room, where he spread his mat at night and rolled it up in the morning, so my mother could be installed in there to welcome visitors. My aunt took charge of the cooking, of the house, of my mother and of me. Her parents were instructed to come and gaze on their grandson, and to see how she supervised Uncle Hashim's household. Uncle Hashim himself unprotestingly made himself scarce, though he made sure to give the daily household money to my mother and resisted my aunt's attempts to confide in him her suggestions to improve their lives. It would have been a hilarious interlude if my parents had known how to get rid of her, but they didn't. My father retreated into gloomy silences and my mother had enough on her hands coping with the strange things that had happened to her body and listening to the never-ending advice which people were constantly giving her. In the end, Uncle Hashim told my aunt that it was time she returned to look after her husband, and we would manage as well as we could on our own. She went reluctantly, but in any case came round every day. If anything needed doing she did it, increasing everyone's obligation to her. Then she stayed until lunch-time, took a portion of the food for herself and her husband and left with promises to return the next day. She would feel terrible if she stayed at home, and was not there when her brother's wife and her own son (that was me) needed her. My mother found these daily visits hard, and fought silently to contain them and reduce them. She succeeded to some extent, but never fully, so for years to come my aunt and her husband were served lunch from our kitchen, and I had to agree to be called her son. My mother disliked this utterly, and did what she could to prevent my aunt fondling me or holding me. Her fondling and holding had a ribbed feel to it, so I was on my mother's side on this. By the time my aunt left for the day, my mother was miserable and tired and wanted to be left to weep her frustration and loneliness.

A new silence descended on my parents' lives. By this time my father was teaching in a school in the country, leaving first thing in the morning and not returning until late in the afternoon. It was not that they did not talk to each other, but their affectionate ways with each other were replaced by a habitual politeness and increasing exasperation. My mother was a soft-spoken woman, and her exasperation often took the form of silence and withdrawal. For my father, his misery had hardened and transformed itself into something which no longer resembled its sources.

I said to Emma that I could not quite understand how my father had become like that, why he had allowed his fear of dependence to overwhelm him as it did. But everything was grist to Emma's mill at the time, and without further thought she said, 'He hated himself. Because he had no dominion over his life.'

Dominion! She had words like that even then, words that flashed and glittered and made everything seem different. 'But I don't have dominion over my life and I don't hate myself.' I said *dominion* with exaggerated emphasis, so I don't know if the long look she gave was because of that or because she doubted that I didn't hate myself.

'Men are like that. First they allow themselves to be swept away

53

by the seduction of falling in love. Then when things become difficult they blame the woman for trapping them and then forcing them to give up freedom and ambition. Because that's what he did, wasn't it? He liked the idea of it all, this attractive young woman peeping at him behind her rose bushes. It was because of her that he found himself imprisoned again and delivered into the clutches of your gruesome uncle.'

'Then he should have hated her,' I said.

'He probably did,' she said, flying up (we had been lying down) as if she had now caught me in an immovable vice. 'But he hated himself more for being foolish enough to be trapped, and for minding being foolish. And there was your uncle and his own grasping sister to thicken the Oedipal brew that he hadn't resolved when he left his father's house.' Then she gave me a sharp nod of triumph, and lay down again.

3

I met Emma in a restaurant, the Costmary Grill in Primrose Road, SW19. It was later to become the Ellesmere Brasserie, but I met her there before its transformation. I had been washing dishes at the restaurant for about a month when she came to wait at tables. This is how I came to be working there. At that time I was living in a bed-sit in Tooting, the south end of it, just around the corner from the big intersection to Colliers Wood and Wimbledon. It was in a small terraced house owned by a Jamaican who was a builder, and who had done the renovations in a resourceful and individual style. So although I had nowhere in the room to keep clothes, no drawers or wardrobe, I had a built-in shower. It was what used to be a cupboard, and a less enterprising landlord would have left it alone as a space to hang a coat, or shirts, or to throw dirty laundry. The room also had an electric extractor fan, on a meter. 'No need to open the window now,' my landlord explained. 'This is a motherfucking cold country, boy. And when you fry your snapper, it don't have to stink up the whole house.'

A walk to the Common was cheap entertainment when I could summon the energy, and it wasted a lot of time, and took me away from the grubby though not uncomfortable room I lived in and the stubborn tasks my teachers required me to perform there. Strolling near the park one weekend morning, I saw a sign in the restaurant window advertising a vacancy: Staff Required. My suspicion was that it didn't mean me. I had lost confidence in my desirability, and I just could not conceive of myself as Staff. Also, something prim and solemn in the name and in the shape of the letters on the board over the restaurant's door told me that its denizens would probably be equally glum and bursting with self-regard. But I was desperate for money and was not allowed to work – it said so in my student visa. So I circled the street for half an hour, approaching the restaurant from different angles to make it look less alien and unwelcoming, and trying to talk myself out of my feebleness. Then on one of my sorties I saw a scrawnily thin man walk up to the restaurant door and begin to fiddle with a bunch of keys. He glanced at me and smiled. 'All right?'

Smart as a paratrooper I stepped up to him. 'Is that job still going, then?' I asked.

'Washing-up,' he said. 'Starting right away. Six till eleven.'

By the time Emma turned up, my excitement about the job had long vanished. Now it was just dirty, greasy water, recalcitrant crockery and feeding on crumbs. (Yes, I used to pick at the leftovers if they had not been messed up too much.) My corner of the kitchen was powerfully lit so I would not miss any of the grease and muck on the dishes. At times the lights made me feel as if I was a prisoner in a camp, surrounded by a mob of irritable, yelping mockers. It had been exciting at first to watch the skill of the cooks, especially their frightening facility with the knife, the economy of their movements and their exhilaration and involvement. But a month later they seemed frenzied and petty, cynical about their customers and vengefully competitive with each other, burning up in their squabbles and feuds while so many dangerous instruments lay scattered around them. The scrawny man turned out to be Peter, the chef, Phut-Phut as the German pastry-chef called him behind his back. Peter was the dictator of this kingdom, a whining, intemperate man and a champion squabbler who treated everyone as a subversive determined to thwart him on every matter. And because he whined at me as he did at everyone else, he made me feel comfortable at first, one of the crowd, even though I did not get to eat a meal with the other staff before the restaurant opened.

Emma was as beautiful then as she was ever going to be, though neither of us knew this or even thought about it. Every time she walked into the kitchen on that first night, whistles and groans met her, and Peter smirked as if this was something he had engineered all along. Emma was so flustered by this display that she stumbled blushingly through her tasks, a fixed, placatory smile on her face. She did not see anyone, nor did she appear to hear any of the flirtatious things that were said to her, so it was with a kind of amazement that she came to a standstill in front of Peter when he began to harangue her in his usual way. After a moment of this, I thought she trembled or shuddered, then she walked away. Peter looked after her for a second and looked menacingly around for more insurrection. By this time it was a busy weekend evening and everyone was at a stretch. I did not notice her leave.

I did not see her again until the following Tuesday, as I had Sunday off and she had Monday. Then she smiled at me and said that she had heard I was a student too. It was probably Peter. He usually waxed lyrical on the theme of student parasites, and although he never raised this interesting elaboration, a *foreign* student parasite must have aggravated all his senses of decency and English fair play. Anyway, Emma stood nearby while I fiddled in my greasy tub (it was a quiet evening) and talked to me. I saw that though her beauty had not diminished, there was none of the wild male display of her first night, only the eyes still loitered on her every move. Perhaps something had happened on Sunday, or perhaps something in her manner made the men feel ridiculous. In any case, she stood nearby, leaning against the counter and lightly tapping the surface with her nails. When it was quiet like this, I liked to dim the lights a little in my corner, to diminish the glare of those imprisoning lights. 'I am at University College,' she said. 'Doing English.'

'I'm at the Institute of Education.'

She tried but could not quite manage to suppress a smile. She was so very beautiful that I forgave her without a qualm. I told her that I was there to train as a teacher, just in case she should begin to imagine that I might be engaged in something more grand, like a research degree or a project on the failure to provide for the educational needs of ethnic minorities or something like that. An intellectual foot-soldier, I told her with a self-deprecating smile. Better to say it yourself, when it might have an edge of modesty and humility about it, rather than receive it in anger and blame and derision. She was in her second year then and living just by Wimbledon tube station. Tuesday evening passed very pleasantly in this way, though Peter did stand in front of me on two occasions with arms akimbo. Phut-Phut. Emma was called away to attend to something, but she came back and stood nearby again, talking about her work and her friends and where she lived. I had not really expected her to come back, or had prepared myself not to expect her back, but she seemed eager to return. I tried to be easy and calm, to chat casually and not to let go.

Evidently something got to Peter in the end, for he stood in front of me again and told me I could doss on the State if I wanted but I wasn't going to doss on him. 'That's the kind of idiot country we have become,' he said, eyes blazing with what looked like the beginning of tears. 'Thousands can just walk off the plane and live off us, but you're not doing that in my kitchen, young man. No way, José. Not on your life. Get your finger out, son.' That burst of poetic speech could not disguise his anguish, though. At that time newspapers and televisions were full of stories and pictures of queues of Indian matrons and toddlers descending aeroplane steps loaded with toys and presents, of airport lounges crowded with saris and turbans, of lean young Pakistanis with downy moustaches who had been discovered in crates consigned from Rouen to Darlington (or it could be Boulogne to Deal), of passport frauds, of overcrowded tenements, rising crime and drug overdoses, of bogus fiancées, and of reports of the congenitally low

IQ-ratings of people from coloured lands and predictions of the end of civilization as we know it. So I understood Peter's distress and was sorry to be even partly the cause of it. I might have said something encouraging. *Chin up, old Phut-Phut, they are not really as many as they look, and they come here full of love for you.* But he looked as if he was on the edge of one of his harangues, despite the melting in his eyes.

He glanced at Emma, and with a sharp motion of his head sent her away. Every time she came into the kitchen Peter glared at me, daring me to defy him, so I kept my eyes lowered or away from her. Eventually she came in when he wasn't in sight, and I looked into her eyes and saw that she was laughing. She left at ten-thirty, calling out good-night and giving me a small wave.

She came back to me at various times throughout the next day, and I smiled when I thought that I would see her later that evening. I did not expect that she would really be interested in someone like me – why make problems for yourself? – I was just looking forward to her company and to gazing at her while she spoke to me. The first time she came into the kitchen after I had arrived she gave in her order and came smiling up to me.

'What time do you call this?' she asked.

'I start later,' I said.

'I thought you weren't coming,' she said and then rushed off. When she returned, and came over to say that she had gone past the Institute today and that we should meet for lunch in town one day, Peter could not bear the sight of me any more. 'You're out,' he shouted at me. 'Now.' He expelled Emma from the kitchen and then proceeded to utter a stream of filth at me, whose metaphors attempted to evoke my degraded and uncontrollable lust. I could feel myself tumescing as his description acquired detail and definition. I did not contest any of it, but hung up my plastic apron, kissed him on both cheeks and departed without even asking for any pay. Who needs a carving knife between the ribs? I had seen Peter slice a whole cucumber into ribbons in less than a minute.

Did I expect Emma to rush out after me? Perhaps, but of course she didn't. I considered hanging around until she finished for the evening, or going for a drink and returning at ten-thirty. It was a pleasant evening, autumn just turning into winter, with a subtle chill in the air that was ideal for a brisk walk along the margins of the Common. But someone might turn up while I was hanging around, and start a conversation full of aggressive charm. And I didn't really want a drink, and only nutters, muggers, rapists and suicides walked around the Common at night. So I walked back towards my room, feeling that this was one of those decisive moments in my life, and lamenting that Phut-Phut's biologized vision of existence had determined its sad outcome. And that would have been that, no doubt, though I can't conceive the thought that Emma might not have happened to me, that everything could have been different, that she might have been leading another life, that I might at this moment have been living on the other side of the world in some upside-down place doing something quite other. In any case, as you well know, that wasn't that, and Emma did happen to me.

She transformed everything. I woke up in the morning thinking myself smart and enterprising, instead of alien and depressed. I caught myself in unusual acts of jauntiness: humming as I walked, smiling broadly when a polite twitch of the lips would have done, trying on sunglasses in Boots. When I felt myself unfairly or discourteously dealt with, I swaggered to claim restitution rather than walking away with a sinking heart and averted eyes. My contributions to class-room discussions increased and were even-tempered and thought out instead of being rare, impulsive outbursts that left everyone bemused and at a loss. My seminar leaders beamed at me and I glowered self-importantly. Even my essays acquired a more confident voice: I took a stern position on creativity and learning, for example, whereas before I would have just repeated the wet-liberal orthodoxies about self-expression spouted in tutorials. My tutor, twisting and turning like an angel on a pin, described this position as classicist, by which I took it that she meant intolerant, but she graded the essay highly.

I could not credit the affection Emma showed me, the praise she heaped on me. I struggled to cling on but it seemed I could do no wrong. Every evening (she had given up the Costmary Grill) she came to my room and we cooked some nameless concoction and talked and worked and played. It seemed the talk could go on and on without end. There hardly seemed a pause, everything merged seamlessly and effortlessly. These evenings were so regular that Emma's landlady, a loving woman with endless rules about what her student guests could do, began to feel guilty about charging her for dinner – though she still continued to do so. Sometimes she stayed the night, and we murmured away through the long hours, well into the night and sometimes until dawn, as if there would be no tomorrow. She brushed away my embarrassments and temerities and made me laugh about the most improbable things, the most painful things. It was love, headlong stuff.

She took me into places I had passed with only a sideways look of misgiving: specialist second-hand bookshops, vegetarian cafés, jewellers, jazz clubs – places I expected to be evicted from with guffaws of derision, places which intimidated me with their undisclosed rituals. Even my alienness seemed heroic to her, in the first place because I was a victim of historical oppression, which earned me automatic sympathy, and in the second because (so she said) I was calm in the face of all the provocation, unperturbed and clear-headed about the seductions of scapegoated radicalism. She even made me feel that I was calm, unperturbed and clear-headed rather than feeble and unnerved, as I suspected in my weaker moments. She drew me into her circle of friends so completely that at times I forgot myself, and I imagined that I looked as they did, and talked as they did, and had lived the same life that they had lived, and that I had always been like this and would go on unhindered way beyond the sunset. But this was only at times, as a kind of fulfilment of the moment of communion. For my alienness was important to all of us – as their alienness was to me, though it took a long time for me to say that even to Emma. It adorned them with the liberality of their friendly embrace of me, and adorned me with authority over the whole world south of the Mediterranean and east of the Atlantic. My word, unless it was utterly implausible, superseded all others on these regions. It was from these beginnings that it became necessary later to invent those stories of orderly affairs and tragic failure. I was allowed so much room that I could only fill it with invention. I did not think that the messy contortions of my own experience would do the trick in the way that stories of strangers on a moonlit terrace could.

In those first months, Emma hardly mentioned her parents, though I knew they lived in Blackheath because she went to stay with them for some special family events. She waved them away when I asked. No, it wasn't them she was interested in, but my parents, my friends, my country. And I was only too happy to oblige, to retell stories, dwell on them, elaborate. In my stories I found myself clarifying a detail, adjusting it so that its impact was unobscured, even at times adding a variation that added irony and a note of bitterness to what might otherwise have seemed banal. I found the opportunity to rewrite my history irresistible, and once I began it became easier and easier. I did not mean to lie to Emma, dupe her out of contempt or disregard while I exploited her for her affection. I don't exactly know why I began to suppress things, change other things, fabricate to such an extent. Perhaps it was to straighten out my record to myself, to live up to her account of me, to construct a history closer to my choice than the one I have been lumbered with, to cling to her affection, to tell a story which would not bore her. Later, she would sometimes catch me out in an inconsistency and would give me a long stare while I flopped about like a beached creature, wriggling in a tangle of my own making.

Uncle Hashim and my father came to me out of the midnight air, when my voice had hit a weary timbre and found its echo in the story of love's petty failure.

I must have been in school for a few years when Uncle Hashim built himself another house on the other side of the road, with a large shop-space on the ground floor and an airy apartment upstairs with a stone-balustraded balcony looking out on the main road. One window in the reception room of the old apartment looked towards Uncle Hashim's new house, though at something of an angle. People began to talk about Uncle Hashim planning a wedding, but it was as much for business reasons as for anything else that he decided to move. He opened his electrical-goods shop first before proposing marriage to a daughter of another merchant called Nassor Abdalla, a man for whom Uncle Hashim felt respect and friendship. It seemed only a very brief time before Uncle Hashim's new wife had a son and a daughter, one after the other, by which time her husband was acquiring a reputation for a new restlessness when women strolled by. People smiled at the appetites his wife must have awakened.

My parents lived in the old apartment rent-free. My father was a teacher of history at the school I attended, the largest primary school in the town. He taught the senior forms, Standard Seven and Standard Eight, and at the time when Uncle Hashim moved out I was still in Standard Six, so I had not yet come under his tutelage. He was a serious and stern teacher where work was concerned, although he also had a reputation for being indulgent with his favourites, who were always the quiet hard-working students. The two always seemed to go together then, the clever ones were quiet and small, and the difficult ones were big and loud. I was quiet and small. There was talk that my father would be sent to the university in Makerere for in-service training so he could be promoted to teach in a secondary school. It was then only three or four years before Independence, but the majority of the secondary-school teachers in the country were European, mostly British, but a handful were from the settler colonies in the south. They had the necessary expertise, it was thought, and the lads and ladies had to have jobs, or what was the point of having an Empire? Their salaries were levied on the colony, of course. So the Colonial Office despatched scores of genial (so they thought themselves), mostly Oxbridge graduates to the far corners of the globe, to awe and succour the natives with simultaneous equations, Shakespeare and Romans in Britain. My father never did get to go to Makerere, but he did get to teach in the secondary school.

Our family spread itself after Uncle Hashim's departure. The three of us – Akbar, Halima and me – shared Uncle Hashim's old room. It was unusual to allow a girl to share with her brothers but Halima was very small, only three, and in any case thought she was a boy. My father bought himself a transistor radio, which occupied a new corner table in the reception room. He also brought out some of his books and hung a framed print of the Kaaba and the mosque at Makka. In the evenings he occupied this room in solitary splendour, trawling the short-waveband for any likely items of interest, reading his books, marking school work. He would sit there alone all evening. It was what we thought he wanted. If he was out for some reason or was late at the café, we profaned this solemn space by listening to the local radio, which at that time of the evening played listeners' requests and repeated the serialized story broadcast earlier in the day.

My mother sat with us then, though she never sat in the reception room in the evenings. When she had cleaned up after supper, she did other little jobs for a while – mending, soaking clothes for the morning wash, ironing our school uniforms at the beginning of the week. After that she went out on the terrace and stretched out in the gloom as she always used to. The roses and lavender bushes were gone. A blight on the roses and the presence of little children had combined to kill them off. The rusted kerosene tins were still there, still full of soil but now dried up and caked into bricks, and one of them contained a spiky and bitter aloe which my mother had planted from a cutting years ago and whose white sap she had later rubbed on her nipples when she needed to wean us from the breast.

She was always deliberate and soft-spoken, with a bubble of teasing humour in her voice, and a way of pressing her lips together which made her seem as if she was suppressing a smile. When I was smaller, I loved this calm in my parents, the silences they carried around with them, the way they shuffled around each other so accommodatingly. It was only later that I realized that they rarely said very much to each other, and just as rarely sat anywhere near each other, that they avoided each other to keep the peace.

As a government employee, my father could not openly join a political party or be an activist. Since politics consisted largely of agitating for the departure of the colonial authority, it was not hard to see why the administration thought it right to act in this headmasterish way. It did not make that much difference. Politics was what everyone did and talked about: in the streets, at the café, at school, at home. Some people blustered and gloated gleefully at the colonizers' diminishing manoeuvres, shouting obscene remarks when European officials drove stonily by. It was not treatment the officials were used to, and both they and our European teachers dealt with this hostility by ignoring it with set faces. Even the few tourists from the cruise ships making their customary one-day stop caught some of it, being followed around the streets by jeering boys and meeting stroppily unhelpful natives when they stopped to ask their smilingly ignorant questions. Others, like my father, were always at hand to offer a more considered opinion. My father liked to say that you had to retain a sense of history and see what lay behind all this, rather than just assume that a bunch of noisy marchers and loud-mouthed café lizards were going to drive away armies with guns and warships and jet planes. He did not say this at the café, for there he would only have received derisive howls of laughter for reply. What was happening in Algeria then? What else did he think was driving the oppressor away if not the determined protests of the oppressed? Did the French look as if they wanted to leave? He said his cautious words about a sense of history at home, when something he had heard elsewhere would return to him and make him indignant.

We kept track of other colonial departures like keeping score in a game: Ghana, Nigeria, Somalia, the Congo, Senegal, Mali, then much nearer home: Tanganyika, Uganda – many of them places where spectacular disasters were waiting to happen. In the streets people bickered over the details of constitutional conferences, with their special clauses on this and that, over new flags and anthems, over designs of stamps. Heroic leaders indiscriminately filled the imagination: Kwame Nkrumah, Ahmed Sekou Toure, Patrice Lumumba, Jomo Kenyatta. There were new maps to be studied, new names, new countries that seemed to surface with incredible solidity out of the featureless mass that had previously been Africa.

But politics also brought shocking things to the surface. We liked to think of ourselves as a moderate and mild people. Arab African Indian Comorian: we lived alongside each other, quarrelled and sometimes intermarried. Civilized, that's what we were. We liked to be described like that, and we described ourselves like that. In reality, we were nowhere near *we*, but us in our separate

66

yards, locked in our historical ghettoes, self-forgiving and seething with intolerances, with racisms, and with resentments. And politics brought all that into the open. It was not that we did not know these things about ourselves, about slavery, about inequalities, about the contempt with which everyone spoke about the barbarity of the savage in the interior who had been captured and brought to work on our island. We read about these things in our colonized history books, but there these events seemed lurid and far away from the way we lived, and sometimes they seemed like self-magnifying lies. So when the time came to begin thinking of ourselves in the future, we persuaded ourselves that the objects of this abuse had not noticed what had happened to them, or had forgiven and would now like to embrace a new rhetoric of unity and nationalism. To enter into a mature compromise in everyone's interest. But they didn't. They wanted to glory in grievance, in promises of vengeance, in their past oppression, in their present poverty and in the nobility of their darker skins. To the nationalist rhetoric of their opponents they proclaimed a satirical reprise of their despised Africanness, mocked the nationalists for their newfound conscience, and promised them an accounting in the very near future. All of which came to pass with incredible promptness.

Before then we still had to go through our own constitutional conferences at Lancaster House, our finely tuned protection clauses for every vulnerable minority, our debates about the possible dates for our release, and in the far future (as it then seemed in our impatience), the ceremonies of the great day itself. There were still election riots to take place, commissions of inquiry to be held into the causes of the riots, conspiracies to uncover, trials for sedition to take place, elaborate handover plans to be made, and a new flag and an anthem to be created, both of which appeared miraculously from an office in London.

My father secretly donated money to the party of the nationalists, afraid of doing so openly in case he was dismissed from his job. My father's sister became one of the stalwarts of the women's wing of the party, organizing, haranguing, getting people out, leading the chanting and ululations, and, as rumour had it, having herself a thoroughly good time in every way. Actually it was more than rumour, as I found out for myself. My mother sent me to her house with a message one afternoon, not the one room in the poor quarter where she and her husband used to live, but a third-floor apartment in a quiet area of the town to which they had recently moved. Time had been good to both of them. And as the custom was never to lock the front door if you were in, I walked unhesitatingly into her apartment calling out the word for seeking admission, *hodi*. She could not have heard me, so with another cry of *hodi* I pulled aside the curtain to her bedroom. As I did so she leapt naked off the bed and I dropped the curtain, but not so quickly that I did not see the coach of our local football team lying on the bed with nothing on. I also saw how unexpectedly graceful my aunt was in her nakedness, how flowingly curved and full her body was. I ran away before she came out, and told my mother that she was not in. Until I told Emma about it, I kept her secret.

But despite her busy life, my aunt did not ignore my mother, who with her insistent encouragement attended every rally the nationalists held in the town, which was more or less once a week. My mother joined a crowd of women who would walk singing to the opposition's deepest stronghold if that happened to be the rally's venue. And it often was, more to aggravate and provoke the enemy than to recruit or seduce. It was a wonder that it did not lead to violence. My mother did this as she did everything else, with an unhurried, stoical air. It wasn't fun but it was necessary. She listened to the endless speeches with the same unflurried air, clapped at the abuse of opponents, and abuse is mostly what it was, and laughed her silent, bubbling laughter when some meanness had struck home.

Two evenings a week she attended literacy classes organized by

the party, and on those two evenings my brother and I were required to volunteer our services as teachers at the branch office
where the classes were held. So at last my mother had her chance
to go to school, to be taught how to write her name by children the
same age as her own. Her enthusiasm diminished once she had
learned to write her name, especially when it became obvious that
literacy was not to be a condition for the vote. This was just as
well, as I was about to go to secondary school and I found my
affiliation with the branch school embarrassing. Secondary-school
boys were supposed to be serious and above such things as politics.

That's where we were, a year from where we weren't, a year
from the brutal climax of our self-deceptions. At that year's end,
there was the midnight drama of the lowering of one flag and the
raising of another, the handing over of a rolled-up parchment,
and the playing of a brand-new anthem – smug ceremonials conducted with practised hauteur after the rehearsal of all those other
colonial departures. For our departing masters it was just a bit of
fun, really, even if slightly embarrassing. There was hardly time to
get used to the flag before the uprising, a matter of weeks. All the
lurid promises of an accounting suddenly came true: murder, expulsion, detention, rape, you name it. Weeks and weeks of it,
months, years, some of it. The bits of paper with their protection
clauses and their defence agreements and their assurances on
pensions and other such civilized paraphernalia were as quickly forgotten as the anthem and the flag. Instead, the radio blared mocking, gloating speeches, issuing detailed prohibition after detailed
prohibition like a demented bully: six-o'clock curfew until further
notice, public gatherings of more than three people are illegal
until further notice, cafés, schools, cinemas are closed until further
notice, all passports are invalid, all travel is illegal, all land is na-
tionalized. Gangsters roamed the streets with gleaming guns they
had liberated from the riot-police arsenal, plundering where they
chose, demanding a display of timid submission from everyone,

seeking out those with whom they had scores to settle, making a point of calling on the proud and arrogant to humiliate and abuse them. And we had to learn to get used to another new flag. In the centre of this flag was an axe, to intimidate and cow with its threat of brutality.

Where my father had given his support to the nationalists secretly for fear of dismissal, Uncle Hashim had done so openly and prominently. On occasion he had even sat on the platform at branch meetings or had been part of a welcoming delegation when a party notable came on a campaigning visit. He did not do these things with any great enthusiasm, but he was one of the eminents of our community, and it was his part to share in its undertakings, and to do so conspicuously. His display was remembered now, and within days of the uprising, after the ministers and the deputy ministers, the party leaders and their advisers had been taken in and humiliated before being summarily sentenced, it was the turn of the lesser notables. Three men dressed in plain clothes and carrying guns, who did not bother to identify themselves because Uncle Hashim already knew who they were, took him away to detention. They roughed him up a little, but nothing remarkable for those times, just a few slaps and a tongue-lashing. It was difficult to imagine Uncle Hashim's solemnly stern person being misused in this way, but his wife witnessed it all and reported it tearfully when my mother went to visit her at her father's home. Uncle Hashim's house, its contents and his electrical-goods shop were expropriated with immediate effect. That meant at once. On the following day someone moved into the upstairs apartment, and a truck arrived to empty the store. He was to spend eighteen months in detention.

On the same day that Uncle Hashim was arrested, my father's sister came to our house. My father had wanted me to go to her apartment to see that she was unharmed, but my mother would not allow any of us to go out, not even my father. We had enough food for a few days, she said, and we'd just keep our doors locked for as long as we could. She even thought the terrace was risky, in case someone should see one of us from the road and demand entrance. My father rushed downstairs to open the door when my aunt knocked and called out. He recognized her voice. Even before she had climbed the stairs, the house was filled with her wails. She sat on the floor at the top of the stairs, sobbing as if her heart was broken, her face streaming as she wailed. 'They've killed them all,' she cried, and began heaving with sobs again.

'Who? Khadija, who's killed?' my father asked, on his knees in front of her, trembling.

'All of them,' she said, gulping and swallowing as if she was drowning. 'Everyone. Ma . . . Ba . . .'

A neighbour who had managed to make the trip to town safely had brought her word. This woman had heard a rumour from some of the other people they had travelled with on the truck, but then she had received definite news here in town from someone who said he had heard it from one of the killers. They had entered the house on the first night of the uprising. It had been planned beforehand. They had killed her father, her mother and her two brothers, and had thrown their dismembered bodies in the well.

My father sat down beside his sister, staring at her with disbelief, his lower lip trembling out of control. My mother turned to me, nodded towards my brother and sister and said, 'Go to your room.'

4

The first time she took me to meet her parents, Emma said, 'Don't tell them those kinds of stories. They'll just lap them up and start up on their racist filth. You don't know what they're like, they fatten up on that kind of thing. It makes all their obscene complacencies seem perfectly justified. I don't mean you should make anything up or something, but don't give them any more ammunition. They get enough of that off the TV.'

'Ammunition for what?' I asked, playing dumb, and earning a look of amazed disbelief.

'I'm serious,' she said. 'You don't know what they're like about these things.'

Oh yes I do, I could have said. *Unless they're something special.* But she needn't have worried. Mrs Willoughby was not interested in hearing any stories from me, although she might have condescended to listen to a couple of anecdotes on torture or starvation or child marriage, or some vital and contemporary narratives about drugs, prostitution, illegal entry or armed robbery. Anybody would. But she had her own way of dealing with me. She made polite conversation when she had to, and did not seem at all concerned with my share of the exchanges, hardly ever raised her eyes to meet mine. It was not that she was rude or openly unpleasant – she has never been that, not in all the years I have known her. But she had worked me out to her satisfaction early on and left it at that. In her presence I often felt like a third person, as if I was absent and the conversation was being reported to me later. She had an idea of the degree of intimacy she wanted there to be between us and she maintained that without too much clumsiness.

I admired this calm arrogance in her, which she made seem like tolerance, a mannered cultivation.

Mr Willoughby was only interested in my Empire stories. It made me wonder how he could have got through his life so far without the steady supply I provided him with, but perhaps I misjudged his resourcefulness. I could see the hunger in his eyes every time we met, and before long he'd find a way of creating an opening for me. Emma and Mrs Willoughby raised satirical eyebrows, but that did not make any impression on him, or at least he pretended it didn't. Sometimes, if we were expecting them to call, I'd work on one of these stories for days, but more often they just flowed.

Under the Empire we had firm and fair rule, governed by people who understood us better than we understood ourselves. Even at the worst of times, when what seemed harsh edicts were being issued, we knew they were for our own good, to force us into the light of civil society, to teach us to defer to rational government rather than despotic custom. The modest and mild-mannered colonial rulers politely but firmly curbed our petty princes from displays of capricious authority. They brought medical knowledge and care, both to succour our ills and wean us from superstition and evil spirits, and to lift from our shoulders the yoke of the witch-doctor and his many devils. Those who were mentally ill among us were taken to asylums instead of being locked in by their families out of shame. The destitute and the indigent were taken off the streets and put in camps where they could learn a useful trade, or at the least find sanctuary. But above all, the Empire selflessly brought us knowledge and education and civilization and the good things that Europe had learned to make for itself and which until today we have still not learned to make for ourselves. Instead of being left in our degenerate darkness for centuries to come, within a few decades we were opened up and dragged into the human community.

The magnanimity and sacrifice of individuals in the British

73

imperial service were both legendary and commonplace, so it was fortunate for us that we were colonized by them rather than by unpredictable and impulsive foreigners. Our rulers did not spare themselves, building roads, hospitals, bridges, prisons. Some of our young men and women found work in their homes and learned to love them. Some of the greatest men in our communities were only able to achieve what they did because benevolent officials had (without show or fuss) given them a guiding hand.

Mr Willoughby's eyes would sparkle at these stories, his lips would part with poignant enthralment. And even when, at times, I thought I had misjudged a detail and expected the sparkle to cloud with suspicion and the lips to close, he made no sign that he had noticed anything. 'Oh why', he would say in the end, 'did they abandon those poor people? It was a blockhead idea.'

'I blame the Americans,' I sometimes suggested. 'It was their misguided talk about democracy in the post-war world that did the damage.' Sometimes the blame went to someone else: Winston Churchill, Gamal Abdel Nasser, the Labour Party. Mr Willoughby effortlessly accommodated himself to any culprit.

'All it's done is to let the few rotten ones among them turn their people's simple minds against everything that happened before. Now look what's happening: chaos, starvation, wars. We have to spend more money sending aid than we would have spent if we stayed and kept a firm hand on the tiller. Blockhead idea.'

Emma laughed at first – *He'll believe anything about the Holy British Empire.* Then she protested that I was overdoing it – *You're exploiting his gullibility and making a fool of him.* Then in more recent times she stopped taking any notice – *I think this just shows what an infantile imagination you have.* In any case, Mr Willoughby and I entered into our own conspiracy, and we often waited until we were away from sceptical ears before we began, though at times of need the moment could not be deferred.

❖

Emma and I moved in together after we graduated. She got a brilliant First and stayed on to start a PhD on the semiotics of dedicated narrative. It was no surprise, her teachers had been predicting it all along. 'What does the dedicated bit mean?' I asked. 'Not all narratives carry the burden of events,' she said. 'They are not all stories.' She wasn't sneering. She didn't use to do it so much in those days but I could hear her restraining herself as she attempted an explanation. In three steps I was lost, and I couldn't tell if it was because I was dumb or because she couldn't make sense of what she meant. I got a middle Lower Second, which surprised my teachers a little but I was too drunk on love to care that much at first. I was pleased to get a job in a comprehensive school in Wandsworth. We rented a flat in Streatham, spent a happy weekend buying bed-sheets and table-mats, and settled down to a life of sin. Teaching was a nightmare, yet those first few years were the happiest of our lives together. In the morning I reluctantly left her beautiful warm body and took the bus to school. I found it hard to leave her, and returned to bed two or three times before finally tearing myself away. Once I got as far as the bus stop and went back for one more embrace.

When I got to school I was too new and too anxious to take my time over a cup of tea in the staff room, and I would go straight to my form room to prepare for the day. I had been given a first-year class in deference to my inexperience, but they were hard work enough. I taught some other years as well, all of them restless and tirelessly mocking. Teaching brought out a violence and anger in me I did not know I possessed. It was fear of being humiliated, of being laughed at. I pre-empted that with glowering looks and a stern voice, and, I have to confess, an occasional well-meant blow, but to my delighted surprise it worked – on most people. I developed a dirty little laugh which somehow took care of them. Whenever they were in doubt, my laugh reduced them to incomprehension. They probably thought I was a pervert of some kind, but it didn't matter so long as it provided small relief. I had my tormentors, but these were children with their own reputations to protect, and they did not succeed in inciting my more docile charges into rebellion. Not for long, anyway. I know I'm giving the best account of these times, so you can imagine how much worse it really was. Later I would learn ways of placating such radicals, but in those early days I had no idea at all how to deal with such sustained disdain. I knew they meant me harm.

I rushed away from school as soon as I could, and on most days I would find Emma already at home. I can't remember the precise order in which we did things, but I would find time to do some marking, then we would cook and talk or go to the pub and then make love. Even now, when I think of that time it recedes into a fug of contentment and intimacy and sex. We did not see very much of anyone, but some evenings we went in to her college because of some event – a dance, a talk, or just to have a drink with her friends. I wonder now that she did not get bored, staying at home with her books most days, and then spending the evenings at home with me.

I told her about how I came to England. By the time I had finished school, the new authorities felt secure enough of their grip on power, and had cowed everyone to such an extent, that travel to neighbouring countries was once again allowed on a limited basis and on a temporary travel permit. The permit was valid for three months, so failure to return within that period meant arrest when or if you did. And you had to cringe and beg for the travel permit as you had to for everything else. The plot we hatched was deep and desperate. Uncle Hashim had been released from detention by this time, even thinner and greyer, but otherwise as capable as ever. I never heard him say anything about the eighteen months he spent in jail, except that it gave him a chance to repay the time stolen from prayer and reading the Book when he had been free and busy with his business. If my mother or my father asked him a question about that time, he waved it away and said *Leave it*. And he certainly never said anything about the daily meals and the weekly change of clothes I used to take to the jail for him. In a very short time Uncle Hashim was back in business again, bringing in – somehow – small quantities of whatever was in short supply, testing the waters. He got hold of livestock, cloth, small hardware items, and whenever he could he dealt in foreign exchange. It was all illegal, but Uncle Hashim knew who to pay to turn a blind eye. He even got his house back, and although when he reopened it his shop did not have its previous splendour – no gleaming table fans and imposing radiograms now, but bags of cement and piles of enamel bowls – he still looked a man of affairs, sitting behind his big desk.

It was Uncle Hashim who suggested I should leave, though he had in mind a neighbouring country or the Gulf, somewhere where his contacts would help me find work and learn about business. Better than to wait here for something to go wrong, he said. The three of us, my father, my mother and I, were summoned to his house to discuss the matter. I said I wanted to study, and he nodded with his usual composure, but then could not resist a mildly mocking grin. Just like your father, he said.

At that time, scholarships to study in Czechoslovakia, East Germany, China or Cuba were easily available since our new state had aligned itself verbosely with socialism, and had accepted the fraternal assistance of several hundred technicians and technocrats in replacing all the people they had expelled or who had fled. The East Germans and the Cubans trained the expanded security forces, the Czechs and more East Germans taught in secondary schools, the Chinese took over the hospitals. Most of these teachers and engineers and doctors did not speak Kiswahili, or English, or Arabic, or even Gujerati, any one of which might have made it possible for them to be understood. It would be nice to say that this created an opportunity for a great deal of fun, but it didn't, not if you needed your tonsils seen to or you were in a diabetic coma. Anyway, Uncle Hashim must have thought I was interested in a scholarship to one of these fraternal socialist states when I said I wanted to study, for he said that I would come back a communist and an atheist, and then murder my family and commit abominations against God. Communism is evil, he said, and God will cut its head off one of these days.

'And the education is useless,' my father said. 'They train you to be a guerrilla and a drunkard, and that's about all. Or if they can, they marry you off to one of their ugly peasant women, the ones they can't find husbands for.' He was now working at the department of education, a technocrat, and although he was not directly involved with the scholarships, he knew from gossip (as did I and everyone else) that only the children of party cadres and those most desperate to leave applied for them. Or at least that was what we all said.

'He wants to go to England,' my father said. 'It's the best place to go for an education.' My father's love for his teachers had not faded despite his eloquence on the evils of colonialism. Every night he listened to the BBC in both English and Kiswahili, then listened to the Kiswahili Service of Radio Cairo, and finally he turned to our local station, laughing with derisive laughter at the news it delivered. On the solidity of English education he had no doubts. 'Even America does not compare,' he said.

Uncle Hashim nodded calmly, which I thought remarkable of him. 'How will this be done?' he asked, tilting his head a little with the patient air of a man of the world who was going to have to listen to some wild talk and then offer wise advice.

'We have found an address for Abbas,' my mother said, speaking softly but looking directly at her brother. Suddenly she could not help grinning. (When I got to this point Emma interrupted excitedly, *Your Uncle Abbas lives in England!* – but I waved her down.

A narrative has to have its deferrals, I told her, as you well know.) Anyway, my mother mentioned Abbas and then grinned with minor triumph. For the first time, Uncle Hashim's face registered dismay. 'He has been in touch with some of the people who escaped to England after the uprising, all those people who say they are going to come back and liberate us one day. We got the address from one of their relatives, Habiba Mahmoud, whose niece married that journalist you hear on the BBC sometimes. If Abbas agrees to take him, will you help us with the fare?'

Uncle Hashim was too stunned to say anything for a moment. 'It may be a risky arrangement,' he said at last, and it was obvious that he was thinking of Abbas, because he then turned to me and said, 'You don't know him. You don't know what he's like.'

'Let him take the risk, before they put him in jail or shoot him here,' my mother said. Uncle Hashim smiled thinly at the melodrama. I couldn't imagine that anybody would be interested enough to want to do that either, but it was not the moment to quibble. They could shoot me by mistake. Anything could happen in the shambles we were living in at that time.

Uncle Hashim would not commit himself for several days, but he wasn't idle. He contacted a business friend in Mombasa who owed him favours, and who was the external associate in his deals. This friend was to have a Kenyan passport prepared for my arrival in Mombasa, apparently a small matter for such a capable person, and was to be ready to purchase a ticket at the most advantageous rates, which in their language meant some kind of crookedness. My mother dictated a letter to Uncle Abbas, who either did not bother to reply or did not receive the letter. The address was somewhere called South Shields, which at that time sounded an unlikely place, too explicit to fulfil the romance of an English sanctuary for an absconder, so I assumed it did not really exist. Then there came a piece of luck which nearly made my mother blaspheme: *Perhaps God has not forgotten us after all,* she said. One of my father's colleagues at the education department, whose name was Ahmed Hussein, was awarded a British Council scholarship for an advanced administration course at Leicester University (the British government was in the process of rebuilding bridges with our government). He told us that I was young enough not to have to pay any tuition fees for a year or so, and that if my family could find a way to send me money, he'd help me out in England until I'd sorted something out. It was a madly generous offer, but in the general secrecy and misery of that time, people took risks to help each other out. I like to think it was some kind of assertion of human care, a sort of tribute to what had been lost, and perhaps the only way there was to protest against our impotence and cowed submission. But, he said, we had to understand that if I left in this way I would never be able to return. It was mad, but that's how I came to Blighty: a travel permit to Mombasa, a fake Kenyan passport, a tourist visa to England, and then secretly living in Ahmed Hussein's college room for a year. At that time, despite hysteria in the newspapers about naked foreigners taking over the land, the immigration services were not as efficient and brutal as they were to become later. We lived in a college house with twelve postgraduate students, all of them foreigners, and nobody betrayed me, not even the cleaning ladies.

Ahmed Hussein was only interested in work and saving as much of his allowance as he could. (He had come to some arrangement with Uncle Hashim which I was never party to, but the only money I received was from him, and that was just enough to buy books or a new pair of shoes.) We never went anywhere: we cooked for ourselves – mostly curry and rice, watched a little television and then worked. It was a bewildering picture of England. Most of the students at the technical college I went to were *Asian*, and most of the graduate students at the house, including Ahmed, were either Indian or Pakistani. Everyone shopped at the market and bought meat at the halal butcher. And although there was strict division in the kitchen between the vegetarians and the meat-eaters, the mingled aromas that rose from there were of spices and frying vegetables. The graduate students were all men, most of them with their families left behind. They talked of England with a mixture of derision and grievance, but gave their teachers and supervisors all their proud honorifics: Professor and Head of Department so-and-so, BA, or Senior Research Fellow Dr so-and-so, BA, MA, PhD, MMBA, RSAD.

Apart from the teachers at the technical college, who did not seem real anyway because they were so mild and understanding in their treatment of us, not like teachers at all, the only English people I came across were passengers on the bus or comedians on TV. Ahmed allowed us to watch one comedy programme an evening, and then we both had to go upstairs to work. His regime was so severe, and my fellow students were such a diligent example, that our teacher persuaded six of us to attempt our 'A' levels in one year. This was only incitement for Ahmed to redouble his efforts to pin me down on the floor, which was where I worked and where later I slept. The comedy programmes would have gone if Ahmed himself was not so addicted to them. He was also addicted to giving me inspiring lectures, which in the new circumstances became more intense and more ambitious.

'If you're doing your 'A' levels this year,' he said, 'you might as well apply to go to university next year.' What about money and a residence permit? My tourist visa had run out after six weeks and someone was bound to ask about that. There was no stopping him. He got the grant forms and the information booklets, was undaunted by the shattering news that if you were not a *home* student you needed to have worked for three years to qualify for a grant. '"The Authority may, in some circumstances, award discretionary grants,"' he read out to me from the booklet. 'What's the matter with you? Don't you have any ambition?'

Because he was so passionate about studying education and

about his profession, and because he thought I would have a better chance of getting in, Ahmed persuaded me to apply to do a teaching degree. It all seemed too fantastic to come about, whether I put down education or astronomy as my intended subject, so I did as he said. I applied for a discretionary award and was invited for an interview. And then the incredible happened. Oh yes, it did. The chairman of the panel that interviewed me had been an education officer in Zanzibar until the moment of the uprising. He told me this as soon as I entered the room, rising from his chair to shake my hand with an air of condolence. The rest of the panel was made up of two white-haired women, one a local councillor and the other someone who worked in the education office, and a small man with a bristly moustache who said nothing throughout the interview but whose eyes clung to every word I said. Later I was to see the same clammy look in Mr Willoughby. I was mostly asked to speak about the horrors of the uprising and its consequences. I did the best I could to make every atrocity as abominable as possible – I did not have to try very hard. The chairman did what he could to egg me on, and even added one or two stories of his own. A few days later, I received a letter informing me that I had been awarded a discretionary grant. 'You see,' Ahmed told me, 'this is England. Anything can happen. Now the residence permit.'

And I got that too. Armed with my grant letter, my university applications, glowing references from my college, a letter from a JP whom one of the graduates in the house was related to, and a letter from my local GP (Ahmed's idea), we went to London for an interview at the Home Office. Ahmed came along, and discreetly but firmly insisted on being allowed to sit in. He was, after all, my guardian, he said. The plan was that I was to be calm for the first few minutes of the interview, and then, as soon as was decent, I was to break down in a flood of tears and Ahmed would do the talking. The man who interviewed us was in his thirties and wore dark-rimmed spectacles which made him look like Clark Kent before he changed into his Superman gear. I found this reassuring, and so it turned out to be. I don't think it was the tears that did it, or Ahmed's wheedling account of my diligence and utter brilliance, but Clark Kent's innate sense of justice. Here I feel free.

Although it seemed impossible that he could do so, Ahmed intensified his surveillance of me even further. He neglected his own work to sit and revise with me. He gave me endless advice and hectoring speeches, invoked God, my parents, a luminous future. I didn't stand a chance, and passed brilliantly. Because Ahmed's course did not finish until September, I was able to stay in the hostel until the last minute (working in a launderette which belonged to another relative of one of the graduate students) before I arrived at the Institute to start my course. That's when I began to understand how much Ahmed had protected me, and how frightening England really was. I probably also understood then that I could have chosen something more interesting than education. It was all so unlikely – the grant, getting to university in that way, the course I was embarked on – that I found that without Ahmed around I was not all that concerned with excelling. I had proved myself to him, and his pleasure and praise kept me buoyant for longer than they should have done. Before I moved to London and the cramped room in Tooting that the university accommodation officer directed me to (after I told her what I could afford for rent), I had strutted to the admiring audience of the people I had been living with, who had treated me with the indulgence and flattery of a younger brother. But in no time at all after I moved, I was overcome by the enormity of my abandonment, like someone weeping in a crowd. I was astonished by the sudden surge of loneliness and terror I felt when I realized how stranded I was in this hostile place, that I did not know how to speak to people and win them over to me, that the bank, the canteen, the supermarket, the dark streets seemed so intimidating, and that I could not return from where I came – that, as I then thought, I had lost everything. Then Emma came and filled my life. I can't describe that.

So the middle Lower Second did not bother me too much when it came, though later I did think that I might have done more to take charge of my life, not have allowed everything to be consumed in a seductive brew of sentiment and a despairing openness to unpromising possibilities. And then I became a schoolteacher. I did not fulfil myself.

It was a good story, and most of it was true. It made me sound a little heroic and a little weak. A nice balance.

It was towards the end of the second year of her PhD, around August, that Emma became pregnant with Amelia. It was a time when the first delighted reception of the Pill was beginning to be replaced by gloomy forecasts of cancer of this and that (breast and cervix, I think) and unspecified damage in old age. Emma was converted to the new austerity and came off the Pill, saying she understood her body better than anyone else and knew how to prevent herself from becoming pregnant. But after too many ciders, or whatever we could afford in those days, the result was Amelia, and the end of the first Arcadia, although we did not know it at the time. I am still awaiting the second. In fact, after the initial shock and the agonizing over the timetable for completion of her thesis (it looked hopeless), we started to become excited about the pregnancy, playing with names, rearranging the furniture, making wild promises of unique cooperation in child-rearing. Nothing like what we were planning had been heard of before. In our lifetime we were going to lay low all the nasty mythemes about bastards and mestizos, expose the cruelty that attended the figure of the mulatto and the half-caste (our child). I even suggested we get married, for the baby's sake, but Emma laughed at my bourgeois anxieties.

Amelia brought Mrs Willoughby into our lives in a big way. We needed the help, we couldn't have done without it. The baby turned out to be a sleepless, noisy brute, as I have already intimated, capable of consumption and excretion in a big way, and all the advice books we had been given did not work or seemed unworkable. Ignore her. Fat chance. We reassured each other, but Emma began to feel inadequate and miserable, no good as a mother, no good as a student, no good as a human being. So we made another plan. Emma no longer received a grant, but she would extend her registration period and take a year to write her thesis. This was what most people did anyway, it's just that they did not have babies in their third year.

Mrs Willoughby had been aghast when the news of Emma's pregnancy was delivered. I was present, was required to be. She listened to Emma's explanation, sat in silence for a long minute and then turned to me with a look of, well, hatred. I deserved that look, I suppose, though it wasn't me that came off the Pill. To be honest, I don't think I would have worried whether she was on the Pill or not. I was just so in love with her that I couldn't imagine anything going wrong, never thought any harm could ever befall us. But I thought I understood something else in that look: it wasn't just to do with Emma's PhD, or that she lived with me in moral squalor, but that now she would have to live with a kind of contamination for the rest of her life. She would not be able to be a normal English woman again, leading an uncomplicated English life among English people. I think even Mr Willoughby was affected by the tragic dimensions of what had happened, though he mostly smiled through Emma's account. But after Emma and Mrs Willoughby had retreated to the kitchen for some hard talking (we had gone to Blackheath to break the news), there was no eager gleam in his eyes, no hunger for our usual transgressions. In the circumstances, it might even have felt obscene to give way to such a desire. He sat looking at me with his lustreless eyes, watching me with pity and disenchantment. I could feel the stirrings of a tragic story: confused offspring of mixed parentage (meaning European and some kind of hubshi) doomed to instability and degeneration as the tainted blood coursed through generations, waiting to surface in madness, congenital bone weakness, homosexuality, cowardice and treachery. But I thought I would sit this one out. He was bound to come round later.

'What are you going to call him?' he asked at last. His voice was without its usual crisp egotism, was almost feeble with uneasiness. It must have seemed to him that life at times could deal quite unfair blows.

Shaka Zulu, I thought, or perhaps the Mahdi. Or Mau Mau. Was that what he was afraid of? Or was this one of his subtle flanking attacks, when what he really wanted was for me to say that we would name the baby after General Gordon or Captain Cook?

'It's going to be a girl,' I said. 'And we were thinking of calling her Pocahontas.'

'Oh,' he said and invited me for a stroll in their spacious garden. When we were outside, he stood for a moment staring at a flight of birds strung out across the sky. 'They're flying in the wrong direction,' he said. 'They're going south. What do they think they'll find there?'

But this contention and dejection could not last, of course, and long before Amelia's awaited appearance we had received several of the necessary items from them. When the time came for Emma to have another try at getting her thesis written up, Mrs Willoughby offered to come over to stay with Amelia for the day whenever she could, and on other days Emma would drop her off in Blackheath on her way to college. Several days a week I would come home to find Mrs Willoughby in full charge, the flat cleaned and altered in some subtle way, perhaps by the addition of a new ornament, or the removal of an old tin that we had used as a flowerpot, now replaced by something more seemly and expensive. She bought us gifts of frivolous foods that we would not normally think to get for ourselves, or thought we could not afford: a meringue pie, or a box of Danish pastries, or a pound of grapes (I suspected they were South African), or over-decorated cakes that she and Emma would then exult over. More likely than not, the evening meal would be cooking or only awaiting insertion into the oven, and Amelia would be crawling around the floor as contented as a slug in late spring. Sometimes Emma would be at home too, absorbed in baby business or knee-deep in arrangements. I tried to get into this stuff, I really did, to join in and seem unconcerned by Mrs Willoughby's overbearing presence, to persuade my heart to melt at my daughter's antics and roar with laughter along with them, but my smiles and chuckles were underlaid by bitterness at the havoc my life had become, and I guess my heart not only did not melt, but was not really in it. I say this with some degree of shame.

It was not that I did not feel affection for Amelia, or disliked being left with her or resented caring dutifully for her, but she was a stranger who had taken my love away and brought Mrs Willoughby to mind and menace my life. And Emma's thesis was not going well, she could not concentrate on it, was not convinced there was any value in it, could not imagine herself finishing it, and what was the point of it all, anyway? Her supervisor was a wanker, the college was such a long way away, but she could not work at home because of Amelia, she was fed up of being short of money, of having to get up so early, and why couldn't I wake up more often at night? Because I was tired, and she was always out of bed before I had even stirred. My work was as nightmarish as ever: the endless malice of the pupils was depressing, the marking seemed relentless, the very idea of teaching in a school, of school itself, seemed senseless. And so voices were raised for the first time since we had known each other, and some nights we lay in bed bickering in lowered voices so as not to wake Amelia, who slept in the same room as us.

In a burst of extravagance, Emma walked down to Tottenham Court Road one afternoon on her way back from college and bought a camera, a Pentax. It was a dynamic way of dealing with being short of money, but when I told Emma this she said that I was not the only one who worried about money, but maybe I should worry a little less. Listening to her talk about me, sometimes I felt that my life was a story and that I was playing my part in events that were beyond me, that were already set out in a pattern I had not been observant enough to comprehend. Yes, I worried about money, and about the bills that always turned up, which Emma would throw to one side saying, *Let them wait. We'll deal with them later*. I thought everybody worried about money. We only had my pathetic salary to live on and it surprised me how many things Amelia seemed to need and how their cost seemed to mount. So I looked at this expensive object I was being introduced to with some dismay. This was long before the days of three rums, of course, but there was always an excuse for a bottle of wine at some stage during the week, and that camera represented several weeks of impending thirst.

'We must take some pictures of Amelia, otherwise we'll forget her as she is now,' Emma said. 'It'll be fun to have a record of all the stages of her life, then we can all laugh together when she's grown up. There aren't any pictures of me before I started school, and I wish there had been, so I could see what I looked like . . . you know? And anyway, your parents will want to see pictures of her, won't they? Or don't you think they would? Have they written since you told them?'

I shook my head. She snorted with disappointed hurt. *And you complain about how my parents resent that you are the father of my child.* She didn't say it, she did not always then, but I guessed that was that she was thinking. She waited for me to say something, to put up a

88

defence, and when I did not she returned to her new camera with an almost imperceptible sigh. I remember wounding moments like that which we did nothing to ease, and how later they festered and turned evil. This was one of mine.

Because the truth was that I had not written home about Amelia, and the other truth was that I had not written home about Emma, either. As far as they were concerned back there in Nativity, neither Emma nor Amelia existed. It was to go on like that for years. I did not know how to tell Emma this – I still haven't. I usually only ever wrote to my mother, but she can't read and can only write her name. When she received my letters she would have to find someone to read them for her and then to write out a reply, some child who would be happy to do the lot for a shilling. Over the years, the exchanges between us had turned into a rare ritual: every several months she would send me a few words about everyone's health and regards and best wishes, and some months later I would send something back. *The weather has been very cold recently, my job is fine, and recently I moved to a house in a place called Battersea.* In any case, I did not know how I could write to her that I was living with an English woman to whom I was not married. In the world I came from, such things were not spoken about. To my mother, Emma would be something disreputable, a mistress, and such matters, if they could not be avoided, were best dealt with discreetly. Not announced in a letter which would probably be read aloud to her by a gossipy child. I thought of lying, of writing to say that I was *married* to an English woman, but I never did, afraid of the havoc that would let loose, afraid of the litanies of blame that would follow. *Now we have lost you, she has stolen you away from us,* and so on. God, home, culture, history would all come into it, boom doom, blah bah. As if I was not already lost and stolen and shipwrecked and mangled beyond recognition anyway. As if home and belonging were anything more than a wilful fiction when there was no possibility (at that time) of them being real again. As if they were anything more than debilitating stories that turned everything into moments of reprise that disabled and disarmed.

So I said nothing. If Emma asked me how my parents might respond to whatever it might be about us, I reassured her as imaginatively as I could. With more complicated questions I was evasive or gave any kind of answer that would do. After a while she mostly lost interest in asking, she included them less frequently in her concerns, and in the end she forgot them, except as figures in a story. I think as time passed and our lives became fuller and more involved, it became harder and harder to imagine them living a life as real as our own. Anyway, I never told them about her, and the longer I remained silent, the harder it became to tell Emma.

As I waited for Emma to come home on the day that I had been to see the doctor about my heart, I knew I would tell her as soon as she came in. I always told her everything, blurted it out like an idiot. Usually I got in first and would have started the cooking by the time she came home from the university. (No, she wasn't still doing her thesis, she *taught* there.) On that day, she came home earlier than usual.

'I've been out to lunch with a publisher and didn't bother going back,' she said. She looked as if she'd had a good lunch, her eyes were shiny and her cheeks were a little flushed. I felt a pang of jealousy which I struggled to suppress, a surge of envy which I knew I would not be able to keep quiet about. 'Is Amelia home yet?'

'No, so we have the house all to ourselves,' I said, flashing eyebrows at her. She snorted dismissively and smiled with what seemed like friendly disdain, or perhaps mild contempt, I forget now, then went off to shower and change. It was impossible to talk to her when she came in with those slightly sickening aromas of rich food on her breath and that glint in her eye.

'I went to see the doctor this morning,' I told her when she came back, pausing briefly to get a decent bit of tension going. 'He told me my heart was buggered.'

She stood very still for a moment, waiting. 'What do you mean, buggered?'

'That's what the doctor said. Perhaps we should look it up in a medical dictionary. I just assumed he meant it was defective in some important way.'

'But didn't he say what was wrong?' she asked, looking quite distraught. That was nice.

'He told me not to worry because Afro-Caribbean people have dickey hearts, so my condition was perfectly predictable,' I said, looking forward to an outburst from her in defence of my traduced brethren. It was the kind of thing you could usually rely on from Emma, and sometimes it was quite fun when invective and indignation burst out of her. But she wasn't in the mood.

'What? But you're not Afro-Caribbean. Did he say what was wrong?'

'More tests before they can say for sure. In the meantime, no rum and no cigarettes.'

'I should think not,' she said, looking almost shocked. 'But didn't he even give you an idea of what was wrong?'

'He did,' I said, feeling that I had once again disappointed her with my feebleness in the face of officials and authority, in the face of life. 'He said it was buggered.'

'Stop saying that. That doctor is useless, and so are you. I bet you didn't even ask him to explain what was wrong. You'd better go and see someone else.'

'I'll wait for the specialist,' I said.

She started to say something and then stopped with a little shrug. *It's your life.* Perhaps I shouldn't have told her about the rum.

91

'You'll have to be careful from now on,' she said. 'At least until we know for sure.'

'Anyway,' I said, before she got too interested and began drawing up a list of life's small pleasures that would now be denied me, 'I also had a letter from home.'

Her eyes lit up with new attention when I said that. It was a rare event and that was reason enough to look alert, but my mother's letters always perturbed her, as if she expected them to contain blame and demands, as if she was about to be troubled unfairly, as if she had been reminded of something shameful and long-past. I'm guessing, because whenever I asked her she always said, 'Nonsense, I worry for you. Her letters always seem to upset you.' I saw her watching me with a poised attentiveness, a look I knew well, as if she saw more hazard in this new information than that about my poor buggered heart. So I smiled and began to talk in what I hoped was a genial and friendly voice, but as soon as I started I could hear resonances of my teacher tones: informative, seeking to persuade, holding things back. I pressed on. I was a teacher, that was what I was. I was unfulfilled.

'I told you there's been a change of government – well, a change of a few people at the top,' I said. 'New president, new vice-president, new prime minister, new deputy prime minister, new ambassador to the United Nations, new director of protocol, that kind of thing, but the same old crowd below them screwing everything up and menacing everyone. This new government is trying to loosen things up, get rid of the more spiteful decrees of their predecessors. They came in on a wave of popular disgust against the previous president, who had foolishly or maybe vaingloriously opened the airwaves to citizens with grievances, promising that no one need fear reprisal. So the letters poured into the radio station and the announcers gleefully read out every single one. It was such scathing, furious stuff that the president began to fear for his authority over his band of jolly knights, and must have suspected that one of them was going to use the opportunity to get him locked up or worse. That he was going to be roasted over a fire of clove-wood and served up as the main dish at a state banquet. In any case, he got into his private jet and fled to the neighbouring country, making speeches when he got there about the ingratitude of his people. The new government came in on this wave of popular triumph and they wisely began reversing or tempering some of the things their predecessor had been most reviled for. They spoke a rhetoric of austerity and public integrity, emptied the jails, and among other things they have declared an amnesty on those people who left the country illegally over the years. If this is for real, then I can go back . . . whenever I want.'

I did a kind of virtual bow when I got to that, inviting her to appreciate the significance of the punch-line.

'That's wonderful,' she said, her eyes shining. At first I took the light in her eyes to be pleasure at the thought of my being able to return, but then I imagined I saw a glint of anxiety in it. Did she think I was suggesting that I wanted to go back and live there? After all these years? After all the transformations, the silences?

'For a visit,' I said, grinning at her. 'Some time soon. Just for a visit, for a few weeks.'

'Of course you must go,' she said, rousing herself. 'It'll be wonderful for you, to see your people again, and for them to see you. It must be nearly twenty years now. God, you're full of surprises today.'

'I'm not sure about wonderful. The thought fills me with all kinds of terror. Everything will be different, and I don't know what they'll think of me. When I thought about it this morning I had to rush and sit on the toilet for a good few minutes afterwards. But I have to go – soon, I think. My mother says she has been very unwell in recent times. Her diabetes has got worse, what with all the shortages of medicine. I didn't even know she had diabetes.

And she now has problems with her eyes – I am not sure what. They're probably buggered.'

'Yes, you must go soon,' Emma said, ignoring my little joke. 'It would be sad . . . if you could meet and you didn't go. We can afford it, can't we? You must do it, and Amelia and I will be fine here.'

'Perhaps it's just a lot of emotional waffle,' I said, 'after all this time. Feeling this attachment out of a kind of habit.'

'Don't be stupid,' she said, her voice bristling with irritation. 'How many times have I seen you sitting here in tears while you talked about her?'

I didn't tell Emma what else the letter said. *All these years you have been living in that country on your own, like a ghoul in a ruined house,* my Ma declared. *You'll say this is not how it is, that your life is not like that. But when I think of you I see you like that. This has pained me more than I can tell you. I want you to come and see us now that you can, and I want you to marry before you return to that country, if that is your wish. I know you are a grown man, and you may think this is no longer my business, but it will give all of us pleasure and you will have a companion in your life, and God willing, a family of your own. I have already spoken to a nice family you may remember, the Hilalis who used to live in Mnazini, and they are willing.*

A grown man. I'm forty-two years old. You can imagine what Emma would have thought of it all if she knew. That my mother was planning to break up our lives together, that she was *arranging* a marriage for me with some unfortunate *child* who had no choice in the matter and who was going to be landed with some old brute with a buggered heart and much else buggered besides. And what was wrong with me that I couldn't just tell them that I didn't want to be married to anyone? What was wrong with me? Why was I so spineless? *I don't care if she's dying. What kind of clumsy, heartless love could make her act like that? You'd better write to her at once and tell her to get stuffed or I'll do it myself. How dare she!*

Best not to say anything, because to do so would mean . . . oh, having to say so much more, to open up a stinking tomb full of writhing lies and dead stories. It was not the first time my mother had mentioned marriage, nor was it the first time she had described my condition in England as a ghoul in a ruined house, an eater of dead bodies (it must have been one of her childhood dreads), but she had never gone so far as to suggest a someone before, a person, a woman, let alone find her, approach her parents, and probably agree a dowry, plan the festivities and think about the jewellery she would give the bride as a wedding present. Of course, she did not know about Emma, but it still seemed a dynamic move. I wasn't going to have anything to do with it, needless to say. It was only a matter of deciding how best to deal with it. I could write to her straight away and tell her to drop the whole thing, but why should she listen? It would be the least she would expect of me. She has already spoken to these Hilalis, and is she now to go to them and make a humiliating retreat because of a ritual demurral, or would she think it better to sit tight and wait until I got there? Alternatively, I could say nothing, and then on my arrival tell her in no uncertain terms that this was out of the question – and I guess the only uncertain terms I have in my possession are Emma and Amelia. I would have to tell her about that. I think.

Amelia astonished me with her response. She was then a brusque and distracted young woman of seventeen, but of course she had not always been like that. Despite all the hours she spent with Mrs Willoughby, she turned out a beauty. By the time she was ten months old she could walk, talk and charm her devoted audience at will. And as she grew a little older, she dealt with most things that came her way with a casual tolerance that would have been impossible to predict from her angry arrival among us. Perhaps Mrs Willoughby was good for her, after all, and passed on some of her capacity for calm without the treacherous spikes she kept hidden under the surface. All was well with Amelia so long as she was not left to play alone, or was not expected to go to bed while there was still a light burning in the flat. She had a handful of peculiar dietary preferences (jam with her fish fingers, for example, and a passionate dislike for the taste of beef, however cleverly disguised), but she took to nursery rhymes with relish and spent hours with crayons and paper, carolling her pleasure in life as she peopled her world. School was fine, her health was fine — except that she peed often –and by the time she was ten she had read dozens of the books on our bookshelves. Some of them she had marked out with wax crayons as a baby, as if she was scenting them for later recognition. Her teachers gloated over her talents for schoolwork, for music, for friendship. She also had a talent for affection which her teachers could not have known about. We reminded ourselves that it was her doing, nothing to do with us, but we still glowed with pride. I suspect I bored my colleagues with all the bulletins of her endless triumphs, and I know that I talked about her to the barbarians I taught, because sometimes they asked for a progress report on some undertaking I had mentioned her being in the midst of.

I remember a holiday in the Lake District as a kind of high summer of our lives together, the three of us. It was nothing special, just a lot of laughter and uncomplicated meals, and reading the Lake poets aloud late into the night, and disappointment at the absence of daffodils (it was August), and long walks by the banks of the endless beautiful lakes of the region. I have photographs of that time and I know I don't imagine the impossible contentment they portray.

Then she grew up, I suppose. She spoke to her mother about things that she must have thought I would not be able to help her with. It was predictable, but it was also oddly painful. She wanted to do things differently, in ways that seemed strange to me, and when I said this to her I felt a distance growing between us. I suppose I was slow to realize that she did not want to be treated as a beloved child any more, who would listen avidly to my wise thoughts and advice and then change her plans accordingly. So the first time she shouted angrily at me, I cried. I remember her distress then, but perhaps there was nothing either of us knew how to do to prevent the distance growing. Maybe it was more my fault than hers, because I was slow to learn to make room for her, to withdraw gracefully and with affection. And the distance grew into a habit, with only moments of wary fondness breaking into the hurtful watchfulness. Perhaps I exaggerate, because as I recall this I cannot restrain the disappointment. I suppose, then, I learned to leave her to herself, except when she overcame my attempts at taking defeat honourably with what seemed like provocation I found impossible to ignore. Yes, I know, all this was predictable too, but at one time it had seemed as if it would not turn out like that.

Anyway, when she came in I was still sitting in the same chair (longing for a rum), while Emma was in the kitchen cooking. I had told her there was no need – I could just make an omelette for Amelia and myself. Emma had already said she was too full to eat. But she insisted, telling me I needed to rest in my enfeebled state, and she would prepare something appropriate to the occasion. I hoped she would cook a quiche; she did that beautifully. Amelia strolled in in her frayed clothes, her tarty make-up smudged and smeared, probably because she had been mauling someone for the last hour or two. She stopped by the living-room door and gave me the satirical smile that was her usual greeting. Then she unhooked the muddy backpack that masqueraded as a school bag and in which she carried the daily paraphernalia of her degenerate young life, and made off towards her room, dragging the bag along the floor.

'Hey, skinhead,' I called out, 'I'd like a word with you.' I called her skinhead because she had recently had her hair cropped, and in some ways she liked the name. It made her feel bad and in touch with the streets. She strolled back and leaned against the door again. 'That is, if you're not too busy.'

'What is it?' she asked with a long-suffering sigh.

I grinned at her, and she raised her eyebrows in derisive enquiry. 'Come and sit down. This will take a few minutes,' I said.

I told her about the doctor first, and she was silent with astonishment, staring at me with a look of horror and pity. Then she said 'I'm sorry,' as if I had just died. 'Perhaps the specialist will find it's all a mistake,' she said. I hadn't thought of that, and I was grateful for the brief comfort it offered. Then I told her about the letter and she smiled with pleasure and excitement.

'Oh, you can go for a visit,' she said, standing up and coming towards me. I thought she was going to give me a hug or a kiss or something. That would really have been going too far for her. She hadn't done anything like that since she was fifteen, and sure enough she managed to control herself and stop a couple of feet away. 'That's brilliant news. After all these years . . . after missing your home for so long, and talking so much about it, you'll be able to go there again. When are you going? Is Emma coming with you? Have you told her yet?'

With that she rushed off to find her mother, and I could hear her excited voice as she related the *brilliant news*. 'Can I come with you?' she asked when she came back.

I shook my head.

'Why not? It's my country too,' she said. She looked so serious and ardent that I didn't dare laugh. 'What are you smiling about? If it's your country, then it's mine too.'

'I think I'd better go alone this time, after so long,' I said. 'Let me see how things are, first.'

In the days that followed, and during the weeks of preparation for the trip, while Emma helped with practical details, with shopping for gifts, with reassurance and advice, lending an ear to all the terrors and humiliations I anticipated, it was Amelia who gave my journey a stamp of romance and adventure. She astonished me with her excitement and her selfless joy. Emma looked on with a smile at her daughter's absurdities but she did not say anything to dispel her fantasies, did not mention anything about the deprivation and want I expected to find there after so many years of chaotic and malevolent rule.

Mrs Willoughby smiled when she heard the news. 'Well, that will be nice for your Mum,' she said. She wasn't interested, couldn't care less. Perhaps she would have been more excited if she suspected that I might not return, but she knew well enough by now that I was not capable of anything as decisive as that. Mr couldn't take it in at first. His hearing had gone and he was rapidly declining. Only his eyes still roved and darted with the old hunger. But when he finally understood that I was returning to the lost Empire, he shook his head sadly at the futility of my mission. 'Too late,' he said.

Whenever Amelia caught me looking pensive (that is, silently panic-stricken) she would say, 'Hey, what are you thinking about? Remember the trip. Why don't you think about going back? That will cheer you up. What season will it be there now? Will it be really torrid? I wish I was coming too.'

'Next time.'

PART TWO

'Your Self's grown gross, a dog that sleeps and feeds.'

Farid ud-din Attar,
The Conference of the Birds (1177)

After the frenzy of preparation, and all the terrors of anticipation, it was with a subdued and resigned calm that I sat in the departure lounge awaiting the beginning of the journey. It was like the moment before a persecution. There was only the thing itself now. Besides, there were so many other matters to worry about. I had not really travelled much since my first arrival in England: a week's holiday in France and another week in Spain, in both cases part of a huge, obedient crowd herded together and facing the same direction. In a state of heightened analysis, everything in the departure lounge interested me. There seemed to be many Indian and African travellers, but that may have been the coincidence of the destinations: most of the flights at that time of night seemed to be heading to dark places.

A man with large hair sculpted to a blunt point over his fore-head came to sit nearby. He was dressed in a pin-stripe, diplomatic-corpse fancy-dress suit for our guys, but in his case there was a kind of urban, streetwise toughness overlaying an inappropriateness in his manner, and there was a certain stutter in the language his body spoke in that costume. When I glanced at him again, casually, our eyes met. His seemed to leap with interest, while I looked instantly away. There was something of the flabby devil in his appearance and in his parasitical airs, something of the government flunkey on a spree. I feared people like him, in-stantly and perhaps unfairly. I could imagine him alighting at whatever hell-hole it was in which he had gained the ascendancy to travel the world in this state of privilege, taking his monkey-suit off, donning his gum boots and overalls, and strolling off to the torture room to pull off testicles with pliers and attach electrodes to other vulnerable parts of the human body. And if he didn't do precisely that himself, then he knew people who did or who ordered others to, and he would sit laughing with them over the duty-free booze he had brought with him from his travels while they chatted about the hilarious scam they had all been able to pull on their pathetic victims.

My neighbour on the flight was friendly, with a shiny round face that seemed incapable of restraining a grin. The shine was mostly sweat, which he wiped with a large hand-towel he carried over one shoulder like a shawl. I expected not to enjoy his company, but he was so charming and pleasant that I found myself telling him of my trip and of my life in England, talking to him with a freedom that was mildly intoxicating. I even told him about Emma, though I made that uncomplicated. He, in turn, spoke about the law school he was attending in London (he seemed a bit old for that) and his forthcoming marriage. That was why he was going home. I asked him which number wife this was, and he laughed good-naturedly and said that he was too poor for that kind of thing. Even now, the marriage was not his idea, but his parents were worrying that he was leaving it too late, so he had agreed in order to keep the peace. He was free with advice and news when he discovered how long I had been away, which I didn't mind as much as I thought I might. But when he touched on my paranoias – *everything is different, everyone's gone, don't feel guilty about not coming back earlier* – it made my stomach turn to liquid and I had to dash for the toilet.

It had been dark when we left London, so there was nothing to see as we flew over Africa, just an occasional light which from that distance looked like a flaring bonfire or a spume of burning gas. In the morning, the land below looked barren and empty, forbidding in its starkness. We flew over what seemed like a dirty rivulet in hard-baked, brown flinty sand, and the pilot informed us that it was the Nile. Tiny clusters of houses adhered to its edges here and there, like lumps or disfigurements on the straight line of the river. Later, the sight of Lake Turkana was shocking for the rocky, bare emptiness that surrounded it in all directions. Then the landscape changed suddenly as we left Kilimanjaro over to our right and approached the coast, dotted now and again with copses and, at times, vast expanses of green. Eventually we caught a glimpse of the limitless ocean and saw regiments and battalions of coconut trees marching towards the empty beaches. Then we crossed the grey still waters of the channel between the continent and our island. Everything seemed so familiar as we flew low over the island that I felt my eyes watering at the clarity of memory which had preserved these pictures so effortlessly, without renewal or exertion.

As we were waiting to disembark, my companion was back at work with his towel, smiling at my nervousness and wishing me luck with benignly malicious glee. The heat and smell of the earth struck me as if for the first time. I didn't remember it like that, not the humid fumes of decomposing vegetation and baking earth which made me heave for breath. The terminal building was new, squat and anonymous, all glass and steel, with a viewing balcony on the first floor. Some way to the right was the old building, looking small and decorative with its crenellations and red-tiled roof and heavy wooden railings, like a pavilion in an ornamental garden or a villa on a Mediterranean hillside. As we walked across the tarmac I felt as exposed as if I had stepped off the plane naked, or as if my clothes were too baggy or too tight, or too colourful and ridiculous, as if I were a refugee from a circus. I looked out for familiar faces on the balcony, and I saw one that seemed as if it could be my stepfather. After such a long time, and from such a distance, I could not be sure, so I waved to be on the safe side. The man I had waved to stared for a moment and looked behind him, then turned back towards me with a look of surprise. He was too young to be my stepfather, I could see that now.

My half-brother Akbar clapped me on the back as I stood waiting for my luggage. I hadn't noticed him approach from behind me, and after the mistake with the man I had taken to be my stepfather I had stopped searching the faces so hungrily, in case I embarrassed myself again. He looked so much younger than I expected. We shook hands as if we were meeting again after only a brief absence, smiling shyly at each other, and speaking the ritual words of greeting without emphasis or exaggeration. He pointed to the gate and through the bars I saw my mother jumping up and down with excitement, smiling and waving, and saying something I could not hear. Beside her was a young woman I did not recognize, but I knew it must be my half-sister Halima. She had been so young when I left. She was waving too, frantically. Suddenly I felt overwhelmed with relief at this welcome and affection. I don't know what I expected, but I think it was blame and long looks.

I sat between my mother and Halima in the back of the ancient taxi while Akbar sat in the front beside the driver. My mother, too, looked less changed than I had expected. Her head was covered with a buibui, though it was pulled back far enough for me to see that her hair was thin and white. But her face looked firm and full of life, and her laughter and her voice seemed as familiar as my own. She had lost a little weight, and seemed leaner and more assured than I remembered her. She kept her eyes on me as she talked, telling me their news, asking for mine, touching my grey hair between sentences and smiling. I caught the eye of the taxi-driver in the rear-view mirror, a man as old and grizzled as his motor, and he looked tense and preoccupied, apparently not at all touched by this reunion scene.

We ran into the first road-block about half a mile from the airport. There was no one by the barrier, but beside the road was a building which I remembered as a police station. This area, three miles out of town, had been a European enclave before independence. It was no doubt on the airport side of town for convenience, but perhaps also to expedite matters should a hasty evacuation prove at all necessary. I remember cycling past at times to visit the ruins of Sultan Ali bin Humud's palace, which were by the sea about a mile or so from the main road. Ali bin Humud had abdicated the Busaid throne in 1911 while in Paris after an imperial junket in London, a royal wedding or a coronation or some such, to which all the boogie chiefs and rajahs and sultans of the greatest empire the world had ever seen were invited so that they could look on England's works and despair. Sultan Ali had already seen England's works, having gone to school and grown up there, and having only come back to his island kingdom to reign over his puritanical Omani barons and their black vassals when his father died. No more parties, no booze, no Ascot, no excruciating dalliances, just flowing robes and family intrigues and prayers and prohibitions. After two years of this, during which the Sultan built himself a modern palace by the sea, he returned to Europe to attend the celebrations of his suzerain and protector, and refused to come back. It was fitting in some curious way that the district around his abandoned palace should become home to a colony of the people he had chosen as his own. The ghosts in that ruin would probably have found their company convivial and fitting.

He wasn't the first in his family to make a dash for Europe. His great-aunt Salma had run off with a German diplomat some years before. The German had caught sight of her on a terrace of the house next door to the one he had rented, and he had fallen in love with her. They both feared that discovery would mean horrible retribution for the dishonour her affair would bring on the family, and they were right to do so. Her crowd thought a great deal of such things. So they ran off together. She changed her name to Emily and they went to live in Berlin, but within months

Herr Reuter was run over by a tram, and Salma was left with her memories and her loss. She had the good sense to write a best-selling autobiography, though, which Ali bin Humud did not.

Right next door to the ruins of Ali bin Humud's modern palace were Bishop Weston's church and hostel. Frank Weston had been a hero of his time, a righteous Victorian churchman who had scoured the countryside, both on the island and across the waters, for slaves he could rescue and convert. He sheltered those who chose to escape, preached to them the words of the God he so loved, and taught them to read so they could study the Good Book. It caused him great distress when he came to hear of the wanton practices that his young charges indulged in in the hostel where he offered them sanctuary, but he did not despair. Nor did he think it necessary to pass this information on to the good people back home who raised funds for his mission at church bazaars and such like. I used to visit the church when I went to wander around the ruined palace. The warden of the church grounds told me once that there was a tunnel running from under the palace to the port, so that Sultan Ali bin Humud could bring in slaves for his pleasure, even though the traffic was illegal by 1910. If there really was a tunnel, and the warden became under-standably evasive when I asked for its whereabouts, then it was more likely that the Sultan had had it built so he could make his escape back to Europe one dark night. In the museum there is a photograph of Frank Weston at dinner, and when I saw it I could not forget that he was an Englishman in a colony, dressed as if he was in Hampshire and eating pudding.

As I cycled past the villas all those years ago, I used to admire their neat gardens and bright colours, pinks and blues and even one (I remember) which had a chequer-board design. They were all built by the government's public works department, probably to a plan drawn up by an architect in a London office, and were only occupied by European staff. Naturally, they had needed their police station nearby, in case of rowdiness or worse. The police station had then looked as neat as the villas, brilliantly white-washed, and with plump bushes and the radiantly colourful and papery flowers of the bougainvillaea lining the driveway to the front porch. Even the policemen at this station had looked decorative and crisply turned out, their ironed khaki shorts stiff and shiny with starch, the tassles of their carefully brushed tarbooshes glistening and full. And I have a memory of a flagpole which one of the policemen was always running a flag up, though I could only have seen that once or twice. Now the walls were spattered with mud and the yard in front of the building was as bare as an earthen floor. No bushes or bougainvillaea or flagpole or white-washed stones to mark out the drive, not even the spiked ornamental chain which I realized now had been a jaunty attempt to suggest an English suburban garden in these tropical climes.

Akbar gave the taxi-driver some money at the road-block, then we waited in the car in tense silence. Beyond the station, by the dirt track which eventually led to Ali bin Humud's palace, a group of people stood under a tree as if waiting for a bus, a small crowd, not speaking, all looking in our direction. 'What's the idea?' I asked, just wanting to know what was going on.

'Wait,' Akbar said, as if to warn me from doing anything rash.

'It's a check-point,' the taxi driver said bitterly. 'If you don't stop they shoot. They're in there watching. When they are ready they'll come out, and if you don't give them money they search the luggage and confiscate this and that. Then they know you, and next time you come through here in your taxi they make trouble about the car, about your licence, for your passengers . . .'

He stopped abruptly, for someone had appeared on the porch. The policeman stretched and then strolled capless towards the car. When he was nearer I saw that he could not be much more than twenty, and I didn't think there was any pretence in the way he was rubbing sleep from his eyes. His uniform was clean but crumpled, no sign of starch or the shining blisters of a hot iron, and of course there was no tarboosh. That had gone even before independence. The taxi-driver greeted him effusively, jumping out of the car and going round to open the boot. It must have been then that the money changed hands because he was back in a moment, shouting his farewells to the policeman as he started up his ancient Austin. 'Mal'uun. They are nothing but thieves,' he said. 'But what can you do? If you don't give the dogs something they take everything.'

'At least you don't have to pay it out of your own pocket, Mzee Hamza,' Akbar said, smiling but firmly reminding the driver that his loss was less in this than the passengers'. Mzee Hamza laughed happily, almost with a kind of pride.

'Who did you think you were waving to?' Akbar asked, twisting in his seat to grin at me. 'When you were walking across the tarmac, who did you think it was? He looked astonished.'

I shrugged. 'I don't know, I thought I recognized him.'

'I was up there on the balcony, and I can tell you he looked astonished. Who did you think it was?' He was still grinning, but underneath the grin I thought I saw something harder, a willingness to be awkward. I couldn't remember that about him, that he had a hardness in him. Perhaps it was an expression of his self-confidence and maturity, or the inkling of an antipathy to me.

Then my mother began talking again, until we reached the next road-block and had to go through the same performance again. I realized as I looked out of the car window that I had expected more change. Everything looked familiar, if shoddier than I remembered. I was not to see the changes until later, when we got into the old town, and later still when I went across what used to be the old creek. The old town was where the Arabs and the Indians and the more prosperous of the rest used to live. The houses there were built in the traditional style of the coast, out of coral stone and plaster. Some were huge, rambling mansions, with balconies and courtyards, and even enclosed gardens. Even the more modest houses were built to last, with huge, carved doors ornamented with elaborate knockers and sometimes brass chasing along the edges of the frame. All the government offices, the hospitals, the schools were on this side of town, which jutted out as a headland, surrounded by the sea. This headland had at one time almost been cut off by a creek, and the only way to get to the other bank was by boat. The district was called The Other Bank. On the far side the houses were mostly made of wattle and mud, although people built sturdier houses as their fortunes improved. Some areas were not electrified, were without running water or a sewage system. The British filled in the creek, so that by the time I was growing up it had almost disappeared, but the differences did not go away. What I saw when I went wandering in the old town was what I had already been warned to expect: whole areas where houses had been allowed to collapse, gloomy, shut-up streets which had once been clamorous bazaars, broken drains releasing sewage into the narrow streets, where it snaked in little stinking streams through which people walked. It was far too deliberate and pervasive to be neglect, it was more like vandalism. The Other Bank had broad, well-lit streets, new blocks of flats, parks and so on. I would have been lost there within minutes if Akbar had not been with me. It did not take much cleverness to see the sweetness of the government's petty revenge.

When the taxi reached the house Akbar said, *Go greet him. He's in the shop. I'll take your things upstairs.* My stepfather was already coming round his desk as I reached the wide doors of the shop, his face impassive and unsmiling. I stepped forward quickly and bent to kiss his hand. He touched me on the shoulder, tentatively. I thought I felt distaste in that touch, but perhaps it was only my paranoia. I know I cringed with guilt and shame, and tried to imagine which of my crimes was uppermost in his disgust. Then he turned and shuffled back behind his desk. Welcome home. He looked unwell, so much thinner than he used to be, so feeble. 'Go wash,' he said, making me feel like a child again. 'Get some food. They'll have food ready for you upstairs.'

I turned and did as he said, and wished I'd resisted, had asked how he was, told him that I would go up in a minute but could I just have a seat and chat with him first? And while we are talking like this, I would say, will you explain to me why you could not even manage a smile to reassure me that I was not just something repulsive which had turned up in your life again? Could you not even say Alhamdullilah for my safe return? He looked so ill. Why had nobody said anything to me? The shop looked so empty, bare to the bone. Was everything that bad? But I said nothing like that, said nothing, just turned away and went round to the side of the house where the front door to the upstairs flat was.

'What did your father say?' my mother asked when I went upstairs.

'He said, "Go wash. Get some food,"' I said, and they thought this hilarious.

I am going to have to go to an earlier history. It can't be helped, because I will now have to tell this story differently. My father died before I was born. That is what I was used to saying, even thinking, though I knew it was not true. I have no image of him, no description, no photograph, not even a scrap of his writing. When I knew about him he was no longer there, and my mother had a way of speaking about him as if he had died. All I knew was that he had been a teacher, and we had lived in the apartment with the terrace where the rose and lavender bushes had once grown in old kerosene tins. I still see glimpses of that apartment we had lived in until I was seven, and the reception room with one window that had a view of the sea. I remember that some evenings my mother would spread a mat on the terrace and stretch out in the dark, with the light from the kitchen thickening her shape, her eyes open and staring at the crowded sky. And that from below us in the street would come the noise of people talking and distant music from the radio in the café down the road. Though these were public noises, there was something intimate and inclusive about them, like the sounds of a house.

And if I felt like listening to my mother as she lay in the dark, if I was not fidgeting and running about and making a noise, she would tell me stories of her life in the country, of her father who would not allow her to go to school, of her elder sister who had died in childbirth, of her beloved mother who had died soon after. Such calamities one on top of another had seemed like a judge-ment, like a curse visited on them. When she said this to one of the relatives who had come to mourn with her, she was asked *Have you no faith in God's mercy? That would make you an unbeliever.*

My mother's father, whose name was Nassor Abdalla, was heart-broken and filled with despair by the loss of his wife, his companion for a generation. In an impulsive attempt to escape reminders of the life he had lost, he sold his land, and decided to move to town and go into business. He rented the apartment with the terrace in which they lived and then he started to trade. It was the first time my mother had lived in the town. There was so much to see, processions and music in the streets, the promenade by the sea, but her father would not let her go out of the house on her own because by this time she was too old to do that.

There were only the two of them for a while, but then Nassor Abdalla decided to marry again. My mother suspected that he would. It was the way men were. It was done quietly, almost secretively, just a handful of guests and the sheikh to say the neces-sary words, then a small meal afterwards. Her name was Nuru, a widow in her thirties only recently out of mourning, a small, angu-lar woman with a passion for jewellery and perfume. She came with her own portion from her first marriage, and therefore she could indulge her passion for gold and musk without consulting her new husband. I knew her later, of course, and heard some of these stories from her too, and I can imagine her effortlessly taking charge of the household. She was the kind of person who took everything in her stride, talking unstoppably in her measured way, and was never short of an opinion on any matter that came up. Even later, she talked to my mother as if she were a child who did not know what was best for herself, who was prone to carelessness with the world.

But my mother's father was too old to learn the new work he had chosen for himself and he never succeeded. He lost money on bad deals and even got into debt. There were too many sharks in the business, my mother said, and he never learnt how to deal with them. It was Bi Nuru who started talking about getting my mother married. It wasn't right for a woman her age to be sitting idly at home (I think she was seventeen). She would only get into mischief. My mother's father became obsessed with finding her a husband before he died, which he duly did and duly died.

So Bi Nuru's marriage only lasted a few months and then she was back in mourning again. I was around five or six when my mother used to tell me these things, too young to do anything but listen in the distracted way of a child. Later I found important details missing from my memory of her stories, details which had not lodged themselves firmly enough in my mind or which had simply slipped away under pressure from other events. Soon after that time, she was married to my stepfather, and never repeated the stories about her father and Bi Nuru again, hardly ever mentioned him except briefly and in passing. Bi Nuru had moved out of the apartment some time earlier. I don't remember precisely when she left but it was not very long before we moved out. In any case, I shall always have a memory of the watery fish stew with large segments of slushy green mango in it that she served with lumpy rice every lunch-time. She left to get married again, this time to an ambitious young boat-builder several years her junior, and because I addressed her as grandmother, I was required to call this dashing young man grandfather too. Though she left the apartment, Bi Nuru was never very far from our lives at first. She used to come back every day, and stay until after lunch, but her visits grew rarer and almost completely stopped after my mother remarried and we moved out of the apartment. Perhaps she was revisiting her time there as much as my mother and me.

I knew who my stepfather was before he became that. Everyone did. His name was Hashim Abubakar, a merchant of means and reputation, with interests and contacts all over the world, as it seemed to us. His bearing and his carriage announced this knowledge, though there was no exhibitionism or vainglory in his self-importance. He never flashed money around and always waited for others to go ahead of him, until they insisted that he go first. He spoke with the care and modulation of someone who knew that people were listening, and he punctuated his speeches with occasional flights of poetry and soaring metaphors. But his greatest renown was that he was a rich and successful businessman. His most recent coup at the time when I came into intimate contact with him was the new electrical-goods shop he had opened, taking up the whole ground floor of a house he had built especially, and with an apartment upstairs in which he lived. Even a child could not help but be beguiled by the new shop and the gleaming gadgets which resided there.

Some time during my seventh year my mother was married to him and we moved to the flat above his new shop. It was bigger than our old apartment, and instead of a terrace it had a veranda which looked over the main road. There was a kind of glamour in living in the house of the famous merchant, though I did miss the room with a view of the sea. Sometimes I went behind the counter in the shop and could not resist a proprietorial feeling as I stood among the exotic merchandise. My stepfather did not serve in the shop himself. He had a young man who did that, while he sat at his desk in a corner chatting with whoever dropped by, or dealing with his papers and the enormous account books. In the flat upstairs there were rugs on the floor, heavy wooden furniture, a ceiling fan in the reception room (which when no one was around could be made to whirl into a blur), a radiogram and a standard lamp, an object of hazard when I was young. The bathroom walls were covered with tiles and the toilet gleamed, so that you felt ashamed of the functions you had to perform in a room so exquisitely bright. My stepfather, whom I was instructed to call Ba but could never manage to, all my life, treated me politely, like a relative who was staying with them. I don't think he worried much about me. He never said anything like that in my hearing, but I imagine he thought I was my mother's responsibility. I felt like a guest there, as if I was on holiday.

Then Akbar came, and then Halima, and after that my stepfather changed. He went straight to his children when he came upstairs, and never seemed to tire of watching them, his face covered with smiles, while they squirmed and wriggled and sang gibberish. He was a thin, usually tense man, with a grand and permissive air in public, as I have described, but he had been terse and precise when only my mother and I were around, as if his performances to the wider world were disguises against the burdens he had to bear in private. So when the smiles broke on his face they transformed him. Instead of sitting in the reception room listening to the news on the radio for hours on end, sipping coffee like a duty and frowning at interruptions, he crawled on the floor with Akbar and Halima, making nonsense noises and giving them kisses. My mother began to tease him, and I saw that their lives together had changed too. He even started to put on weight and was freer with his hugs and caresses, and seemed to forget himself enough in public to laugh with a kind of abandon which was obviously false and intended to reassure and disarm some unfortunate who had come to him for a favour or advice.

Previously it had been for these customers that he had reserved his grandest manner. It was then that he began to seem like an uncle to me, benign and, well, avuncular, and Akbar and Halima like cousins I was often required to keep an eye on and look after.

It was not to last exactly like that, with my stepfather as the besotted family man, but his silences in the house now had a new ease, a kind of contentment. And his persona outside was grander for the generosity his happiness now made it possible for him to extend. When his children threw themselves at him, he laughed and hugged them, smiling at his wife. He brought them little presents of fruit or sweets, and sometimes a cheap toy that had caught his eye. With me he was always gentle and, well, polite, as if I was an orphan he had accepted responsibility for. He was only occasionally short with me, usually if he thought I was fussing about something which seemed clear to him or if I was not attentive enough to Akbar and Halima. The only time he ever hit me was when a bicycle barged into Akbar when he was playing in the road and I was supposed to be keeping an eye on him, and my attention had wandered or Akbar had been reckless. I don't remember. But I do remember my stepfather came to look for me when he heard the story, hours after this little fracas had happened, and he hauled me to my feet by grabbing my head and pulling me up, and then he gave me a luscious slap on my left cheek. I remember that.

And of course I lost my mother, at least as I had known her before. She was now so busy, with her children, with my stepfather, with people who called on her to pay their respects to the merchant's wife and the mother of his children, and to accumulate credit for a day (may God prevent it happening) when need might force them into a plea for assistance. One of the visitors began to grow into an intimate friend. Her name was Rehema, and she was a kind of relative to my stepfather. I am not sure of their precise relationship but I suspect they weren't related by blood. It may be that her mother had been nursemaid to the family. With some people sharing mother's milk is a bond which is almost fraternal. In any case, she looked very different from my stepfather and from his other relatives, and she lived in one room in the poor part of town, across the creek, on The Other Bank, with a husband who was a house-painter. When politics got going, she became a stalwart rabble-rouser for the nationalists, leading mocking chants at rallies and in the forefront of marches through opposition strongholds. It was she that I would find later in bed with the football coach, when I would be roused by the beauty of her body. Rehema came often, for an hour or two in the afternoon, and filled the house with laughter.

My mother could only have been in her late twenties then, and at last her life was full. That is what I mean when I say I lost her. She was still soft-spoken and her warm laughter was never far below the surface, bubbling as always under almost everything she said, but to me she spoke mostly about the errands and the chores she wanted me to do. Somebody had to do them, and I suppose she felt as bad about them as I did. I went to the shop to buy bread and buns before going to school, I went to the market to buy salad and fruit when I got back from school, and I listened with a long-suffering superior air as my mother told me how much better she could have done, she who never stirred from the house, like a slug condemned to a piece of lawn where she slimed her daily exist-ence, or where she lived like an animal captured from a forest and kept in captivity and made to perform tasks that animals do. Then I took Akbar and Halima out to play when I came back from Koran school in the afternoon, went to the shop for sugar, tea, soap powder, whatever, helped with the washing-up, swept and so on. And later, I would go to the prison every day to deliver my stepfather's lunch and his change of clothing, every day after school, while the merchant's children were stroked and had bless-ings called upon them for the evil that had so unfairly befallen their father. My mother wouldn't have a servant in the house – I don't think she would have known how to live with one – even though my stepfather kept on telling her she should. 'A servant would steal, and I wouldn't feel easy with a stranger in the house,' she said.

Sometimes she caught my eye with a look of recognition. Then she would say something anxious. 'Are you all right? You're very quiet. Why the long looks?'

I would have no choice but to lie and tell her that something had happened at school, or that my stomach hurt and could I miss Koran school for the afternoon? or something like that, some small advantage I would gain from her concern. After a while I got used to the way things were, and played the part I was given as courteously as I could, even earning praise from my stepfather for my good manners and docility. Perhaps I even learned not to mind so much as my life became fuller away from the house, with friends I began to make at school, praise from my teachers, being selected for the school football team. But now and then I would remember my mother as she had been and I would miss the swift embrace that had sometimes been my reward for saying or doing something precocious or amusing, and the strangely abandoned way she used to lie in the dark on the terrace while her words mingled with the noises of the world we lived in. I know that I thought then that when I grew up I would not marry, and would not have a child. I could not imagine how a love such as my mother's for me could be lost. It seemed so unfair.

I didn't act like a boy-victim-hero out of a Dickens novel, not that bad. But I could have done better. I could have been resourceful, charming, brave. I wasn't brave, I could have done better. Perhaps that was why my stepfather left me to myself. I had the opportunity, the connection, the forbearance of circumstances, the contacts (his), and I chose to act like a stepson. Nor do I remember that time tragically. There were stories, in the first place, stories to fill the hours and the mind in the contest with life, to lift the ordinary into metaphor, to make it seem that the time of my passing was a choice in my hands, that there was method in the manner of my coming and my going. That is what stories can do, they can push the feeble disorders we live with out of sight.

The walls of the flat looked grimier than they used to, everywhere in need of a coat of paint, and some of the ceiling panels in the hallway had swollen and warped from a leaking roof. But it was when I went into the bathroom to wash as I had been instructed that I saw how changed things were. The toilet was blocked and nothing in that bathroom gleamed. I had already been warned that there was no running water anymore, so I washed as quickly as I could out of the bucket and ran out, revolted to the pit of my stomach by that blocked, stinking toilet. Later, when I tackled Akbar about it, and asked him with a rage I had not felt since my arrival why it was that they did nothing about such squalor, he shrugged. 'There is no water,' he said. 'The waste pipe itself is blocked, so are the sewers. Where do you want me to begin?'

There was only electricity for a few hours each day, soap was short, as was pepper, sugar, toothpaste, rice, you name it. You should have brought us those things instead of the chocolates and the bottles of perfume, Halima said. She said it with a smile, but I could not help hearing the blame in her words, that for all these years they had been living like this and I had not even bothered to find out, or even think of doing anything about it. I expected a murmur of dissent from my mother or from Akbar at Halima's gracelessness, but they kept silent, so perhaps they thought her words were well said. She was soft-spoken and full of smiles like my mother, though she looked nothing like her. But she also had an enthusiasm, a kind of confidence in life, which I could never remember in my mother.

'I didn't know,' I said.

'Of course you didn't,' my mother said. 'And even if you had brought something they would have taken it away from you at the Customs. They take anything they want, they do whatever they wish. There's no law here.'

'Even if you tell people outside about such things, they don't really take it in,' Akbar said, smiling too, being understanding, implying that he knew I would not be one of those people, or at least courtesy prevented him from saying so. 'How can you imagine this kind of petty hardship when you live in a place where you don't give any thought to the possibility of such shortages? If you run out of anything you go and get some more. If something breaks down you replace it or you call someone to fix it. How can you imagine what it would be like to spend a morning looking to buy a few ounces of salt? Or pursuing a carpenter for weeks to have him replace a ceiling panel?'

I sat in guilty silence as they spoke of their deprivations and wretchedness. Despite everything the food tasted good, I said, which briefly made everyone smile. Then when the urgency of their grievance had been slaked, for the moment, they asked me to tell them about my life in England. The room felt crowded. Akbar's wife, Rukiya, was there, with the youngest of their three children in her arms. Their other two children were sitting on the floor, listening to everything as if they were hearing it all for the first time. Halima's husband worked on another island, she had come on her own to welcome me, and would be going back in a day or two.

My stepfather did not sit with us when we talked like this. He went down to his empty shop every morning after listening to the news and sat there for whoever wanted to stop for a chat. The café down the road was not what it used to be. The customers had changed and the café radio was now only tuned to the state station, whose endless commentaries were alienating with their mendacities. I went and sat with my stepfather after breakfast, and we talked without trying too hard, touching on this and that subject warily. People stopped to chat and he asked them to guess who I was, which everyone did. It was a game he evidently enjoyed, because his face broke into smiles even before the question had passed his lips. Then we had the predictable astonished conversation. *How long has it been? We thought you'd forgotten us. You were only a boy when you left us and now you return with a head full of grey. Mashaallah.* I had never seen my stepfather like this, smiling and frivolous amid the ruins of his life, all the tension and intensity gone. It made him seem capable of a generosity of spirit I had not seen in the stern man I had known as a child. When one of his callers had gone, he would sink for a while and then we would pick up our desultory conversation again, and maybe he would gossip a little about the man who had just left us.

In the afternoons Akbar took me around, to visit people he thought I would like to meet, to exhibit me to his friends, to see places that had changed and those I had known before, where he would deliver me as if by magic, watching and waiting smilingly for my gratified words. One afternoon he took me to visit Bububu, and showed me the new houses people were building for themselves out of town. I remembered Bububu, I knew that my father used to teach at the school in that village before he left. For a while, at the turn of the century, a train service used to run between the town and Bububu, which was a kind of heartland of Omani occupation. Now, because the town had grown so much, Bububu was a suburb, a brief ride on the dollar-dollar, which was the deferring name for the fixed-fare bus. Akbar walked me past the new villas, some colonnaded and veranda'd and marbled, and described their provenance with a proprietorial air.

Then, with one of the grand gestures I was getting used to in him, he took me to visit the house of a Seyyid Hafidh, one of the old-time barons. There we met a man, a distant relative of the Seyyid, who had redeemed the old place by pleading and money.

As we walked round the decaying old building with its silent fountains and stinking bath-houses, and its quarters for concubines and suriya, it seemed a clear metaphor for the changes we had gone through. Our new barons have turned out to be spendthrift robbers, dismembering such corpses as Seyyid Hafidh's old house with joyous abandon, but they had their example to start with.

But it was the evenings I looked forward to. My mother would say, *Now tell us more.* Every night we sat in the big room and took turns filling each other in about our lives. Who was dead, who had married who, who had said what or done something or the other. Who had cheated and betrayed, and led his family into shame and ruin. Bi Nuru died six years ago, Rehema has moved to Mombasa and found herself a new husband and so on. When my stepfather came upstairs, he went straight to his room and his transistor radio (the radiogram had died years before), where a tray of very light supper waited for him, which he picked at while he trawled the air-waves of the world. Nobody went to him at this time. The raised voices from his radio were like injunctions to keep away. My mother was always the last to leave, and only when I said it was time to go to bed. Then we would sit for a few minutes more on our own, while I would quietly begin to steel myself for a final visit to the bathroom.

Late one evening, after I had been there for several days and the conversation had once again gone well, I said to her when we were on our own, 'Tell me about my father.'

'What about him?' she asked, a smile on her face which she turned slightly in the direction of their bedroom and the booming voices there. She touched her hair in a gesture which suggested contentment, a lover's display of memory.

'My father,' I said. I had assumed she would understand me from the first, and would dissemble cautiously. I did not expect her unguarded and self-absorbed pleasure in my stepfather. She understood me now, perhaps because I had spoken with a different emphasis. The smile instantly left her face and her eyes widened with surprise. After a moment she looked away from me, and we sat in silence for a long time. She sat there with her eyes on the floor and I felt I had hurt her in a way I did not understand. Yes, I understood something of it, that after all this time, after my silence, my long silence . . . I wished I had found a less solemn way of asking her, but I had been waiting to blurt this out for days and that was how it came out. I'm not perfect. I'm unfulfilled.

'What do you want to know?' she asked at last, her voice soft and her eyes gleaming with surprised sorrow.

'Whatever you want to tell me,' I said.

She rose and pushed the door to, not quite shutting it, and then sat down again. 'After all this time you ask this,' she said, an edge to her voice. She was silent for another moment, then with a look of resolution, her eyes looking directly at me and then away again, she said, 'I'll tell you. We were married for just over a year and then he left. I don't know why for sure. He never said anything. He just left, just before you were born.'

She clasped her hands together gently, and tilted her head slightly as if readying herself for a blow. 'The house we were living in belonged to your father,' she said, nodding towards their bedroom. 'The father of Akbar and Halima. He let us stay there without paying rent, for years, Bi Nuru and I. You were born there. And Bi Nuru paid for the household out of her portion. I had nothing, no money of my own and no relatives to turn to. My father had left nothing but debts, may God have mercy on him.'

I hadn't known about my stepfather letting us stay in the apartment rent-free, or about Bi Nuru paying for everything. I could imagine my mother and Bi Nuru talking about it in front of me, but I had no memory of it. 'Why do you think . . . he did that?' I asked. 'Why do you think he let you stay in the flat rent-free?' I expected her to protest my stepfather's honour, to say that he was a good man who had been sensitive to their predicament and had done what he could to help.

She sighed and then smiled wearily, resignedly. 'You really want to rummage into this, don't you? Haya. Perhaps it's better. You've been away a long time, and these things must have troubled you.'

'I was too young to ask when I left. And maybe you wouldn't have told me anyway,' I said.

'Don't speak like that,' she said. 'You make me think you're blaming . . .'

'No, no,' I interrupted. 'Don't think that. I only meant we didn't talk about things like that. I would have found it hard to ask you, and I am guessing that you would've found it hard to say anything. Why did he let you stay in the flat?'

'Your father was Hashim's relative, his sister's son,' she said, and she paused and looked at me, to see if I had understood. 'His mother was Bi Habibi. Do you remember her? We used to visit her sometimes when you were small. She used to live in Kikwa-juni, just by the old football stadium. Do you remember?'

I shook my head. A look of sympathy passed through her eyes. 'Time has cheated you of so much,' she said. 'Anyway, you were very small, though I would have thought you'd remember her. She used to make such a fuss of you. She must have died when you were six or seven. Her husband had been a man of learning. He had studied at Al-Azhar in Cairo, and when he came back he became a renowned scholar of religion. But he died when your father was still at school, and left his family with little means. So, Hashim used to look after them, in every way.'

She paused, and I thought she would say, *Do you see what a good man he is?* The air was heavy with the words, but she did not say them, and after a moment she resumed, 'When my father moved to town, he traded with Hashim. And when things went bad for him, he borrowed money from Hashim. Then Bi Nuru came to live with us, and all the two of them could talk about was getting me married. So in the end my father went to Hashim and offered me for his nephew, and instead of a dowry for me Hashim agreed to forgive my father's debt to him. It wasn't a big debt, so everyone got something out of the arrangement. That was all, that was how it was.' She smiled lightly, as if the words were not hurting.

After a long silence, when I thought she would no longer continue, when I was about to suggest that we leave it for now, she started again. 'I had seen him, of course. Your father. Although they lived in Kikwajuni, he had friends down here. I remember once Bi Nuru and I were going visiting somewhere, and he passed us in the street with his friends. Bi Nuru called to him and asked if he wasn't Bi Habibi's son. He was full of apologies and courtesies, saying he hadn't seen us, though I don't think he knew who we were. Or maybe he was just embarrassed in front of his friends. Afterwards Bi Nuru teased me about how he had looked at me. "That's your husband," she said. Perhaps that's what put the idea in her head.' My mother smiled at the memory. 'He sometimes walked past the house after that time we met in the street, and if Bi Nuru caught sight of him, she would tease me for days. He was at the teachers' college when he married me, just about to finish. Then a few months later he left. I don't know why.'

Tears flowed down her face for a moment, then she wiped them away carefully, without drama. It seemed grotesquely painful that a woman of her age should be crying silently like that, should be crying so for a man who had left her years ago. 'My father was already dead by then, may God have mercy on his soul, and you were about to be born. Hashim told us not to worry about somewhere to stay, that we could live in the flat for as long as we needed to. And if we had any other need we were not to hesitate from going to him and he would do his best. He told Bi Nuru, who would have known how to make it easy for him to say those things. So we stayed, and whenever we talked of moving he would not have it. We were part of his family now, he told us, because of you. That was how it was.'

And that was where we left it that night. I sensed her impatience the following evening, and thought that she would not stay behind as she usually did. She scolded Akbar's children twice, and at one point left the room for several minutes. But in the end, I think, her impatience was for everyone to go. She seemed edgy and I suspected she would be angry with me for the things she had said, for allowing me to rummage in her life, as she had put it, the previous evening.

'I heard stories,' I said when we were alone.

'About your father? What did you hear?' she asked, her eyes attentive and her head tilted with a kind of detached, professional interest. It was her habitual gesture of concentration.

'That he had stowed away on a ship to England.'

'That's what we heard too. He used to say he wanted to study, and he loved talking about England. He had a picture on the wall that he had cut out of a magazine, English countryside with a lake in it and some palace or something beside it. He used to say he would go there one day. So it may be that the story is true.' She smiled. 'Perhaps somebody knows where he is, and you can go and visit him . . . and his English wife. But perhaps he never got there. You've heard stories of what happens to stowaways if they get caught, of people being thrown overboard or worse, though God forbid that anything like that should have happened to him.'

'I heard another story that he was living in Germany,' I said.

My mother shrugged. 'I don't care if he is living in Hell.'

'Tell me what he was like,' I said.

She must have been ready for the question, for she did not hesitate. 'We were both very young. He was twenty years old when we married, and I was eighteen. Everything seemed possible then. I had lived all my life in the country, I knew nothing. And even when we moved to town, I just stayed in the house. I had never

127

been to school, I couldn't read a book. If by chance I listened to the news on the radio, I had no idea what was being said, or where all those places were. I just listened to what everybody around me said, and I had no choice but to accept it, like a beast or a child. He seemed to know everything. Lo, and he loved to talk. We used to sit on the terrace in the evenings and he would tell me about all the things he had read in books, all the things he had heard his teachers say. The radio said this, at the cinema he had seen that, in Europe they have such and such. Even Bi Nuru used to sit with us sometimes, interrupting your father with sceptical remarks although she was really just as ignorant as I was. But that's the way she was, she would preach at the stars if the mood took her. Sometimes we used to lie in our room talking until the muadhin called the dawn prayers. He made me laugh so much. Usually he was quiet with people, you know, polite and retiring – kimya kimya. Like you were when you were younger. But when no one else was around, he was full of it, stories and jokes and mischief. Bi Nuru spoiled him. She treated him like a favourite son. Everything was for him, and I was always at fault in her eyes for not having thought of this or provided that. It was his courteous, laughing manner. She could not resist that. And his pleasant appearance . . .

'What did he look like? He was slim, in the way young men are, and not very tall. A little taller than me. I used to tell him that he was still growing. His hair was soft and curly, almost glossy, not tangled and ropy like yours. His face too was slim, with a small round chin. When he smiled he looked so young, like a gentle innocent boy. It was that Bi Nuru liked so much, I think. Bi Nuru loved him. She used to tease him that whenever he tired of me she was always available to him. Then he left.

'At first we thought something had happened to him when he did not come home that afternoon,' she continued after what had seemed like an endless silence. 'An accident on his way back from work, perhaps. He was teaching in a school in Bububu, so he had to take a bus there and back everyday, and you know what those buses were like. So at first we thought the bus had broken down and he was stranded somewhere on the way. But when he still had not come back after it got dark, Bi Nuru went to Rashid Suleiman's house to ask for news. He was the headmaster of the Bububu school, I don't know whether you remember him. He used to live just down there by Bondeni, near the petrol station. Rashid Suleiman told us that your father had not turned up for work that morning. He said that he had thought of calling round to ask after him, but he had heard at the café earlier in the evening that someone had seen him at the docks, and later seen him get in the launch which was heading towards one of the big ships that was in that day. We didn't believe it at first, but then Bi Nuru heard other stories, so in the end we had no choice but to face the truth. It seemed as if he had died, and for months I wished I could die too, may God forgive me.'

She sat in such dejected silence for so long that in the end I said we should stop if she was feeling distressed. I had heard my stepfather turning the radio off, and that was usually the signal for her to go to him. But when I mentioned the radio she shook her head. 'Hashim knows I'm talking to you about all this. It's better that you hear all you wish to know. You have been cheated of enough already. Do you know what I did after you were born? I destroyed everything of his that I could lay my hands on. His books, his photographs, his clothes. I didn't want you to know anything about him or even think about him. I wanted him to be dead. I wanted him never to have lived.'

'Bi Nuru told me things about him,' I said, and I saw from her face that she had not known that. 'Not much. Just a few stories, and then I imagined the rest. She said his name was Abbas and that he had died, but I heard people say different things outside, especially when I was older. Why do you think he left like that?'

'I don't know,' she said, suddenly, not wanting to be asked that question.

'But you must have thought about it,' I pressed.

When she began to talk again, it was if she had forgotten my question, or had found a way of evading it. 'We had been married for about three months when he was sent to that job in Bububu. It was a good school and near town, so we were pleased about that. Some of his friends had been posted further away and had to live in the places where they had been sent. He didn't like teaching. The children tormented him and he could not persuade them to listen to any of those things he loved to talk about. When he came home he would sit quietly, going over the things that had happened to him. He said every day made him feel smaller. I couldn't take it seriously. I was negligent. I thought he was just tired, and that when he got more used to the work he would become the way he had been before. I haven't spoken about this to anyone. You come back after all these years and want me to live all those times again. I can't bear the impertinence of it.'

'I'm sorry,' I said, before she could say more, before she could close the conversation for ever. 'Let's leave it. If you feel it's not right . . . if you don't want to. I'm sorry you think it's impertinence, and I don't deserve your truthfulness. I've been negligent too, but I'm glad of what you've told me already. Let's leave it like that.'

So we left it, but not for long. The next night, after the others had left, with Akbar giving me long looks, she stood up as if to push the door to as before – only this time she shut it. I could see that the telling and the listening had become compulsive. We were both in it for our own purposes, but I knew that I had found a reason to love my mother after all. Not as a child who had lost her embraces and had sulked with a feeling of abandonment, but because I saw she could not stop, and she could not hide the hurt of those years, and could not disguise the pain of the failure of her love. There was something genuinely tragic in the freshness of all that pain. Yes, there was. And in knowing that such pain never ends, that nothing which means so much is ever over. It was a hateful sight and hideous knowledge.

'When he left, without saying a word like that, I couldn't think what could have made him do it. I couldn't imagine what might have gone through his mind. All I felt all day and all night was shame and loss . . . and terror. Then as I thought about it later, I began to put things in their place until I could arrive back at that moment when he left.'

'Did you?'

She looked at me curiously. I pictured the two of us sitting there talking about such things, and I was struck by the strangeness of it. We could have been sitting in that half-dark room talking about the beauty of the evening, or about how we managed to find ways of forgetting our ugliness and meanness, or how despite every-thing we could be free to talk about anything without a definite aim, without wanting to know. Instead I was forcing her to open old wounds that I would have no way of helping her close again.

'Did you arrive at the moment when he . . . left?' I asked, and I heard the word booming round the room.

'No, I didn't,' she said. 'But I found a place for some of the things that had happened to us. I remembered how shocked he had been when I told him I was pregnant.'

'Shocked?'

She shrugged. 'He didn't say anything. Bi Nuru was saying enough for everybody and I suppose I took no notice of him. Then later I remembered that he started to go out for walks late at night at that time, and his silences became longer. Or when he spoke he was sharper than he used to be. Sometimes he just sat in the bedroom for hours, with his marking in front of him, doing nothing. I don't know how these things are connected. I didn't think much about any of it at the time. I thought it would pass.

Then he left. I wanted to be angry with him, to hate him. But I couldn't for long. I just couldn't understand why he'd done what he had. It was as if he had killed himself, God forbid.

'I didn't leave the house for weeks. Bi Nuru did everything. I couldn't see how that time would ever end. But it did. It did. Like a miracle. His mother never recovered from it. She became ill, and the hospital doctors had no idea what was wrong with her. Her heart was broken. She never went out, her curtains were always drawn. If it wasn't for the food Hashim had sent to her from his kitchen every day, she would probably not have eaten. Whenever I went to see her, she cried and begged my forgiveness. She grew so thin and gaunt that you thought she would go any day. But she lingered on for five or six years. In the last of those years she was always terrified, leaping in fright at the smallest noise, crying all the time. She said there was a crack in one of the walls of her house, that it was getting bigger every day and that soon the house was going to fall down on her. She had heard it cracking one night. Datta. In the end she refused food, and she refused to be taken to the hospital. Her neighbours and her brother did what they could to talk her out of her madness, but she was determined. She starved herself to death.

'He never wrote to her after he left. I don't know if he ever wrote to anyone. Three months after Bi Habibi died, Hashim asked for me,' she said, and then she smiled. 'It was Bi Nuru's work, and God has been generous to us.'

I tried to imagine what could have made him leave like that. I had been trying to do so for years, but I was always defeated by the magnitude of the act. For it was a big thing he had done, leaving his whole life behind him to hide in the belly of a ship which would take him to an unknown wilderness. Was it to gain freedom or to escape that he had done it? Whatever oppression he was escaping, how could such a departure provide anything but an intolerable aftermath? If it wasn't to escape, if it was for freedom that he ran, what was it out there he wanted so much that he could act with such callous self-assurance? I used to think there must have been someone else, that he had got involved in something which became too big for him, and that he had then just simply run away. Nobody ever mentioned anything like that, and in such a small place such a juicy item would have been hard to suppress, but that didn't mean it wasn't possible.

When I started to think that I would like to leave myself, I used to have a secret fantasy. I would find out his address, someone was bound to know if I was persistent enough. Then I would write to him and he would reply to say, *OK, come.* Those were the worst years of our oppression after the uprising, and we lived on fantasies of redemption and escape. I never did write, never mentioned him to anyone. Whatever I heard about him was volunteered to me by people who had known him, and perhaps wanted to remark on something in me that reminded them of him. When it came to my leaving, my stepfather did everything: the passport, the ticket, the money, even the distant relative of an acquaintance who would keep an eye on me and look after my allowance. And the story I told Emma about Ahmed Hussein, who was studying in Leicester and with whom I lived, was not too far off the truth of what that time was like. (Yes, I know I haven't mentioned Emma for ages, but it is not because I wasn't thinking of her.)

'What are you up to with her?' Akbar asked me the day after that last conversation with my mother. 'And what are you doing to Ba?' We were on our daily afternoon tour, after he had come back from work and had his meal and his mandatory siesta, and washed for an unbelievably long time in the revolting bathroom, and dressed himself in his strolling middle-best in the time-honoured way. I knew he had been restraining himself from speaking for a day or two, and I had seen the lingering hurt looks he addressed to his mother, but I also knew that he would not wait very long. We were

133

strolling along the waterfront, his favourite walk, going nowhere in particular, the postcolonial condition.

'What am I doing to him?' I asked, and saw him frown.

'What is so difficult about calling him Ba?' he asked sharply, looking as if he would say more.

'Ba,' I said quickly, before he could begin on what I feared he was going to say, before he could start talking about my ingratitude and my discourtesy. He had never said it before, no one had, but it was what I feared they all thought. And I thought that once he started on that he would be unable to stop himself from talking about my other remissions. Akbar was eight years younger than me. I had spent all those years when he was small dragging him around from place to place, and laying down the law on whatever I could get away with. Now I could see and feel his assurance with me, that it was he who could act with unforced authority while I felt alien and at fault.

I have been writing about the conversations with my mother as if nothing else was happening between them, as if we were Scheherazade and her monstrous Shahriyar, living the day in a blur before returning every evening to narratives that were really contests of life and death, to stories that neither of them wanted to end. But my mother was no Scheherazade, no virgin princess trying to save the life of a dissolute despot. She spent her day praying, helping Akbar's wife in the kitchen, receiving visitors, hectoring, advising everyone within earshot, smiling. And after so many years away, my days were full of impact, full of intricate negotiations with people and places I had known differently. I felt that I had to be alert all the time, as if everyone was looking to catch me out in some dereliction, probing my account of myself, the way I spoke, my observance of social rituals to see how I would reveal my distance from them. I was keen not to be seen to have changed beyond recognition, not to be thought alien. But I wanted to tell my mother's story of her abandonment, in one piece, as I reconstructed it in my mind afterwards, to deliver something of the force of the cumulative telling.

'What am I doing to Ba?' I asked Akbar.

'You tell me,' he said.

On the day I arrived, after washing and eating as I had been instructed to do, I went and sat with my stepfather, and we talked in the desultory fashion I have described. He talked about the hardships they had had to put up with over the years, but not in the tone of personal grievance I was to hear later upstairs, but that of the man of affairs: the incompetence of the authorities, their mindless bullying, the endless fiascos, their irrational vengefulness. It was a public conversation, and as people stopped by, and after they had gone through the routine of wide-eyed greetings for the prodigal, they could sit down and join in without intrusion. My stepfather's shop was on the main road, and this traffic of casual callers was heavy in the middle of the morning but gradually diminished as the sun grew fiercer. By the time the muadhin began calling the faithful to midday prayers, we were sitting on our own while I was giving a lightly discreet account of my life in England. We fell silent during the muadhin's call, then my stepfather rose and put on his jacket and started to walk out of the shop and towards the side of the house. I walked alongside him for a few steps, picking up my story where the muadhin had broken into it, when my stepfather said without looking towards me, *Go and say your prayers*.

He said this harshly, with something like disdain. I should have expected it. He was, after all, a Wahhabi, those lovers of the unadorned word of God, zealots of the Sunna, the muwahhidun. The original Wahhabis were the fundamentalists of fundamentalists, and could proudly take their place among the fanatical crazies of any religion. They banned music, dancing, poetry, silk, gold and jewellery, and probably a few other little pleasures which it

135

would not become their holinesses to mention aloud. They abhorred begging and the veneration of holy men. If their greatest historical act of vandalism was to destroy the tomb of Imam Hussein, the Prophet's grandson, at Kerbala, their most persistent persecution has been reserved for sceptics and philosophers, for the Sufi orders. Some of their modern ikhwan have doubts about whether God would have sanctioned the telephone or television, let alone rockets to the moon.

My stepfather was not that kind of Wahhabi, but I should have known that there would be no messing about with prayers. I guess I was just trying to put off the moment. In any case, after he snapped his command I turned on my heels and made towards the mosque. It was only a few hundred yards behind our house, past the old baobab tree which domineered over the clearing, and then a few steps down the narrow street on the right with its shut-in smells of gutters. I had not been in a mosque in all the time I lived in England, had hardly said a prayer except in parody. I knew this moment would arrive and feared that I would disgrace myself, would make a hideous blunder which would reveal my long neglect. I left my sandals on the wide, stone terrace and walked to the stone water-tanks to wash. I washed my hands, my face, my arms up to the elbow, behind my ears, my brow and my feet up to the ankles. The three steps leading to the door of the mosque itself were wet from the feet of others who had preceded me, and the mat just inside the door was dark and spongy from those same feet. People were scattered round the small space, sitting on their own, leaning against the squat pillars in the middle of the mosque, or sitting against the walls. Occasionally someone would get up to greet a new arrival and exchange a few words, but there was no conversation.

I sat against the back wall, keeping my eyes on the floor, afraid that I would catch the eye of someone I would fail to recognize and who would take offence at my lack of greeting, or that I would greet someone I did recognize but who would have no memory of me, and who would look as astonished as the man at the airport had done. I sat there sinking gently with anxiety, awaiting exposure, ashamed of myself for my feebleness. When the call to rise to prayer came, we formed lines behind the imam, repeating his words silently to ourselves, then bowing and kneeling in satisfying unison. As I rose to leave after the prayer, a hand tapped me on the shoulder. And a moment later someone else I had known years ago also came to greet me, and others whom I recognized walked past with a smile or a word of welcome. The prayer and the mosque had brought with them a surge of the familiar, so that despite my anxieties about blundering I had been secretly smiling at the memories brought back by the smell of the mats on the floor, the bluish whitewash which covered the walls, the gentle hum of muttered prayers. I felt a surprising pride, for a man of my age and history, when I overheard someone saying in a loud whisper, *That's Hashim's son. The first thing he did when he got off the plane was to come in here to say his prayers.* They did not think me alien.

After that I needed no encouragement to go to the mosque whenever the muadhin called, except I could never rise for the dawn prayers. I could not rise until ten in the morning, even though I had given up (had had to give up) my three rums in the evening and slept deeply and exhaustedly through the night. For years I had been used to waking up at six to finish off some preparation or marking before setting off for school. Now I found I was keeping adolescent hours and felt shattered when I got up. To get to the crusted bathroom I had to walk past my mother's and stepfather's room, and their door was always kept open all day and all evening, until they went to bed. My stepfather's chair, with a coffee table and his transistor beside it, was positioned right opposite the door, so he could see the traffic that went up and down the corridor. My first visit to the bathroom inevitably (so it seemed) coincided with his final cup of coffee before he switched the radio off and went downstairs to watch the traffic that went past the shop. It was as if he was waiting for me to rise before he left his station. Because the bathroom was so loathsome, I undressed in my room and put on a bathrobe, to avoid getting my night clothes soiled. But the bathrobe I had with me was a skimpy, towelling number, the kind of thing you might wear on the beach (not that I ever wore it like that because I never went to the beach in England). Strolling past my stepfather's room every morning in this state of undress, at my age, knowing that he would have been up since four and would have said his prayers before listening to news bulletins on half the world's radio stations, made me feel that I deserved the disdainful look I imagined him casting on me as I hurried past. I never looked.

But my regular attendance at the mosque did win me smiles and approval, even from him. And as the days passed and we sat together in the shop every morning, drinking endless cups of coffee from the huge thermos I was given to take down with me, our conversations changed. In the interstices between visitors, some of whom I began to understand were on a regular and daily round of calls, he spoke with a fullness I had not anticipated after our desultory beginning. It was not so much that he talked intimately or said things that were completely unknown to me (though some were), but that he spoke about them without intensity and in generous detail. And when I asked him to explain something, he seemed to do so without evasion.

I hadn't known that his father was a grave-digger, or that his family had been shunned for this. His father was hafif, feeble, and you wouldn't have thought he could do work like that, wielding picks and shovels with such precision. But the mosques always came for him because grave-diggers were rare, and especially ones who felt a need to placate their betters, who felt such desire to deflect the contempt in which they were held that they did not argue about what they were given for their labours. His father

138

carried a certain smell on him, and when he was younger my stepfather used to think it was the smell of death, maiti, the stink of flesh drying out and decomposing in the heat, or the high fragrance of the wet earth of the graveyard. That smell, and the clumsy tools, and the casual mockery with which he saw his father treated – those were the things that determined him to take on whatever work came his way, to find honour and prosperity in this life as well as God's forgiveness and mercy in the next, but never to follow in the path his father had trodden.

Later he found out that the smell was not that of death after all, at least not in the way he had thought it was, but of a tumour on the inside of his father's right thigh, which he nursed for the last twelve years of his life. In the end the doctors cut the leg off – my stepfather said this with a brutal side-swipe motion of his flattened palm – but it was too late. He died right there on the operating table.

My stepfather wasn't at home when that happened. Business was bad in those years, and in some desperation he had found work on a dhow tramping along the coast towards the Gulf and Persia. He was away for nearly two years, living on scraps and millet, like the savage people of the interior. *At least that's what they ate at that time. Nowadays, these people we are not allowed to call savages any more eat whatever Europeans send them in sacks and tins.* He left the dhow in Bombay, because the merchant who had chartered the ship wanted the nahodha to go on to Siam and Java, and my stepfather had had enough of working as a sailor for a while. After he was paid off, he spent three months sightseeing in India – Delhi, Agra, Hyderabad, Madras. Pictures of those cities were still very clear in his mind, even though it was such a long time ago and he had never had the opportunity to go back. At Madras he joined another dhow which was making its way back in the monsoons.

It was not until the years just before the war that business began to pick up again, he said. And during the war itself, with all the shortages, an alert trader could always make something here and there. The real money was in the hands of the Indian merchants and creditors, of course. God has given them a gift for business but has denied them charity. They were the only ones who could afford to bring in the goods that were needed, which traders bought from them on credit, and repaid with interest. From the beginning, when the Omanis made themselves lords in these parts two hundred years ago, they brought Indian bankers to look after their affairs. The merchant Topan, in his day, was richer than the sultan, and half the petty princes of the islands had their land mortgaged to him. They knew their work, these merchants, and they knew the vainglory of princes and sultans. So they financed their extravagant display – lavish mansions and opulent weddings and grandiose schemes, pedigree horses and gilded scabbards for their long knives – and held the deeds to the lands the Omanis had granted themselves after the conquest of the islands. Sooner or later, the creditors owned the land and the princes and the lords lived in a pretence of prosperity which the Indian merchants prudently and wisely financed. While the sultans and their nobles arrogantly strutted in their tarnished finery, and intrigued and plotted endlessly, the merchants were in control of affairs. By the time the lords wanted their property back, the creditors' lawyers had tied everything up and the British were here to ensure that the law was obeyed.

When the war came it was possible to do a different kind of business. (He grinned at this point, and although he did not say so, I knew from somewhere I can no longer remember that in the early Forties he had spent a month in prison for smuggling.) Everything was short and rationed, the British needed it for their own people, who were far more important than us. So whatever you could find – rice, sugar, simsim, millet – even if it was of poor quality, there was always a good market for it. People learnt to eat jaggery and brown rice and shellfish when before they would have spurned such food as fit only for servants and heathens.

It was difficult to get news of the war. There were no radios then, or very few, and those who owned radios kept quiet about it because they were afraid they would be confiscated. The British were nervous about everything, so we guessed that things were not going well for them. It was not a surprise. We knew the Germans and how they made war. Some of the riff-raff here joined up, and some young people who were still at school did so too, because they were promised that they would be sent to a big college when they returned, and would all become doctors and lawyers. It's a good thing you didn't become a lawyer, their business is to cheat. Or a policeman, because if you are a policeman and they order you to arrest your mother you have no choice but to obey, and God has said *Honour your father and your mother after Me*. So if you become a policeman, you are also saying that you are prepared to disobey God if the need arises. Anyway, they were sent to Abyssinia to fight the Italians and to Burma to fight the Japanese, and we didn't see them again until the end of the war, those who came back. The ones who had joined up from school asked about their big college, and they were sent to the teachers' college in Beit-el-Ras, and others became policemen after all.

We knew the Germans and how they made war, but we didn't know the Russians, and didn't know that they were even more savage and brave. When the war turned in favour of the British, we began to get more news, and that was when we first heard about the Russians. Some people refused to believe that the Germans were losing again. We knew the Germans. Even after the war was over, and cinema vans went around everywhere showing pictures of the German surrender, of the destruction of their cities, of those camps where they had murdered Jews, some still refused to believe it. British propaganda, they said. Propaganda, that was a big word in those days. The end of the war was propaganda, the victory of the Jews in Palestine was propaganda, as were the killings in India and Pakistan at their independence. But the end of the war also brought prosperity, for a while, until politics came.

'I'm not doing anything to him,' I said to Akbar. 'He talks about what he likes and I sit and listen. Today he was telling me how the family of Mohammed Thani persuaded the authorities to give them back their house. It was a blow-by-blow account, and he played all the parts himself: at one time he was the family, then he was some minor clerk at the Housing Ministry, then the Permanent Secretary, then the Minister, until eventually he was the President himself, the Seyyid Rais in person, the zimwi of Kiboni Palace.'

Akbar grinned. 'Has he told you the story of when they were summoned to Kiboni? It was at the time when girls from various communities were being forced to marry black Africans, especially fat old black Africans who were senior officers in the government, the Members of the Revolutionary Redemption Council, may God curse them.'

'I remember,' I said. 'I heard about it.'

Akbar looked at me for a moment. 'I wrote to you to ask if you could get any publicity for this . . . crime. I sent you some documents and photographs.'

'I tried to. I wrote to newspapers but no one was interested.' I had written to the *Guardian* anyway, which had replied guardedly, and sent the material to their correspondent in the region. Later I heard that he was a personal friend of our Federal Rais, and was a regular visitor at State House. So it was then easy to imagine what had happened to those documents when they reached him. For a while I had worried about Akbar, and whether the papers would all be traced back to him, but I should have known that the pathetic bullies who ran our security services were unlikely to be capable of such cleverness. Their real talent lay in plunder and torture and petty persecution.

'You never replied to my letter,' Akbar said, and then looked away and chuckled as if he was amused by me. 'The sight of those beautiful young Iranian or Arab or Indian women who were unavailable to them drove the old lechers crazy. Their pale complexions and long, glossy hair tormented them. So they had one of their mad conversations in the Revolutionary Council for the Redemption of the Nation, and decided that these women were racists, God's truth. That was what these racists to shame all racists arrived at as a way of forcing those women into their beds, may God strike them with vile diseases in old age. Racism is an evil which our nation cannot tolerate, the radio announced the same evening. This was the preamble to naming names and requiring the delivery of so-and-so to the house of Member of the Revolutionary Redemption Council so-and-so, where the marriage ceremony would then take place. The monsters even expected the parents and relatives to deliver their own daughters to this cannibal feast.

'Anyway, as you may imagine, most of the women refused to go. Their fathers grumbled and their mothers wailed, and marriages were hastily arranged to pre-empt this catastrophe. But the old lechers, may God rot their mean souls, were having none of it, and army trucks came to collect the lucky brides from their homes. The Father of the People himself came to hear of these grumbles from the women's fathers and mothers. He was marrying and unmarrying at will, without need of army trucks. Just a quiet word and the parents would deliver the lucky daughter to the beast's lair, to be violated and dallied with at the Redeemer's whim. But then the Rais had the power to torture and maim and worse, without stirring from his divan. When he heard of the grumbling, he summoned representatives from all the various communities, by locale, religious sect, country of origin or any other category they could dream up. His Chief of Protocol or Head of Security or whoever does these useless things must have spent a whole week at it. Of all things, Ba was summoned, though I don't know who he represents, and his one daughter was already married. So there was this crowd of greybeards sitting around a banqueting table or something up at the palace, muttering their prayers while expecting God knows what. The Father of the People strolls in, and the sight of those cowering old men makes him laugh that rumbling, ghoulish laugh of his.

'I hear some of you are grumbling,' Akbar said, making his voice deep and menacing, and then bursting into laughter. 'You should hear Ba do it.'

'I will,' I said.

'So then, while his voice is still rumbling round the room, the great man unzips his trousers, pulls out his cock and puts it on the table. He lets everyone have a good look before he says: *What's there to grumble about? It's not that big. They can swallow that whole without any difficulty. Now go home and stop making trouble. Do you think you're something special? Those days are over. My government abhors racism, and will remove it by any means at my disposal, including this.* Then he taps his cock and puts it away, and gives his audience his rumbling, fiendish laugh before returning to whatever debauchery he had interrupted for that bit of fun.

'That was our big man. Nothing was too much for him. No meanness was too petty for him. Perhaps those who cut him down with machine guns, mean bastards though they were themselves, will receive just a tola of mercy from God when their day comes. But I hope that right now our big man is burning in Hell, admitted early as a special privilege, and that he is already sampling those impossible punishments God has promised some of us in the next life.'

Later, as we walked back home with the muadhin summoning everyone to evening prayers (no one stayed out too long after dark in these times), Akbar said, 'You say he talks. I know he talks. He sits there with those other old men every day and does nothing else. But now when he comes into the house he says nothing. He just sits in his room. That's not how he is usually.'

I had noticed that when Akbar wanted to say something harsh he looked away, and his face became a grimace of ferocity and disdain. That was what happened now as he spoke. 'I saw him sitting in there a couple of evenings ago and I went in and said to him, What's today's news? Something like that. And he gave me that long, mean look of his, as if I was the world's biggest fool. Then he said, I'm just thinking. What about? I asked. Do you know what he said? Things that cause me pain. I've never heard him say something like that. Things that cause me pain, and with a blank look on his face. That's what I meant when I asked what you were doing to him. And all those secret talks with Ma, I can hear you two rumbling away until the early hours. What's going on? What are you up to?'

I could see and hear his anger, and I guessed that what he wanted to say was something more brutal, something to make me stop unsettling their lives. Or perhaps it was simpler than that. Perhaps he was simply wounded by the exclusion, by what might seem like the rekindling of old affections whose consequences would be alienating for him.

'I asked her about my father,' I said. 'My father Abbas who ran away.'

Akbar did not glance at me or break his stride. I expected him to turn to me, aghast, as if I had drawn back a curtain on an intimate embarrassment.

'That's what we've been talking about mostly,' I said. 'I just wanted to know about all that. When I left before, I was too young to ask.'

He nodded, and although he did not say anything, I could feel his censure. *Have you come back after all this time to make her rake over all that old stuff?* Then he nodded again, so perhaps he was not disapproving after all, just uncertain what he could say about something so fraught with wounding possibilities. Unbeknown to him, his face began to change. His frowning sneer gradually slackened, and I saw him take a deep breath and release it in a slow sigh.

'I thought you'd come back to get married,' he said with a grin. 'Not to carry out an archaeological project.'

'Cut out that getting married stuff,' I said, and in this way we smilingly slid past the troublesome moment.

2

Sometime during my second week at home I received an unexpected visitor. He turned up just before lunch, full of apologies for the awkwardness of his timing, but he had just heard from Akbar that I was back and so he thought he would call on his way home from work, and he was sorry he had not had time to bring me even a small token to welcome me back. Just about all he had been able to pick up in the the rush were these few prints of the old waterfront before it was destroyed by the Royal Naval bombardment in 1890. Had I come across them before? A researcher from the university history project had found them in the Ministry archives and had had some copies made. In one of the prints, three barefoot Marines from an Irish regiment posed with their guns across their chests, in front of the trophy of a sprawled black body. One of them had his naked foot on the dead man's head.

My visitor said he had seen me at the mosque the other day, from a distance, and had been unsure, but this morning Akbar had confirmed that it was indeed I, and he thought he had better come and greet me, empty-handed though he was. How kind, but no, he would not stay for lunch, shukran. We were standing just inside the front door, and no, he would not come upstairs and intrude at such a time. Would I have time to call on him at his office the next day? Or the day after, if that was more convenient? It would please him very much if I would. There were many things for us to talk about. La, la, no, he really would not stay for lunch. His family would already be waiting for him to begin lunch, ahsante sana. Until tomorrow then, inshaallah.

My visitor was the Permanent Secretary at the Ministry of

Culture, and although I had heard his name mentioned and had been to school with one of his younger brothers or cousins, I had never met him before. I couldn't imagine the many things we had to talk about in his office. No one upstairs was interested in my visitor, except Akbar.

'He could be useful,' he said. 'I'll come along.'

'What for?'

'You won't know the way,' he said.

'What about your work?' I asked.

'What work? We won't do any work here. We just turn up at the office and hang around and then go home.' He worked at the Ministry of the Environment, and it was true that he did not seem to spend much time there. He turned up at the house two or three times every morning, on the thinnest of pretexts. He had heard that there was some good fresh beef at the market, so he was going to get some before it was all gone. Or one of the fishing boats had brought in a large catch of tuna out of season, and he was going to the beach to see if there were still a few slices going. Or he thought he would go and pay the electricity bill, or try to get the builder to come and have a look at the ceiling panels which seemed on the point of collapsing. He almost never went back to work after lunch, although in theory the working day did not finish until four in the afternoon.

The Permanent Secretary's name was Amur Malik. He was a short man in his early fifties, just inclining to plumpness. His office was in the former house of an Indian family. I didn't know the family, but the house was near the Post Office, and years ago I had walked past it several times and seen the family at their affairs, coming and going, washing a car, chatting at the threshold with a caller who was not intimate enough to be invited inside. The house would have been confiscated after the uprising, as were so many houses and farms and businesses and cars and anything that was not paltry or useless. The state had an insatiable appetite for plunder then, and many barons and knights who convetously sought their portion. A wall ran round the front of the house, enclosing a courtyard that was paved but was also planted here and there with jasmine bushes and dwarf oleanders and an ornamental palm. Against the wall was a rampant creeper with tiny mauve flowers I had never seen before. I reached for a flower, but Akbar told me not to touch. Its sap will stain your clothes, he said. I was only going to pick one of the little flowers, not roll around in it, but I pulled my hand back in case he had meant something I had not understood.

We went up the wide, stone staircase that led on to the veranda, and then into the sudden cool of the building. Amur Malik came out with hand extended, and if he was surprised to see Akbar there with me, he gave no sign of it. I doubt he was – government offices were like bazaars, and every transaction was conducted in the public gaze, as I had already discovered when trying to change money or ask about making a long-distance phone call. Amur Malik's office was a large, comfortable-looking room with a view of the sea. Perhaps in its earlier usage it would have been the family room, where parents and children would have sat in the evening to catch the gentle breeze which blew off the water and to listen to the music on the radio.

Amur Malik waved us to our seats and then sank back into an easy chair behind his huge and empty desk. For a moment he held a large, genial grin on his face, then with a look of concentration scratched the edge of his neatly trimmed moustache with a crooked index finger. I watched with mild envy as he and Akbar slipped effortlessly into a cheerful, light conversation. I knew it wasn't something I would have been able to do, but perhaps that was because they were at ease with each other and with themselves. Living among strangers for such a time, I had long ago lost that casual assurance, that ability to lean back comfortably, scratch my moustache and chat.

Akbar began talking about the project he was working on, the renovation of the old colonial hotel and the restoration of the European quarter around it to its period splendour. There were to be some structural repairs, but not many, considering the neglect of recent years. Eyebrows were raised here in mutual commiseration. They knew how to build houses in those days, Amur Malik said, and Akbar made a deep, rolling noise like a male pigeon on its lustful rounds. The real cost was in replacing the fittings and the decor. In that department everything was run down and neglected: frayed rugs, filthy showers, broken light switches, and you should see the state of the toilets. The kitchen was disgusting. The elephant-foot umbrella stand listed in the inventory had disappeared, the hotel library had been pilfered, and many of the books that remained were infested with bookworm. All those first-edition classics of English literature which so many visitors had been surprised to find there and had written about in newspapers in Europe, so many of them ruined. And that was only the hotel, let alone all those other houses nearby where people like Livingstone and Stanley and Burton had lived as they put together their expeditions to the interior, buildings which were part of history but which had been turned into hovels by people who cared nothing about their past.

'It will take a lot of money to get all that sorted,' Amur Malik said. 'But it's necessary . . . It's a pity the Aga Khan Trust wasn't interested in the project. I mean, there's tourism potential in this.'

'But we're confident UNESCO will sponsor it. We're expecting a fact-finding team quite soon.'

'Hard work, it's all such hard work,' Amur Malik said. 'There's nothing tougher than attracting international sponsorship.'

'We do our best,' Akbar said.

I kept my eyes on both of them, to see if there was any way in which the conversation was ironic, if they were making fun of themselves, or just taking the piss. Were they soberly talking about

throwing money at colonial curios when the whole town was falling down about their ears, food was short, toilets were blocked,
water was available for two hours in the middle of the night and
the electricity was as likely to be off as on? And when the radio
and television were blaring lies at all hours of every day and night,
and for every simple thing that you wanted you had to lie belly-up
on the floor and play the clown? I looked for a glint of cynicism or
a tone of mockery in their faces and their voices, but they seemed
absorbed by the weightiness of their concerns. Whose history was
it they were renovating? Then suddenly it came to me that they
were talking like this for my benefit, that it didn't matter what was
being said because it all amounted to the same thing: project,
sponsors, UNESCO, the work of nations. Not to impress me as
the visitor from Europe, but as an expression of their engagement
with pressing and urgent problems of the world they lived in, we
lived in. I don't know.

'Yes, we're all doing our best,' Amur Malik said, turning to me.
'Which is why I'm so glad you've been able to come in today, akhe,
my brother. There's a lot to be done, and we need people like you
to come back and do it with us. I am going to try my best to
persuade you of that. All our capable people have left to work for
other countries, leaving only us boneheads here. We need them to
come back and help us rebuild the country, wallahi bwana.
There's a job right here in this Ministry which you can have
tomorrow if you want. I hope when I tell you about it you will feel
excited enough to want to return and join us.'

I was flattered, of course – they need me here – but not for a
second was it a suggestion to be taken seriously. My life was elsewhere, principally Emma was elsewhere, and I could not in my
wildest imaginings picture her agreeing to give up her university
job and the conveniences of Blighty to come and unblock toilets
on a tumble-down raft floating on the edges of the Indian Ocean,
with captain and crew that to an unimplicated eye could only

seem like a cannibal rabble. None the less, I asked what the job was, and saw a small, cynical smile cross Akbar's face. I could have done with that a few minutes before when they were talking so seriously about the elephant-foot umbrella stand and the history which was to be renovated by international sponsorship.

'We're setting up a translation project,' Amur Malik said, leaning forward and resting his elbows on the desk, the dynamic ideas-man-in-action now taking on the gravitas of the patron with a job up his sleeve. His voice, which had in it a quality of genial clarity, now took on a husky timbre, a secretive, confiding intensity. 'We've put in a bid to a Scandinavian cultural foundation and expect their agreement to come through any time now. They've helped us in the past, and they are usually very generous. They'll fund the whole thing: staff, equipment, publication, marketing. There'll probably be a couple of trips to Copenhagen as well, to coordinate the details. I'd like you to be part of that project.'

Amur Malik glanced at Akbar and gave him a radiant smile, mischievously revelling in the bounty of his patronage. *This*, I imagined him saying to Akbar, *is what it means to be a Permanent Secretary to a Minister. To be able to hand out such luscious prizes to the deserving of your choice.*

'But the funding hasn't yet come through,' Akbar said, speaking to me, cautioning me not to get over-excited about the prospect of a visit to sunny Copenhagen. Perhaps calling it funding made it seem less like begging and dependence, less like taking the guilty money of our betters to throw away on trinkets and petty exhibitionism. Funding. Words like that transcend hypocrisy. They become like liturgical language, solemn and layered with intimations, but no longer precise enough to resist proliferating meanings.

'What will the project be translating?' I asked. 'Assuming that the Scandinavian cultural foundation comes up with the funding.' I wanted to try the word aloud, to see if it soothed to speak it.

'They will,' Amur Malik said earnestly. 'We've dealt with them before. I'm sure they will be understanding, akhe. Have no fear about that. The Scandinavians and the Dutch are among our most reliable donors. Actually we've submitted the same bid to a Japanese foundation as well. We're trying to bring them into the picture too, though this is only a recent development and we don't have any results. As I understand it, the Japanese are very generous once they're convinced. But as I say, this is a new project for us, at least on the cultural frontier.'

'So . . .' I began, wanting to take him back to the object of this labour, but he cut me off with a bright, knowing smile.

'I know what you're going to say,' he said, broadening his smile to take in Akbar and then the whole room with its demure light and the cool breeze off the sea. 'You've struggled all these years to make a successful life for yourself, and now you have a good position, with all the comforts and conveniences you desire. Don't think I don't know how difficult it must have been to achieve that. Some people here think that living in those places is just a matter of turning up at the bank once a month to collect your salary, and the rest of the time you can put your feet up in front of the TV. Listen, I know it's not like that, and that it required hard work and dedication to get to where you are. And now that you have, why should you give it all up and come back here to begin the struggle all over again?'

His face was earnest again, an understanding man of experience. I would have liked to have told him that he was overestimating my success, but it felt good to be spoken to as a conqueror of circumstance rather than as one of its minnows.

'All right, I'll tell you why you should come back,' continued the tireless man. I felt Akbar stir beside me. I wanted to say to Amur Malik, *You look vigorous and well fed. You have a neat, impressive moustache, and a pleasant face which is probably responsive to most of your commands. I'd say that you appear to be coping sensibly with the difficult and humiliating estate you find yourself in. This stolen room in which we sit, and in which you spend your days, is pleasant and even beautiful, and no one can prevent you from saying whatever you like, from weaving whatever fantasy appeals to you, from toying with whatever significances your words can accommodate. So why do you have to talk to me as if there is a purpose to what we are likely to do, to what you pretend you require of me? Can you not just say, Isn't this a pleasant room I've acquired for myself? Have I not done well? Isn't it a beautiful day?*

He couldn't. 'Because we need you here. Forgive me for saying this, but they don't need you there. They have enough of their own people to do whatever is necessary, and sooner or later they will say that they have no use for you. Then you will find yourself in an alien land that is unable to resist mocking people of our kind. If you come back, you'll be with your own people, of your own religion, who speak your own language. What you do will have a meaning and a place in the world you know. You'll be with your family. You'll matter, and what you do will matter. Everything that you have learned there will be of benefit to us. It will make a difference here, rather than being – once again, forgive me for saying this – another anonymous contribution to the petty comfort and well-being of a society that does not care for you.'

I couldn't have put it better if I'd tried, although of course he could not know the fertile subtleties and complexities that enriched my condition. Of course they needed me there. It helped them know who they were. Amur Malik glanced at Akbar, who took up his cue and said, *It's the truth.* There they were again, after the truth. Amur Malik approved the terse concreteness of Akbar's contribution, for he nodded firmly, once, and then leaned back in his ample chair and nodded again.

'I might add', he said, growing expansive now that he was content to have come so close to delivering the truth, 'that this approach I am making to you was initiated by the highest authorities. I mentioned to the Prime Minister a couple of days ago that I had heard' – a nod towards Akbar – 'that you were back for a visit. He remembered you when you were at school together. He was several years ahead of you, but he remembered your reputation for brilliance. We all do, indeed we all do. He said to me, Do what you can to persuade him to return. We need people like him to come back, to rebuild the country to something like it was and to move it forward into prosperity. This project would only be the beginning. We would expect you to move to bigger things after a while, and that is no idle chatter.'

Amur Malik sat still for a moment, his eyes lowered, contemplating what he had done, no doubt assessing in his mind's eye whether it was enough. Yes, of course I was flattered. Brilliance. Well, anyone can do with a bit of that. It beats standing in a cold, muddy pool eating worms any day. And one of my fantasies in the early days of England's cold depressions was that one day I would return to preside over my knackered land. At first I would resist the endless pleas to return and take charge of matters, but in the end duty would overcome my understandable reluctance and I would agree. The President-Elect, I sometimes named myself in my youthful day-dreams, before even day-dreams became too ridiculous to entertain in the face of life's true decline. But I was also puzzled. What did they think I could do? There must be some mistake. I'm a schoolteacher, for God's sake. I'm unfulfilled. I know that I perform this unthrilling task in the land of giants and wizards, and 24-hour porno TV channels on cable, and the mother of parliaments and the most exciting metropolis since Nineveh, and at the heart of the Holy European Empire, but none of that makes me deserving of such expectations. And in any case I spend most of my time there on buses, or waiting for buses, or in a smelly school building, or fretting in a bed with a woman I'm beginning to suspect despises me. Why such a heavy pitch to persuade someone as sunk in mediocrity as I to return to a squalor which was evidently beyond their powers and mine to do anything about? Was it just an irresistible desire for moral superiority? Give up your treacherous comforts and come and suffer like us? Perhaps if I told them about my buggered heart they would realize their error.

Emma. How I missed her.

'Please thank the Prime Minister for me,' I said, and chuckled at the improbability of it all. 'I am honoured by his invitation. It was kind of him to think me worth persuading.'

'It's not a joke,' Akbar said, affronted by my levity. *Yes it is,* I wanted to say. *It's a joke. And isn't this stolen room beautiful? I'd expect the Prime Minister's to be even more lovely.*

'You can thank him yourself, in person,' Amur Malik said, smiling to make light of Akbar's intensity. 'He'd like you to ring his office and fix a time when you can call on him. In fact, you can call his secretary right now.'

He reached for his phone, ivory and silent for all the time we had been there, but I shook my head vigorously. He stopped in mid-action and looked at me steadily for a few seconds. No more Mr Nice Guy in a minute. I could sense his irritation, and for a gleeful second or two I thought he would threaten me, or start reading some miserable lesson of duty to me. It would have been amusing to see all that genial sliminess peel away to reveal the cynical bully I suspected dwelt beneath it.

'What is it that the project will translate?' I asked. 'You still haven't told me about the details yet.'

'The great books of the world,' he said, I think with some relief and certainly not with a triumphant bark of appropriation, but in a voice of mildly beseeching modesty. 'We want to make the profound thoughts they contain available to ordinary people. Of course, the project will work out its own priorities but I would've thought it would probably want to begin with Shakespeare, Marx, Tolstoy and Hemingway. As perhaps you know, the Rais of our Federal Republic is very fond of Hemingway, and he is himself a translator of Shakespeare. Marx we need so that people can have

156

a firmer understanding of the democratic socialism which is the governing ethos of our state, and Tolstoy for his sympathy with the peasants and the masses.'

I should say at this point that *the Rais of our Federal Republic* is no relation to the cannibal lout who dangled his cock to the venerable greybeards at Kiboni Palace, nor to the somewhat more placid incumbent who replaced (after the abortive radio campaign) the man who replaced the founding Beast. The island part of our republic had been forced into marriage with the big state next door after the uprising, but we retained our own Rais, and our own Revolutionary Council for the Redemption of the Nation, our own jails and a myriad of picnic sites where our psychopathic authorities could play their dirty little games. We shared the same flag, though – yet another one – and used the same money, with a picture of the same man on the bank notes. And that man was *the Rais of the Federal Republic*, who had presided for decades over the crumbling state while his carefully modulated commentaries on the African nation soothed liberal consciences in Europe and North America (as well as in one or two advanced institutions in backward nations). In the earlier years of his reign, before he became seriously indispensable to the stability of the world, he had translated two plays of Shakespeare. In my last year at school (he was already on the throne then), we were required to put on a performance of his translation of *Julius Caesar*, which everyone from the stage hands to the leading actors sabotaged. Even the audience played their part, booing us and smashing louvre windows in their exasperation with our ineptitude. That was the Rais that Amur Malik had in mind, though I hadn't known about his love of Hemingway.

'These great thoughts all seem to be from Europe and its dispersals. Would you consider translating great thoughts from anywhere else?' I asked.

Amur Malik smiled. 'I understand what you mean, but we have

to be contemporary.' He said the word in English. I nodded meekly and waited, mulling over *contemporary*. Perhaps that was another liturgical word, like *donor* and *funding*, perfectly understandable to Scandinavian cultural foundations.

We left Amur Malik's beautiful office with me promising to think about his proposition (I suggested that it would be best to leave it until the funding came through), promising to call at his office whenever I had a spare moment, promising to ring the Prime Minister's secretary for an appointment, and just generally making promises about staying in touch, about caring for our people and their future prosperity. That, after all, was what mattered above everything else.

'That man is just words,' Akbar said, after he had got over the transition from the office to the heat of the streets.

'I thought you liked his words. *It's the truth,*' I mimicked.

'It *is* the truth. It's just that with the bunch we have sitting over us here it would just be a waste of energy. Anyway, I had to say something. You were frowning so hard at him I thought you'd do something silly. And don't forget to ring the Prime Minister's office.'

'Yes, he could be useful,' I said.

Akbar told and retold the story of our morning. My stepfather nodded uninterestedly and rolled himself another cigarette. That's what government is now, begging for alms, he said. May God have mercy on us. My mother looked interested but then became afraid that it was a trick to get me to come back so they could lock me up. Why should they want to lock me up? I asked. You don't know these people, she said. They've gone crazy with malice. Look at how dry their faces are. God has emptied their hearts of pity, astaghfirullah. On our afternoon stroll later that day, Akbar regaled every acquaintance with whom we stopped to exchange greetings with the story of the morning's play, and everyone scoffed at the idea, telling me not to waste my talents and my opportunity. For God's sake, there's nothing here, they said.

Later that evening, when the television had been switched off and the children had been chased off to bed, the talk once again returned to the offer of a job. By now Akbar was treating it as an inexhaustible joke, whereas I was beginning to think it had had its run.

'Stay here with us, my akhe. We can then marry you off without any complications,' he said.

My mother looked displeased. It was not how she would have wanted the subject raised. As I glanced quickly around the room – at my mother, Akbar, his wife Rukiya – I knew I was about to be ambushed. This had been planned. They told me they did not want to interfere in my life, to intrude in my affairs. It was only concern that I should be happy, and who could be happy without a family? As the days had passed, I had begun to think that the subject would not come up, that having seen me again after all this time they had decided it was best not to raise the matter. I had determined, in any case, that if it did come up I would treat the whole thing lightly, turn it into a family joke and make my escape. So after the initial surprise of their sudden attack, I put on an amused grin and sat back to listen, not protesting overmuch, relying on my detachment and lack of enthusiasm to make plain to them that they were getting nowhere.

My mother was the most earnest, determined to persuade. This project mattered to her. Rukiya put in dutiful words of support (in these early stages) and was full of encouraging smiles. Akbar was enjoying himself, being satirical and hectoring in turn, relishing my absurd situation but unable to resist acting the worldly man of experience, the responsible family man bringing a libertine brother to heel. You can't go on doing those filthy things you're doing out there for ever, he said.

'Akbar, don't be disgusting,' Rukiya admonished, glancing at my mother.

'Soon you'll be too old, and then you'll make yourself into a clown,' he continued, taking no notice of his wife. 'Chasing after young things who'll spurn you and laugh at you behind your back.'

I must say, I almost unclipped my superior grin at that point, so that I could say a few words to puncture his smug moralizing. But I couldn't do that without talking about things I did not want to, or telling untruths. So I stayed with my detachment, chuckling knowingly, as if Akbar's description of how I lived was not too far off the mark. Yeah, that was me, cruiser of filthy city streets. Then I saw the horror in my mother's eyes and wished I had protested. Akbar too saw her look of abhorrence and laughed loudly. It's only a joke, Ma, he said.

'Soon you'll be too old and no one will want to marry you,' she said, giving me a long, truth-speaking stare. 'Do you think her people jumped at the suggestion? You have been away so long, they had no idea what you had become. None of us had any idea. Then they were worried about losing their daughter. They were afraid that you would take her back there and that would be the last they would see of her. But they were also worried about your age.'

'I don't blame them,' I said, just managing to keep the facile grin on my face. Emma. 'They're reasonable concerns. So why don't we just leave the whole thing right there and put an end to their worries?'

'We talked with them,' my mother said.

'We talked them round,' Rukiya said, wanting to be precise, not smiling this time. 'You must let her study.'

'God, how old is she?' I asked.

That was the deal, that if after she met me she wanted to be married to me, I would have to agree to see her through a medical degree. She had already done a year at the university medical school on the mainland, so she had all the entry qualifications. (You can imagine what the self-besotted over-achievers who run British medical schools would have to say about those entry qualifications.) She was twenty, by the way. I remembered Emma making fun of me, saying that if I had stayed at home I would be taking a seventeen-year-old out of school by now to make her my third wife. The memory and the thought of Emma distressed me.

'We also told them what a brilliant success you have been in England,' Akbar said, signalling with his loud laughter that he was about to satirize me. 'How you write letters to the newspapers, travel in a coach and horses around London, have tea with the Queen.'

'I wish you had not done this,' I said, ignoring Akbar and addressing my mother. 'I don't need a wife. If I did I would've found one for myself. And I *am* too old. Her family should find a young man for her, someone her own age.'

'She wants to study,' Rukiya said. I thought I heard a note of indignation in her tone. At my ingratitude for all they had done? 'She has already turned down two proposals from younger men, because she would not have been able to continue studying if she married either of them. What she wants is to study to be a doctor in England.'

Her name was Safiya. She and her mother were to come visiting the following afternoon. (I was thinking of fixing my appointment with the Prime Minister for then, I said, but was ignored.) They were coming to pay a call as a courtesy at my return, but I was to make myself available for mutual inspection. Then we'd see.

'What does he think about all this? Ba,' I asked. I felt self-conscious using that word for him and avoided catching anyone's eye, but the moment passed and I felt virtuous and self-sacrificing for having done so.

'He thinks it's very funny,' Akbar said. 'Though he knows he'll be laughing on the other side of his face when he has to cough up the expenses of the wedding.'

'He thinks it's about time,' my mother said, smiling. I could see that she was pleased with how things had gone, that I had not proved too difficult.

Later I pondered on why I had not been more difficult, more adamant about refusing even to discuss the possibility. Perhaps I was curious to see what she might look like, whether she might look at me and burst into mocking laughter, or stifle embarrassed chuckles, or whether she might smile at her piece of good luck. But most of all, I was not difficult because I felt sure that I wanted nothing to do with the whole thing, and felt confident that I would find a way of conveying this to my mother unmistakably in due course. I would tell her about my bad heart, and if that wasn't enough I would invent a disease that had made me sterile. That should take care of it. As I lay in bed that night I toyed with the idea of a young wife and found it horrifying. I would fail her in every way. If necessary I would have to tell them about Emma. Emma. I had not been able to call her since arriving because there was no phone in the house, though I could have found one some-where, I suppose, if there had been something urgent. I had not even sent her a postcard, distracted by the things that were hap-pening to me, but also so eager to return to her that I could not imagine that a card would get there any quicker than I would. But when I thought of her my body emptied with anxiety. Had we neglected each other for too long? Would she be relieved at my absence?

Safiya and her mother came late in the afternoon, the customary time that women made courtesy calls on each other: the day's chores were done (though there was still supper to warm up), the men of the house would have had their siestas and gone out for a stroll or to sit at the café, the children would be out playing in the

162

streets, so even the women could take it easy for a couple of hours. Akbar had gone out for his habitual walk, so I went to sit with my stepfather until I was called to greet the guests. My stepfather spent the late afternoon in the shop too, though as a concession to the more relaxed nature of the time, he sat on a bench outside rather than at his desk. He was too old and ill for strolling or the café, but some of his morning callers would stop by to pick up the threads of conversations they had left trailing earlier on. When the coffee-seller across the street saw a new arrival, he would stroll over and pour him a cup, and on most occasions would refill my stepfather's cup. He settled his bill with my stepfather in some mysterious way I never witnessed. They consumed a prodigious amount of the stuff. When the coffee-seller was not around, there was always the huge thermos that was sent down for my stepfather on demand.

When Rukiya came for me, my stepfather grinned but did not say anything. The two visitors had not taken off their buibuis, and were sitting beside each other on the sofa. The mother rose slowly to her feet as I walked in, languidly, confidently. She gave me her hand and I bent towards it as if I would kiss it and then released it. She could have been anybody's mother, of medium height, matronly, smiling pleasantly. I turned to Safiya, and she gave me her hand without rising. As we shook hands she glanced up and looked away again. I sat in the chair opposite my mother and listened to her conversational courtesies as if they were the knottiest propositions. After a few moments Saifya's mother took over, and I felt myself growing less tense as I listened to the two women talking about things I had heard a thousand times before.

She did not look twenty, more like seventeen. Her face was slim and still, everything held in and out of sight. When at last she smiled, she did so slowly, as if holding herself in check. Rukiya had walked into the room, carrying a tray of snacks and some tea, and the two of them had glanced at each other and smiled.

Rukiya's presence changed the pace of the conversation that the two older women had established, and before long they were talking and smiling among themselves as if they had completely forgotten about me. Safiya's voice, too, was low and measured, as if she had considered what she was saying. Her eyes moved about now, lighting up when something amusing was said, and then turning sombre and steady as the conversation moved. I felt ridiculous sitting among them, on such an errand as I had been called here to perform.

My mother brought me into the conversation with the announcement that I taught in London. Who could fail to be impressed by that? It even made Safiya speak. What did I teach? she asked. English, I said, and saw her smile sympathetically.

'You mean a foreigner is teaching English to the English,' her mother said, a joke which everyone who made it seemed to think was original. 'Can't they speak their own language?'

'Where do you teach?' Safiya asked.

'In Wandsworth. Do you know London?'

She shook her head, and smiled embarrassedly, as if I had caught her attempting to pass herself off as knowledgeable about the great metropolis, I think. 'No, I don't,' she said. 'Do you teach in a college?'

'A school,' I said. I wish I could have said that I taught neurology at University College London, and in my spare time took a clinic at Guys Hospital, and at times appeared on TV when one of my cases caught the public imagination. Perhaps then I wouldn't have got the disconcertingly crestfallen smile she gave me. This would have been the moment to say something about the *kind* of school I taught in, and the barbarians who were my students. And then perhaps towards the end of this description I could slip in that the work was so crushing that I had suffered a heart attack (God forbid). That should take care of all talk of marriage. But I couldn't. Pride forbade it, I think. But in addition I certainly found myself beginning to enjoy the idea of making this young woman like me – in a hypothetical way, of course, because I was bound to say it was impossible in the end. It helped that our acquaintance predisposed us that way, allowed room for us to like each other. That made it less arduous in some senses, more abstract.

'Schools in London are even better than our colleges,' Rukiya said, loyally coming to my rescue. 'And the universities are the best in the world.' Imagine getting a medical degree from London! This was what was left unspoken. I beamed at Safiya, to confirm Rukiya's perspicacity. To my surprise, she laughed delightedly. Smiles spread round the room and looks were exchanged. Emma, how I missed her.

After they left, I asked for more time. 'What for?' my mother asked in exasperation. 'Didn't you like her?'

'She seemed pleasant, and attractive, but ... well, I hardly know her,' I said.

'Know her! What do you want to know about her? I had hardly spoken to your father when I married him.'

Yes, and look what happened to you, I wanted to say but didn't. That really would have been to put the whole thing on a different plane of seriousness. Anyway, I think the same thought crossed her mind, for she retreated, fell silent. Akbar shrugged and Rukiya looked disappointed. Why should she care? Perhaps it was just the project of getting two people married off that appealed to her. Perhaps she just wanted everybody to be as happy as she was, seemed to be.

'What do you mean by time?' she asked. 'How long?'

'I don't know. Long enough to know what to do. And anyway, I expect that she'll send word tomorrow to say that she is not interested.'

'That's not your problem,' Rukiya said, bristling for the first time.

It was wrong of me to ask for more time. I should have said I was not interested in marrying her or anyone else. And could they please stop looking for someone for me? But even before Safiya and her mother had got up to leave, I had found myself thinking about her as a woman I might be attracted to, and after they left I was unable to stop. I liked the self-assurance with which she kept parts of herself out of sight, out of harm's way. There was in her manner a suggestion that danger was nearby. It was not that she seemed frightened, but as if she was conscious of being at risk and wanted to act calmly when the assailant broke cover. Yes, a kind of powerlessness in the face of circumstances. *Who is the third who walks always beside you?* Perhaps I am wishing this on her because I feel so often like that myself, but to be sitting in that room, having your life sized up by an infirm mediocrity like me, must seem a little like coming face to face with the mugger who has been stalking your life. Yet I could not resist toying with the idea of her, even though the thought of her youth was horrifying. I would fail her in every way. Yet I lay in bed that night imagining what it would be like not to feel such an alien in England, to be able to live with someone to whom I could speak casually about things without having to give long explanations, what it would be like not to live in England at all, but here, in a crowd, rather than always being and feeling on the edges of everything.

I was only toying with the idea, but once I began I found myself imagining more: where I'd live if I returned, what work I'd do – perhaps the translation project was worth considering, after all. It would only be for a while, until the Prime Minister had had a word with someone and had me moved to do something more exacting. For if I came back it would be to do something exacting, otherwise what would be the point? And my wife would be a young doctor devoted to her profession as all doctors are, unconcerned about the meagre pay, rewarded by her people's gratitude and affection.

✧

My stepfather was gloomy the following morning when I went to sit with him, uncommunicative. I assumed he had heard about my prevarication and was irritated with me, but I was wrong. 'Have you heard the word that's going round? The Prime Minister has been arrested,' he said. 'Now they'll start locking people up again.'

'Why?' I asked. *What about my appointment, Your Excellency?* or however Prime Ministers are addressed. 'What has he done?'

'Nothing, probably. They don't do these things for a reason. It's just a sport to them. They lock people up or kill them as they feel like. This one was beginning to sound sensible.'

Further reports came throughout the morning. Each of my stepfather's callers had something to add on their arrival and something to take away. The reports were not just delivered, but their sources and credibility also examined, hadithi sahihi au si sahihi. The excitement of my stepfather's callers, most of whom were as old as him, was in dramatic contrast to his supernatural calm. Some of the stories would have stirred a well-fed sloth. It was said that the Prime Minister had been planning a coup with some elements in the army. (Coup against whom? He was the Prime Minister.) Or that he had been selling state secrets to our enemies. (What state secrets? What enemies? Who cared enough about our state to pay money to know about it?) Or that he had been implicated in an embezzlement ring, had made the mistake of getting caught. Or, most dramatically, that he had inadvertently insulted the Rais of our Federal Republic, who is notoriously incapable of suffering insults, inadvertent or otherwise.

There were variations on these luscious stories, and my stepfather listened to them and transmitted them calmly, while his visitors grew increasingly excited as the morning wore on. It was only later that I learned that he was on tranquillizers which he had prescribed for himself, for some reason, and which he obtained in his old ways. When I came back from the midday prayers I went into his room, where he sat leaning towards the transistor, listening to the news. 'Have they announced anything?' I asked, sitting down by his other side. 'No,' he said, leaning closer to the radio. 'Go and have your lunch.' He could be a charmer when he wanted to be, my stepfather.

Over lunch, Akbar delivered his own stock of stories. His sounded more authoritative and were more detailed than the lurid tales the old men had carried from shop to café to office. The Prime Minister, according to Akbar in his technocrat mode, had tried to hurry through a law legalizing the formation of political parties, other than the Revolutionary Redemption Party, of course. The Rais of our Federal Republic did not like the sound of this. It went against everything we had been working towards for a generation, he was reported to have said. It betrayed all our principles. So he ordered our own little Rais to have his Prime Minister put under house arrest on whatever charges he cared to concoct. 'It's been coming for a while. He's been pushing hard for this law. All those Ministers and Members of this-or-that Council of the Revolution were sitting on their plump arses not liking it at all, thinking of all the cheap thrills they would be denied and all the money they would no longer be able to steal. They weren't going to let him get away with it. This was coming. Everyone knew that.'

'Well, I didn't know that,' Rukiya said, irritated by Akbar's smug tone. 'What's the point of legalizing political parties? We'll only have all that nasty bickering again, then these monsters will get provoked and start their business as they did before. Anyway,' she said, turning to me, the hardness still in her voice, 'Safiya is coming this afternoon.'

She came on her own, looking as elegant and untroubled as before. I wondered if her mother knew where she was. When I shook hands with her, she smiled. Rukiya fussed around for a while and then left. Presently she called for my mother from the kitchen, so they even contrived to leave us alone for a few minutes. We talked mostly about studying in England: fees, entry requirements, that sort of thing. It was depressing talk, but I suppose it indicated the drift of her mind, the direction in which she was leaning. I liked her, and because I felt stirrings of longing for her, I also felt ashamed for my betrayal of Emma. By the time she was ready to go, I felt sure I knew what she would say about the proposal. Not that I knew anything about these things, about women. Emma was the only woman I'd ever known. She still is. What could prompt a beautiful young woman like Safiya – yes, she was beautiful – to want anything to do with a man like me? Just an education? I am not saying that because of my age alone, although that is advanced enough compared to hers, but because I would have thought it obvious to anyone what a spiritless hulk I am. It was only Emma who moved me, and at times she moved me to tears.

Perhaps it was a habit of submission that made Safiya agree, or appear to agree, to an arrangement so clearly unjust. And perhaps it was the same habit, learned in childhood and transported to England before I had had chance to learn the full might of male adulthood, that made me retreat in so many of the confrontations I had with Emma. In any case, it was clear that I was going to have to stop the whole thing going any further. Not because I was afraid that I would forget myself and be unable to resist the seduction they had organized for me, but because I feared they would feel even more betrayed if matters progressed any more. I thought of saying that I simply did not find her attractive, but I could imagine the look of incredulity on Rukiya's face. I had seen her glance at me with a secret satisfied smile as I stared unguardedly at Safiya.

So that left telling them the truth about Emma. Somehow, I had thought all along that I would, and perhaps I wanted to. I was leaving at the end of the week, and would have preferred to delay the telling until as near the leaving as possible, but I did not think I could do that now that they had brought the whole thing with Safiya to a head. 'I'm going for a walk,' I said, before either my mother or Rukiya could ask me anything. I wished that I was away from there, that I was back in Battersea with Emma, back home. It wasn't England that was home (so you can roll back the red carpet, or file away, if you care, reproaches against the alienated native), but the life I had known with Emma. It was the secretest, most complete, most real part of me. I knew that now, and wanted to finish with what needed to be said and done and return to her, return from here that is no longer home.

3

The Prime Minister was on TV that evening, hale and hearty, if a little indignant. He said nothing about the rumours of his arrest, and the proliferating tales of his misdemeanours and misjudgements, but there were several significant pauses in his address, and the general emphasis was on wounded self-vindication. His government's new development plan would come into operation as scheduled. All the formalities were now complete: the Revolutionary Council for the Redemption of the Nation had approved it, the Rais had signed it, and the Rais of the Federal Republic had rubber-stamped it. And earlier that morning he had received several representatives of the diplomatic corpse who had come to express their support and offer assistance. The people, the people's representatives, the people's leaders and the donor's delegations were all in favour of the new plan. All that remained now was for the people to address themselves to the task before them with the necessary zeal and self-sacrifice, and commit themselves without reservation to their patriotic duty, and prosperity and progress would be inevitable. It was no small thing he was promising, but the fulfilment of all our dreams: better schools for our children, better hospitals and health care, enough food for everyone to eat, adequate shelter, electricity and running water to every home in the land, and the end of dependence. If we were to put our backs into it and pull together, this was not an impossible dream. And with the help of God, and the funding he had been promised by the donor's representative, it was a dream which was likely to come true in the very near future.

As I listened to him speak, earnest and growling with the

duplicitous truculence of the truth-speaker, I felt the fun-loving part of me diminish and quail. It is a faculty of limited value, and I only have a small charge of it in normal circumstances, but watching the man on the screen hectoring the world to save his paltry life made it cringe and squirm into something submissive and self-contemptful. He made me dislike myself so much that I could sit and listen to him, and feel unease both that I would fail his lying vision, and that I did not get up and leave or spit in the general direction of his whining image.

I remembered him from school now that I saw his face. He would have been in the senior form when I was starting, a tall, lanky boy (when I was a stumpy squirt) who seemed gentle and courteous compared to the swaggering prefects and house captains and head boy in the same year as him. Perhaps I *should* go and see him, and tell him how much I preferred that civil prefect to the hectoring Prime Minister. *Isn't it dry for the season? When are you going to get the toilets unblocked?* He finished his address with a short prayer: May God bless our endeavours. And I in turn said a little prayer for him: May the donor deliver enough funding to make the burdens of office bearable.

The Prime Minister was followed by a man dressed as a sheikh of Islam, wearing a long juba with a silver lining and a thin turban wrapped round a hard cap. The studio was back-lit with a picture of the Kaaba, and the sheikh issued from that Holy Stone like an emanation. You could tell just by looking at him that he knew his lines. He had mean-looking lips, or in any case they looked as if they were used to saying hard words, and he had the regulation stubble around his chin. From the size of his ears I could tell that he wasn't a listener. This man was not joking, and as soon as he opened that mouth you had to lean back as the authoritarian blast issued from it. And what he had to say was simple and implacable, like the heaving breath of a dying dragon. (Not that I have met many dragons in this condition, but I mean that these were gasps

172

of spent might clinging to a memory of power and sounding only like terror.) God has chosen our rulers for us. That is why they are our rulers. Our duty before God is to obey them.

'What shall we say to Safiya's parents?' my mother asked.

It was in this casual way that I was invited to put the noose around Safiya's neck and drag her into the shambles of my life. In reality, my mother's question was forcing the matter to a crisis, my crisis, not the resolution she thought she was bringing about by firm insistence. No escape. My audience waited: Rukiya, Akbar, my mother. Should we not fetch my stepfather? Should he not be here at the execution, to hear me ask forgiveness before submission? They waited, words of approbation lying coiled alongside sour words of blame.

I gathered myself and gave it to them, relishing the impact that I knew I was going to make. Here it is, this is how it really is, a lot worse than you could have imagined and nothing much can be done about it.

'I live with a woman in England,' I said. It sounded odd when I said it, so cruel. 'Her name is Emma. We have been together for twenty years, and we have a daughter who is seventeen, Amelia.'

The man on the TV fell silent for a moment, and I looked at him to see if he had a view on the matter, but he just swallowed hard and continued. 'I love her very much,' I said. 'And I can't wait to return to her.'

Akbar laughed, as I might have expected, an ugly man-of-the-world bark. Rukiya made a face, something between disappointment and disgust. I forgave them both. My mother dropped her eyes.

'Why didn't you tell us this?' Akbar said, his anger mounting as he spoke. 'You could've saved us a lot of trouble. What did you mean by keeping silent while all this was going on around you? What are we to tell her people now?'

173

PART THREE

'Wee goe brave in apparell that we may be taken for better men than wee bee; we use much bumbastings and quiltings to seem better formed, better showl-dered, smaller wasted, and fuller thyght, then wee are; wee barbe and shave ofte, to seem yownger than wee are; we use perfumes both inward and outward to seeme sweeter then wee bee; corkt shooes to seeme taller than wee bee; wee use cowrtuows salutations to seem kinder then wee bee; lowly obaysances to seeme humbler then wee bee; and somtyme grave and godly communication, to seem wyser or devowter then wee bee.'

Sir John Harington, 'Treatise on
Playe' (about 1597), in *The Letters and
Epigrams of Sir John Harington together
with The Prayse of Private Life*, Edited
with an Introduction by Norman
Egbert McClure (1930)

My flight from home was frantic. The taxi was late, decrepit, and at every road-block sounded as if it would judder to a terminal halt, but somehow struggled and dragged its knackered hulk to the airport. The check-in was crowded and chaotic, everyone pushing and jostling from every direction, stumbling over luggage to reach the one official who sat calmly behind his podium, unhurriedly scrutinizing the documents which were presented to him, looking every inch a man contented with his work. Customs were awkward, wanting luggage unpacked. (I got through after only a brief interrogation to which I responded with beaming smiles.) Immigration studied my health certificates with great care, perhaps out of concern about whether I was well-enough protected from the pest-ridden land I was heading for. Then Security insisted I hand over all the local currency I had on me, since it was illegal to take it with me and since it was no longer possible to get out again to the bank counter and change it. As we waited in the crowded departure lounge, people sat in silence or paced the edges of the herd, smoking and looking out of the windows. It was as if we were waiting for the last plane away from an approaching disaster.

There was more frenzy on the plane itself, with arguments over seats and luggage space. The boarding cards showed every passenger's seat reservation, so it could only be a habituated fear of being short-changed and screwed by officials that prompted the anxiety, though perhaps some of the more obstinate contestants were in it just for the love of hassle. The staff of the Kenya Airways flight kept well out of it for a while, then moved in with ruthless courtesy and managed to get everyone seated in a little less than half an hour. I found myself in a middle seat with a beautiful Indian woman on the window side of me and a plump man in his sixties (I'd guess) in the aisle seat. When I sat down next to the man, he gave me a long, unwelcoming stare, and punished me throughout the flight by releasing a series of foul-smelling farts. After a while I could see them coming. He would make a small shuffling movement, and that would be the signal that something was on the way. It seemed that every small adjustment he made to his body released poisonous fumes. As you may imagine, life became even harder after he had had his airline meal. I learnt to respect that man's quiet assurance over the next seven hours.

The Indian woman was much more interesting, though when the farts began I was afraid she would think I was the perpetrator of the evil deed. I must say that until I located the source of the pollution unmistakably, I did wonder if she might be the culprit, so she must have wondered the same about me. Her name was Ira, and as I quickly found out when we began to exchange a few remarks, she lived in Ealing and worked as a systems designer for an international communications firm. So I told her that I lived in Battersea and had been working as a drudge in a school in Wandsworth for all my adult life. I had a sense in our exchange that we were two strangers meeting up a long way from home.

'Were you here on business?' I asked her, just making conversation, for I couldn't imagine that anyone would think to construct a system on our little island that required such dedicated design. I would guess that the usual practice is to set up whatever comes as a job lot from a Scandinavian cultural foundation.

'No, visiting relatives,' she said.

'Relatives! Are you from here?' Her hair was cut short and styled, though I couldn't tell you what the style might be called, not being familiar with such things. She spoke firmly and unhurriedly, and her face had a look of assurance and cultivation, the kind of face that you would expect to know how to get about in a theatre, or an airport, or a restaurant.

'No, I was born in Nairobi, but I have an aunt who still lives here,' she said. That *still* hung in the air for a few seconds, then she picked it up. 'All the family has left Africa now, except for her, gone to England and Canada. She says she is too old to start again, and she doesn't like the sound of the cold.'

It was a face that had seen something of life, by which I simply mean that I guessed she had known some pain. I must have been studying her unawares, because after saying that about her aunt not liking the cold, she looked back at me for a longish second and twitched her eyebrows the slightest fraction, which was the most elegant demonstration I have seen of the question *What are you staring at?* I retreated in confusion.

'When did your family leave Nairobi?' I asked, when a moment presented itself to reopen the conversation.

'A few years after independence,' she said. 'When I was about ten.' That made her about thirty-eight, though she had the kind of face that could have turned out five years either side of that. 'My father trained as a geologist. In England. I think he hoped to work for a mining company or something like that, but when he came back to Nairobi, his father needed him in the business. Selling farm machinery, motors and so on. It was a big concern but it wasn't really what my father wanted to do. He felt it was his responsibility to the family. Then when my grandfather died, he ran the business until after independence. It became much harder then.'

She glanced at me, to see if she should continue. She had spoken easily, as if talking about banal everyday matters, about a visit to a garage or the virtues of Swissair over British Airways, not about intimate family history. I have no great experience of travel, but I did wonder if sitting together on an anonymous aeroplane has that effect on people. I had done the same thing with the grinning man on the flight from London. 'You mean because of all the petty persecution of Indian businesses?' I asked.

She nodded. 'There was a lot of restrictive legislation, that's true. But it was also difficult to get the stock, and every official, right up to the top, wanted a cut. Three years after independence my father developed a heart problem from all the stress. He was only forty-three. It was then that he and my mother felt it was time to get out.'

I wanted to tell her, *I'm only forty-two, and I have developed a heart problem. A buggered heart, no less, with unstated consequences which I'll hear about in due course upon my return to civilization. Do you hear me moaning? Do you hear me planning to leave?*

'How did you get on when you first went to England?' I asked, suppressing my ridiculous irritation for the pleasure of Ira's unforced voice and her lovely face. There was plenty in my head which was waiting to burst out, and I was happy to keep it in check for as long as I could.

She grinned at the memory. 'He got a job with a mining company at last,' she said. 'I can't remember how many jobs he applied for. His age was against him and he had no experience, but he got one in the end. It was an Indian company that mined phosphates in West Africa and had its headquarters in London. My father just handled equipment orders and supplies, administration work. So he never got to be a geologist, but it was a mining company. That was when we moved to Ealing.'

'Oh, do you live with your parents then?' I asked.

'No, I live alone,' she said, casually, but I thought to myself, that's the pain that I saw, sharp-eyed blighter that I was. 'My father died about ten years ago, but my mother still lives in the same house they bought all those years ago. My elder brother and his family live there too. But here, you let me go on about myself and you say nothing.'

'I'm not interesting,' I said. God, haven't I got enough trouble without also being interesting? 'I meant, how did you get on yourself when you first went to England? Honestly, you're not going on at all. I'd love to hear some more.'

The fat man next to me must have had an opinion on all this, for he silently released a stunner. He must have had something rotting in him. Conversation was quelled, perhaps we both instinctively shut our mouths to prevent the poisonous fumes from entering our gullets. We sat helplessly gasping and choking in this swamp effluvium for a while, until airline business took us all in hand: a small tray packed with tiny tupperware dishes containing grandly named but evil-looking portions of food, a nasty sharp wine which was none the less welcome, followed by the dimming of the lights and the in-flight movie. Ira hardly touched her tray, and I made common cause with her, two sophisticated metropolitans spurning the crude, processed garbage intended for undiscriminating, beastly plebeians. I was to regret this as the night wore on, especially when I discovered that Ira was vegetarian, and had not been hungry enough to make a fuss when she was given the non-veg tray. My other neighbour methodically refuelled for further exploits in the early hours of the morning.

Anyway, after the lights were dimmed and the video was switched on, Ira curled herself up and shut her eyes. I tried to do the same, but as soon as I did so all the memories of the last few days, which had been squatting patiently in my darkened brain, began to stir.

I didn't mind Akbar's anger or Rukiya's despising looks. What did I care? I listened to Akbar's frothing spite with some astonishment, watched him build himself into a rage. I had misled them all. I had misled the young woman and brought shame on both families, but especially on my mother and father. Is this what England had made me into? An ill-mannered, heartless, dishonourable barbarian? An enemy, that's what I was. *Adui*. And now after all this, I announce the grotesque state of affairs. An

English woman! My mother said nothing at first, but I imagined her thinking that I had left her before and then it seemed I had come back, and now I was leaving her again, as my father had done. When she spoke at last, it was to say that I had been wrong not to tell them about this English woman I had married from the start. She did not know what she thought about the idea. Something in her felt revolted, ill. How could I do it? I couldn't have done worse if I had married a Jewish woman. But I should still have told them from the start. Perhaps after they had had their fill of revulsion and disappointment, they would have sent their blessing, or at least sent word of their feelings. Now what did the poor woman think of them, for their silence to her over all these years? That we were people without civilization or decency? That I was some pitiful vagrant, without home or family? And what about the child, who has not known her people and to whom she, my mother, would never be able to speak with understanding? What did she think of them for their silence to her? All these years they had worried, or at least she had worried, that I was living alone and dejected in a strange land because my home had turned into such a nightmare. But I had already found another home, and perhaps had already forgotten them for an English woman. And through all the blame and the hurtful words her name was silently screaming inside me. *Emma. Emma.*

I wanted to tell my mother that Emma and I were not married, that I had been lying to her for years about them, and that I *was* a pitiful vagrant, living a life of bondage and unfulfilment, a stranger, an alien, without any particular distinction or use in that place, but that I no longer had any choice. It was the only life I knew how to live now, and that more than anything in the world I wanted to get back to her and put right what could still be put right. But my mother's words of anger and hurt silenced me. There was more, and it seemed that her words of blame were endless, though afterwards I knew she could not have spoken for that long. In the end my mother said that since I had managed to forget about her for so long, she would have to learn to forget about me. She would have to learn to think of me as no longer her son. I was forty-two years old and she was disowning me, for Christ's sake!

Then the three of them left and went to my stepfather's room. I heard the transistor being turned off, and the door being shut and bolted. It would have been a good time for a walk, to get away from the distasteful drama that was brewing up, and to give thought to all the words that had been said, to feel the unavoidable potency of what had been delivered and received in a spate. Words are like that. Even taken in in bulk, they lodge themselves in the infinite corners of recall, and then return in their full regalia in ones and twos and threes, each little bunch stepping forward to corrode the heart with venom again and again.

But it was late in the evening, and the night outside was dark and empty. I had gone out on my own on an earlier night, when the TV was showing yet another episode of *Dallas* and everyone in the room was abandoned to its improbable seductions. It could only have been about nine, and I walked the open roads, not the coiled and insinuating alleys, yet everywhere there was a tense and anticipating silence, as if the assailants who throng the darkened path of our petty existence were waiting in the dimness of those gloomy streets. Now and then a figure slid into the open, silhouetted by the secretive shadow which followed it along the wall, and I knew without knowing anything for sure that these stalking figures were hard-hearted connoisseurs of human pain, prowlers after the flesh of the poor and the destroyed. A man staggered towards me, and even in that light he looked young and familiar, perhaps someone I had once known, but his face was puffy with old bruises and his body was soiled and reeking. When he opened his mouth to speak I saw that his front teeth were missing. *Beloved*, he said, reaching out for my arm. *Beloved, my beloved. Don't just walk past me.* I stiffened and glared at him, my body trembling with offence and abhorrence, and some anxiety. *Please*, I said, and hurried away, and heard him break into loud sobs behind me.

I returned to the house to find that my absence had not been noticed. I had not taken a key and had to knock for admission, which caused consternation. No one called at that time of night. When I was allowed in, I had to listen to lectures about the dangers of the streets at that hour. Nightmarish images came to me that night. Not grotesque or frightening shapes, but often faces, that appeared, sudden and looming, the moment I shut my eyes. Not familiar or especially menacing or mocking, but intense and hard, unforgiving, promising pain.

So while my misdemeanours were being discussed with my stepfather, I only considered the possibility of a walk as a desperate option. They might not let me back in this time, and I might have to walk the streets with those other looters of humanity. On the TV was another American soap, but I was too ignorant of these things to recognize it, and for a moment the absurd luxury of the set seemed loathsome and deliberately mocking. But only for a moment. It was nothing to do with me. And perhaps the reason why that fantasy world seemed real and engaging to everyone was because it was removed in every respect from the deprivations of existence in that place. Or perhaps it simply put that existence out of mind, turned it into something impossible and absurd.

I left the TV on and went back to my room to await my fate. Emma was waiting for me as usual when I got back to the room. Whenever I went back into it after I'd been out, it was as if she had been in there all the time, waiting for me to return. And then whole chunks of our lives together came to me and filled me with dread and longing. Sometimes I thought I heard her crying in the middle of the night, not loudly sobbing, but speaking with a broken voice while tears flowed out of her eyes. I don't remember her crying very much. I was the one with the tears, and in recent times Emma had tended to become irritated by my loss of control. How fascinating!

I expected that after the anguished confab about the vile English woman, Uncle Hashim would hobble to my room and wave his cane at me as he pronounced his curses. But I should have known better. I should have known that even in old age and dosed up to his fingertips with valium, Uncle Hashim would not forget to act with his customary decorum, would not soil his honour over a wayward stepson's misdemeanours with an English woman. That night I dreamed that the gas cooker had exploded in the flat in Battersea, and body matter was scattered in generous lumps all over the walls and floor. I dreamed that when I shut my eyes the scene disappeared, and when I opened them again there was the mangled metal and the bits and pieces. So I must have been in there somewhere, but I couldn't see myself.

They sent me to Coventry, in that quaint phrase. They didn't speak to me. When I went to kiss my mother good morning, she gave me her hand with slow reluctance and did not raise her eyes. Usually she sat with me while I ate breakfast (she did not eat in the morning, an old habit), but this time she remained in her chair in the corridor, from where she commanded a view of all the comings and goings in the flat. Rukiya stayed in the kitchen while I ate, and left without a word when I went there with my dirty dishes. There was no greeting nor the habitual struggle over who should wash up the dishes. It was time for a walk. I didn't think I could face an encounter with the grandee in his threadbare emporium. So I went to the Kenya Airways office to confirm my flight, wandered the shops for a few presents and considered calling on the Prime Minister to offer him my congratulations. I didn't care.

I walked on to the old golf-course by the sea, where British officials stranded on the island on call of duty used to play, and then retire to refresh themselves in the clubhouse, and hold forth on their plans for improving the condition of their charges, and plot and plan and continue their polite affairs. The clubhouse had been a wooden building raised on stilts, with a veranda running all round it and green straw blinds that were let down in the evenings to keep out the gaze of the curious. In the day it had looked like a humble wooden house, but in the evening it had glowed with the glamour of Empire, with the exclusiveness of colonial mystique, of abrupt dismissals and stern looks, of secret rites and strange foods, and of loud distant conversation and sudden ostentatious laughter. It had burnt down mysteriously after the uprising, and the pile of ashes and the blackened spurs lay on the ground for several weeks until the wind blew them away or people came to collect the wood for their cooking stoves. The golf-course was now several football pitches, an informal conversion that had required nobody's permission or funding, as was evident from the variety of ramshackle goalposts and corner flags. On the beach, fishermen's outriggers were drawn up under the cypress trees, in which hosts of crows wheeled and bickered and lingered for the fish offal which the fishermen discarded on the sand. In the time of the English, the beach had been a genteel promenade where the prosperous drove up in their cars and walked along the sea to be near their masters. And at night other cars would drive up and cut their lights, and sit in silence for hours.

A thatched awning on a dozen posts now dominated the site, under which an outrigger was in construction. The construction of an outrigger is crude technology, if you ignore the historical eye that is needed to locate the right tree to be felled, its transportation, and the brawny and sharp-witted business of hollowing it out and making it float and respond to the master's guiding hand on the tiller. I was prepared to ignore all this as I looked around that mysterious trysting place we had loved to creep up to to anticipate the next scandal, and lamented its transformation into a ditch where crows and fish offal traded unequally. But this was postcolonial reality, where the living space of the people was appropriated from the marginalized élite who had reserved it for their dramas of sensibility – and the people fished and crows ate offal.

Don't mistake me. I ate the fish, and crows had their uses, though I used to have nightmares about their piercing eyes when I was younger. I lamented that it was this old beach with complicated memories which had to be appropriated for them to get real. It was there, creeping up on a silent car that when you got near turned out not to be so silent, that I heard the Rolling Stones doing 'Satisfaction' for the first time, and saw my Chemistry teacher in an undignified clinch with an unknown woman (at least, unknown to me) who was to be his fifth wife. These things matter, although there is no gainsaying postcolonial reality. It was not just littered beaches that made me lament, not just misremembering what seemed a more orderly way of conducting our affairs than the reckless self-indulgence of our wordy times, when we can chat away every oppression and every dereliction, not just a nostalgia for the authoritarian order of Empire which can make light of contradictions by issuing dictats and sanitation decrees, but because as I wandered over the rubble of the damaged town I felt like a refugee from my life. The transformations of things I had known and places which I had lived with differently in my mind for years seemed like an expulsion from my past.

I returned to the house and went to seek out Uncle Hashim. He was sitting in the shop as was usual at that time of day, and for once he had no visitors, just the young man who ran the shop for him and whom I had hardly ever heard speak. Uncle Hashim accepted my greeting casually, and then looked out to the road for a long moment, his face hard and set, but his eyes brimming with hurt. He spoke suddenly, intimately, coming from a long distance. 'At times like these, memories come back to cause me pain,' he said, his face still turned away from me.

At times like what? It was what he had said to Akbar, and he must have liked the sound of it. But his misery *was* shocking. I had been used to seeing him impassive and calculating, always capably managing, even with the valium and the hollow days of his decline. Look how his day was ordered, how a morning in the shop was followed by prayers and lunch and a spell at the transistor, followed by a siesta and another spell at the transistor, back to the shop until early evening and then back to the transistor. His life was full of chat and worldly concerns, full of global speculation and rumours of intrigue and state treachery. He hardly had time in this unforgiving engagement with the world of affairs for frivolous conversations with his household. And now there he sat, anguished and old, tortured. It was shocking. He glanced over my shoulder at the young man who was probably lounging against the counter with his habitual look of ostentatious discretion, and said *Coffee* with the brusque discourtesy he reserved for employees and the beggars who came whimpering for pennies at the shop door.

'You remind me of your father,' he said, looking at me for the first time.

'Ma said I look nothing like him,' I said.

'Not in looks. In the way you are both afraid,' he said, glancing briefly into my eyes to check that he had hit home. 'When your father left here, it was something incomprehensible. May God treat him with mercy. What was he running away from? Like a thief or a killer. It was not an act I could understand. I don't think there was something he wanted out there, wherever he ended up. I think he just wanted to run away from his life, from us, from here. He could not imagine the hurt and shame he was leaving behind. And now you have done the same. For years you have been silent, I never thought I would see you again. Half a lifetime you have been away. Your return made your mother happy. It made her think that you would marry and be part of us again. But now you tell us that in all this time you have been living this life about which you have told us nothing.

And now you are getting ready to run again, leaving us with the shame and disregard that will come from the miscalculations we have made.'

I could not help it. I began to sob. For the father I had never known, and for his desperate escapade which had filled everyone else with pain. But mainly I sobbed for myself, for the shambles I had made of my life, for what I had already lost and for what I feared I was still to lose.

Uncle Hashim broke into a broad grin, which in a moment grew into chuckles that shook his feeble body and made him struggle for breath, laughing for the sheer disdainful joy of seeing me abject. It helped staunch the tears, anyway. *At your age*, he said through his smiles. I was always prone to tears, from childhood. When we first moved to the flat after my mother remarried, I was ready to turn liquid at a long look from Uncle Hashim, or I would sometimes burst into tears just standing in front of him while he talked to me wisely about something or other. I suppose that was what he meant, and maybe it was the memory that made him laugh so much, that and the irresistible pleasure of drawing blood. In recent years I have learnt to sob, though not usually sitting in a half-empty shop by the roadside while being lectured on my cowardliness, more often sitting in the flat while words and memories of words jostled and rattled my feeble defences. Anyway, it was good to see him looking cheerful and sipping his coffee with some relish.

'You're lost now,' he said. 'Not only to us, but to yourself. Just like your father.' It was obvious he liked the comparison, and perhaps he had been expecting to make it all along, whatever I might have said or done. I didn't care. People like Uncle Hashim can say things like that, even if they are true. They can store them for years, hold on to them and let them harden and solidify, until the moment arrives when they can be delivered as they had been intended to, to crush a bone or bruise the heart. So I waited for more. That's what I do. I'm a waiter. And I know that when hard words begin, there are always more crowding just behind them.

One of his cronies turned up before he could say more, a tall, slow-moving old man who carried his belly ahead of him as if it was something separate from himself. He had been a stalwart of the other party before the uprising, a joke figure in the area in the partisan politics of those days. Children had shouted abuse as they ran past his house, and on one occasion the outside walls, which were always covered with mocking graffiti, were smeared with human faeces. But after the uprising he was appointed chairman of the local party branch in a now one-party state, to rule over an area which had always voted massively for the government so forcibly ejected. He had a direct line to party headquarters, and to many other places besides. He was rumoured to be a personal friend of the President, the founding beast who had laid out his cock on a table to reassure the greybeards. It fell to him to translate and put into operation the government's decrees – to some extent, anyway, because everyone had his say in those days, and every thug had a gun. And all of a sudden he was being called over to come and have a coffee as he passed a café, and children fell silent as they hurried past his house. He remarried and moved to a larger house, and grew a pot to add stateliness to the new distinction in his life. But he was no longer young when all this happened to him, and he never quite carried off the belly. And instead of disdaining the invitations to coffee as transparently stoogy and grovelling, he seemed pleased to be made welcome. It was no surprise to find when I came back that he had become one of my stepfather's oldest friends. It was exactly what you would expect of Uncle Hashim.

He came by every day to bring news from high places. Even though he was now too old to be involved in the daily business of running his fief, he was still the branch chairman, and could rescind whatever he wanted to. He had become the notable of the area, and people went to him as they would to a wise and generous autocrat. To see the dignity of his walk and his address, it was impossible to imagine the days when grown men shitted into buckets and then transported them in the dark, giggling and smirking, to smear his walls while he slept.

He sat down heavily and began to tell the latest on the Prime Minister's crisis. 'It will be on the news tonight, he's definitely out,' he said with satisfaction. To the branch chairman the Prime Minister was a self-righteous meddler. He wanted to make rules about everything, interfere with everybody's business, and as for allowing the establishment of other political parties, where was the need for it? Everyone was happy and satisfied, and what could not be helped could not be helped, and had best be left with God. Tell me, Bwana Hashim, tell me. What will other parties bring us that we don't have already?

'Funding,' I said. I couldn't help it. I would rather have sat in dignified silence, but I couldn't stop myself. 'Democracy is a big thing at the moment, and I am sure multi-party elections will bring more funding.'

'It's true,' the branch chairman said thoughtfully. 'That's what the Prime Minister says and you can see the sense of it. But these parties will take us back to the bickering of the old days, when for so long now we have had nothing but peace and prosperity.'

It's true we have had to kill a few thousand hooligans, and imprison other thousands, and rape and mutilate several dozens, and force a handful of women to marry some old codgers, and we don't allow anyone to so much as fart without permission, humiliation and bullying, let alone vote, travel or speak the sedition that is in their minds. But unlike before, now everyone is in the same situation. Everybody is short of food, everybody is short of water, everybody has to creep and crawl for the smallest thing, and every school has no books and nobody has two pennies to rub together, and of course, everybody's toilet is blocked – except for the senior officers of the government who have to keep the country running, and obviously they couldn't do that if they were hungry, thirsty, poor and unable to use a clean toilet.

The branch chairman looked at me through blearily swollen old eyes, eyes that had seen contempt turn to trembling acquiescence, and waited for me to make noises of agreement. He felt the absence, I did too. His greatness needed them, the moment itself needed them. After an instant of this quivering silence, he twisted his head and spat with sudden violence into the road. Then he turned back to me, grimacing as he swallowed, and asked *Do you understand?* – still wanting homage and submission from me. Somehow I managed to prevent myself from nodding, but I saw as he brooded over my silence that it was flabby devils like him as much as the armed thugs, and the Permanent Secretaries and the Honourable Members of the Council for the Redemption of the Nation, and the Prime Minister and his Secretary, and the rest of the crowd of cannibal louts, who turned our lives into chaos and beggared our societies without clue or purpose. Why do I say *our societies* when we are all so different, from Timbuctoo to Algiers to Havana to East Timor? Because in this we are all the same, that we keep silent and nod – for fear of our lives – while bloated tyrants fart and stamp on us for their petty gratification. (I knew I'd be catching a plane in a few days. I didn't care. But that didn't mean that I would be able to get that *our* from my biography.) In the meantime, the moneybags who rule our world can continue with the anguished business of watching our antics on TV, and reading about our ineptitudes and murders in their newspapers, secure in the knowledge that a small donation here to fund a translation project and a modest shipment of arms there will keep the plague in the thirsty borderlands of their globe and away from their doors.

Uncle Hashim and his friend returned to their conversation about world affairs: the Prime Minister's crisis, a new shipment of rice that had just arrived, the bizarre murder in a block of flats in Mchangani, the derailing of an express train in India, Gaddafi. Just as I thought it was time to withdraw from this discussion of weighty matters, and perhaps go and call on the Prime Minister with my condolences, the branch chairman turned to me. 'How much longer will you be staying with us?' he asked. 'You've been away such a long time.' I told him I would be going in a couple of days.

'He had some news for us yesterday,' Uncle Hashim said to the branch chairman. I never thought he would. He had always been such a decorous, secretive man that I never thought he would talk about Emma. Perhaps the valium was having an effect after all. 'It turns out that all these years he has been married to an English woman.'

'Then you're lost,' the branch chairman said without any hesitation, making Uncle Hashim smile with recognition. 'You've lost yourself, and you've lost your people. A man is nothing without his people.'

It was as if they had rehearsed it. I thought of saying that I wasn't married to Emma, but I didn't. I didn't care. At that moment I didn't think I was too worried about losing my people, if that meant those two cruel old men. I nodded meekly and turned to go just as the branch chairman began on the tragedy of mixing blood. I thought of Amelia and felt shame for the meanness with which they thought of her, even in the abstract. I thought of Emma and my heart sank with a sense of unending vulnerability, and my head churned with exhausted ructions. I realized that I had been hoarding the little things that had befallen me to tell to her, frivolous little things which can only be spoken about intimately. Not the curses and the accusations, *You're lost, you're lost*, but a ludicrous conversation I had had with the airline clerk earlier in the day, or the first time I walked again along the sea front on my first morning and felt the strong warm breeze blowing in from the sea, or a chance meeting with an old teacher who remembered me but whom I had no memory of.

Ira stirred when the video ended and the lights were turned down even further, but it was only to rearrange herself before going back to sleep. The fat man on my other side was asleep with his mouth open, and as is only to be expected of someone whose insides were putrid, more foul smells came out of that orifice. At one time Ira leant lightly against me in her sleep and her head dropped almost on to my shoulder. I could feel her warmth against my arm and thought I could sense her hair grazing my neck. I wanted to lean towards her too, allow myself to relax against her, but I was afraid that would make her jump away, so I settled for the minor comfort. The plane droned on in the gloom, and though my body ached and twitched with exhaustion, I could not get to sleep. So I tried to sit still with my eyes shut, and to keep my mind blank (fat chance!).

They lectured me some more when I got back, telling me not to sulk and take things badly. Or at least Akbar did, while my mother sat in silent rebuke, and Rukiya bustled about all afternoon. It had been hard for them to listen to such distressing news, and to know the embarrassments that would now follow with Safiya's parents. Could I not understand that? I made conciliatory noises in return, which only seemed to invite my mother to begin her lecture again. Hadn't I given any thought to anyone else? What could I have been thinking of to do such a thing? To marry an English woman after everything that had happened! I wondered what that could mean, but I didn't care. My father, I guess. And why had I not told them? Had I not thought how abandoned the child would feel?

Amelia abandoned? Because she had been denied knowledge of their scintillating existence? *Listen, Ma, she has the TV, her CD player and an army of boys with whom she can, if she chooses, indulge most of her excruciating fantasies. The young woman is in her element, she belongs.*

But I didn't say any of that. I just wanted to get away from all the drama, get back while there was still time, and I could not imagine how I would get through the two days before my flight.

There was no announcement on the news that evening, and the branch chairman's rumours of the Prime Minister's fall were obviously exaggerated, for the virile chief himself appeared after the news with another speech full of noble words and synthetic indignation. As before, he said nothing about his crisis, just an occasional ambiguity accompanied by a misunderstood look, a self-pitying pause and a drooping lower lip. I was beginning to become quite fond of him and his ability to keep confounding predictions of his demise, and his nightly appearances in the room made it seem as if we were in the middle of an intimate family quarrel. I tried to remind myself that these were people who sentenced their opponents to one hundred and fifty years in jail, who made them walk barefoot on broken glass, and who pushed garden hoses up their arses and then turned the tap on. But I could not help admiring his unsmiling insincerity, and the utter callousness with which he delivered platitude after platitude with such heavy-handed angst, as if what he was telling us required thought or conviction or unflinching self-exposure.

I like stubborn, wily survivors, and wish I could be one myself. So the next day I walked to his office, to extend my appreciation of his doggedness and to wish him a joyful time of it. I didn't expect to be allowed in, just appearing like that to call on the chief of the nation (and the man had things on his mind, for God's sake), but of course I was. His office was in Vuga, near the hotel with the missing elephant-foot umbrella stand that Akbar spent his working hours planning to restore to its full tourist potential when the funding came through from the donors. There was a kiosk opposite the hotel selling browning postcards of the beautiful sites of our island, some of them buildings and gardens which have since turned to rubble and vegetable patches. I lingered there, breathing in the aroma of stasis and suspension, of a time kept stubbornly whole like insects that have fallen into a jar of oil and been preserved, like nerves twitching in cooling amber.

The office was a large villa set back from the road and surrounded by a low, white wall. Between the wall and the villa was an orchard of full-grown fruit trees: oranges, tufaa, pomegranates. It had been confiscated from its true owners years ago. I forget who they were now, some rich parasites who had built it by looting the people, though I remember the terrible temptation of those fruit trees when I was a child, and the restless dog which prowled beneath the trees just on the other side of the wall. Even if you stopped to take in the fragrance of the fruit and blossom that dog became demented with fury, a comprador lackey of the ruling oligarchy. But now there was no dog, just a man with a gun, his face scarred in a way that made it clear that he was not a native of our shambles, but from the mainland. We talk like that, or used to. He's not one of us, like Lord Jim, though Lord Jim was *one of us*, of course, which was where the whole story turned. How could someone who was so much one of us, the son of a vicar in Hampshire, for Christ's sake, turn against us to the extent of abandoning a shipload of pilgrims to save his own miserable life? It was true that the panic to abandon ship was instigated by the blustering German captain, but none the less, who would ever believe that we had the right to rule over the world if we were capable of such petty concern for our tiny lives? And no one even bothered to tell the pilgrims that the ship was sinking and they were being abandoned on it. And then the ship didn't even sink, was rescued by the Royal Navy and taken to Aden. Shame on the White Man's Burden!

But the soldier at the Prime Minister's villa was not one of us, and he unhooked his automatic rifle from his shoulder with such casual lack of concern that it was obvious that he did not think he would have to use it. I thought I'd have to tell the Prime Minister about that. It might matter to him one day. Anyway, I told him that I had an appointment to see the Prime Minister, and gave him a big smile. He grinned back and asked me where I was from. I said London, which made him grin even wider. Then he hooked his automatic back on his shoulder and nodded. For a Prime Minister in danger, he certainly had chilled-out security arrangements around him. *Don't write lies about us*, he said. Who would believe them? I replied, which made him frown and stroke the strap of his rifle. *Which newspaper do you write for?* he asked. *The African Pioneer*, I replied and strode on. The guard made no fuss, and I could imagine him shrugging to himself. I was past him and was somebody else's responsibility now.

Inside the villa door was another guard, and he was much more stern with his enquiries, which made me feel relieved for the Prime Minister's sake. He was a well-built man in his late thirties, with a firm, well-fed face and a glossy moustache: a man of experience, no doubt, with a family of his own and relatives who depended on him. When I said I had an appointment to see the Chief, he telephoned his secretary, who of course said I was telling fibs. The Prime Minister has no appointments this morning, the guard said, and became even more stern, and seemed quite uncharmed by my wide grin. He remained just as unmoved when I said I had come all the way from London for this appointment. Well, not quite unmoved, perhaps his eyebrows quivered fractionally, but he remained just as firm as before, and if anything his jaw sharpened and his voice hardened and acquired an irritable edge. There must be some mistake, Officer, I persisted.

What would he do if I got on his nerves? Shoot me? Have me thrown to the sharks? Expel me from the country? *Persona non grata*. I remember that we learned that new phrase after independence as foreigners discovered how sensitive to insult our government could be: one European joker was expelled for going to a fancy-dress party in a grass skirt and with a bone through his nose, an

American teacher on a peace corps assignment was sent home for having a live-in rent boy, someone at the British High Commission was discovered to have copies of the bills for furnishing the Minister of Commerce's new villa, which was a bit much, I suppose. Away they all went, *personae non gratae.* So I reflected whether by my insistent behaviour I could become subject to this phrase. That would make me an exile rather than an immigrant, and give me the credibility to sit on platforms and harangue people to give up their small comforts and join in the political struggle. If I cared to.

'Could I have a word with the secretary?' I asked, making one last try for the sake of it. The guard, if anything, seemed to be winding himself down, so there seemed little danger of being martyred. Also, up to now I had been speaking to the guard in English, hoping that this would make me seem more interesting to the Prime Minister in his eyes. But now I spoke in Kiswahili, just a little experiment. He gave me a sharp glance and then grinned, and I couldn't help grinning back. 'Can I see him? Perhaps I can explain.'

'Ala, mtu wetu,' he said. *You're one of us.* 'I thought you were West Indian or an American, one of those black Europeans. Give me your name, and I'll speak to the secretary again.'

When I gave him my name, he considered it and then looked at me for a long moment. I knew what was coming. We were in Darajani Primary School together, he said, his face glowing with joy. Don't you remember me? Mohammed Khamis, I was four years behind you. It's been a long time, brother, but now you say your name I can see it's you. So what was that speaking to me in English, some kind of disguise? Karibu, bwana, welcome. I hadn't heard that you were back, or I'd have come round to greet you. Alhamdulillah, it's good to see you again.

Now that he mentioned it, I thought I recognized him too, but I felt that about so many faces, to which I could not put any names, that I had begun to think that I was just over-compensating for the way time had cheated me of memory, had addled my past after such a long absence. In any case, I was soon in the hands of the secretary, who was such a young man he seemed a mere boy, and who was swept away by Mohammed Khamis's enthusiasm for his reunion with an old schoolmate, and had no choice but to ring the chief and ask him if he had time to see me.

So at last I got to meet the man whose shameless (because so transparent) antics for survival I had been watching every night on TV with reluctantly increasing admiration. He stepped out of his office with a hand outstretched, a broad secure smile resting firmly in his face, his tall athletic body striding effortlessly towards me. I was struck by how much, in this mode, he resembled the school prefect I had known years ago rather than the ranter on the box I had come to know more recently. I remembered at that moment a school sports day many years ago. I had the honour of belonging to the photographic society. At that time I had visions of becoming a world-famous news photographer, though for the moment I did not mind taking passport photographs of my schoolmates for a few shillings, or developing and printing their films at a cut-price rate. In any case, the photographic society ran a competition to see who could come up with the best action photograph of the sports day. It was a project ideal for exhibitionism and the triumph of the will, so I decided to go for farce. I would concentrate on the losers and strugglers, capture their agony and despair as their strength failed them and they anticipated the jeers that would greet them as they gasped and spluttered to the finishing line. Or better still, catch a revealing image of one or two of the fakers, the non-tryers (I would have been one of them if I hadn't been exempted because of the photo competition) who huffed and puffed while they jogged along contentedly half a mile behind everyone else. When I came to process my film, I saw that I had succumbed to the athleticism of the Prime-Minister-to-be and had snapped him winning a thrilling 1500-metres race, his arms flung out in triumph, his head thrown back, an impossible grin on his up-turned face. I put that photograph in as one of my entries, but of course it didn't have a chance. Nobody had a chance, and the prize was duly won by the president of the society, who was a sixth-former, a prefect, and a cousin of the headmaster (who was the sole judge of the competition).

As I walked ahead of him into his large, airy office, with important-looking papers scattered over his huge desk, I reminded myself of the young man who had accepted a blown-up copy of that photograph with embarrassed pleasure, and tried to forget his cynical endeavours to remain chief of the country's empty food-stores and its blocked toilets by persuading us that our betters were on the point of showering us with agreeable funding so long as he was there to receive it. Then we could renovate our hotels, bring in the tourists, enter an era of prosperity and justice for all, and live happily ever after.

'Amur Malik told me you were back,' he said when we were sitting opposite each other in huge chairs. 'I'm honoured that you could spare the time.'

'The honour is mine,' I said.

'Then we are mutually honoured,' he said with an easy, prac-tised smile. 'Do you know the first thing that came to mind when he told me you were here? What a pleasure it was that our best minds were coming back home. That's what I thought. There is so much to be done here, and I remember what a brilliant student you were when we were at school together, and how much you've achieved since then. But it's here that we need all that brilliance, not to have it wasted on the English. I asked Amur to tell you that, and to suggest something to you that you would find impossible to resist. I hope he succeeded.'

I smiled back and waited. Really, I couldn't see what they were up to. Brilliant student was an overstatement, but I was willing to accept it, especially under the present dire circumstances when curses and abuse and heartache were my lot, but the achievement-since-then stuff must be a mockery, or politeness, or just waffle, something to say to pass the time. *Why aren't you getting the toilets fixed instead of chatting me up? Why did you agree to see me at all? Don't you have work to do, a country to run, tonight's speech to ponder over?*

'I can see he did not completely succeed, then,' he said, courteously failing to disguise his disappointment. 'I would, if I may, add my entreaties to his. Not only do we need you back, but there are opportunities here for dedicated cadres. Do not abandon us.'

'I have been watching you on TV the last few nights,' I said, wondering if I was about to do something crass and foolhardy, something that would result in a bumpy flight from my homeland. I am not sure, but I think his eyes began to move sideways before he stopped them, as if he was expecting someone over his shoulder to be listening to our conversation. 'They have been inspiring performances. Will you be doing another one tonight? The funding prospects look good.'

He waved the subject away genially, but his eyes were hard and watchful. I was not surprised. I would have been ranting at the impertinence if I were him, and I knew he could rant. He was, after all, the chief, even though there were bigger chiefs above him, the Rais and the Federal Rais, who could snuff him out between meetings or orgies or whatever they did when they weren't giving speeches at the UN or addressing international conferences on the future of Africa.

'Let me tell you. Sometimes this is a thankless task,' he said, straining at sincerity. 'We do our best to move the nation towards progress, to change things for the better. We do this with our best effort and our utmost dedication. Do you think our efforts are appreciated? Well, by most of the citizens they are, I think. I sincerely believe that – but there are always malingerers, people who would rather wreck our whole future for their own petty gain. I am only trying to renew that enthusiasm for progress that is so characteristic of our people, to persuade them to hold on, not to give up but to labour for the future that we know we deserve.'

'So there is going to be another appearance tonight,' I said, smiling at his hard eyes.

He waved the subject away with a synthetic smile. 'I hear you've married an English woman,' he said, smiling in that arch and crass way that men do when they talk about women on their own. 'I also hear that you turned down Safiya Hilali. She is a lovely woman, much sought after. It's your choice, of course, but I can't say that I think it's a wise one. I understand that your parents are very distressed, and I'm not surprised. Still, everyone has his own life.'

I knew then (not that I didn't really know before, but some lessons have to be learned and relearned, and even then we forget them so easily and talk ourselves into something ameliorating and hopeful) that the food-stores were going to remain empty, and that schools would be without books, and the air would be filled with cruel, duplicitous promises, that justice would be just another word brayed from the mouths of the donkeys who rule us, and of course the toilets were going to remain blocked for a long time. If, with all that was waiting for him to do, our chief found time to concern himself with the intimate and pathetic doings of my existence and the unthinking meannesses of my family, then there was little else to do but hope that the funding from the Scandinavian cultural institute would turn up and keep the ramshackle ship of state afloat. If our chief, who was rumoured to be the best of them, could only fill his head with such gossip, nothing could be expected of the rest. They had long ago turned into organs of consumption and penetration, prehensile tools of self-gratification.

The sky was just beginning to lighten when the airline crew began to bustle around us: turning the lights back up, distributing face towels, promising breakfast. Unfortunately, they also woke up the fat old man, who shut his mouth and began a fresh assault of poisonous fumes from his nether end. Perhaps fresh is to mis-describe it, but potent and energetic, in any case. *Have mercy*, I whispered, but he only glanced round with loathing, parting his sneering lips for a moment to release more stale perfume. No question, the man was serious. It suddenly occurred to me that the man might not have been farting at all, but carrying a colostomy bag round his belly, and that all night long I might have been sitting with a purse of shit by my right hand. I rushed off to the toilet to gag and brush my teeth and generally freshen up in the yeasty atmosphere of an aeroplane lavatory after many hours in the air. I caught a glimpse of myself in the mirror. Mashaallah, I didn't think I had seen anything uglier for years.

'You asked me something earlier which I never got round to answering, but I was thinking about it in the night,' Ira said when she returned from the toilet, and had climbed over the stinking old man, who refused to move a muscle to let either of us in or out – which was just as well. Perhaps it wasn't a colostomy bag, but a meanness and bitterness which had corroded his body and made it rot. 'You asked what it was like for me when I came to England. I would guess there can only be one answer to that question. How would a ten-year-old Indian girl who had grown up in Nairobi feel about coming to England in the late Sixties?'

'That's a question, not an answer,' I said smartly, the teacher in me unable to resist such an obvious opportunity, but I said it nicely, with an exaggerated smile and a twinkle in my eye.

'Which I'm just about to answer if you give me the chance,' she said. 'Though maybe I should reconsider if you're going to be so pedantic.' She was smiling too, and her eyes sparkled. I'm usually slow to take a hint, being naturally generous, but I got the point. It was that *pedantic* that did it, a terrifying insult for someone in my profession, which is popularly assumed to be prone to that tendency, let alone the feeling of personal unworthiness which accompanies it.

'Everything was strange, obviously,' she said. 'Not frightening or anything like that, but strangely quiet and efficient. Everyone seemed to know what they were doing and went about their business calmly. That was my first impression, until I went to school. In Nairobi I had gone to a private Indian girls' school, where we were taught in English and made to think of ourselves as better than the people around us, the Africans. You know, that they were stupid and strong and dangerous, but had no brains. Big penises but no brains. Our parents thought like that, anyway, but the school made us feel special, gifted and pretty. We thought ourselves as good as the Europeans. Well, not as good as, but more like them than not. I couldn't have said that at ten, but I know I felt it, and my parents or some of the other people I knew quite probably said something like it. We even spoke in English half the time at home. So in a way – don't laugh – I thought of myself as kind of coming home.

'You didn't laugh,' she said, smiling at me. 'You should have. When I started school . . . That was terrible. I couldn't understand a word anyone said to me. There was so much noise and confusion, and the smells. Everybody smelled of sweat and steamed food. Dirty necks all around, creases of dirt, necks lined with rings of old sweat. Can you imagine it? All the other children seemed bursting with energy and . . . Then there were the names, of course. Most of them I'd never heard before: wog, coon, Paki bitch. I'd never heard bitch used like that before. The meanness was shocking, as was the casual violence and bullying. It's a familiar story I suppose, but I burst into tears as soon as I got home and wailed to my parents that I would not stop until they agreed to return to Nairobi. My elder brother came home with similar stories, and the two of us must have kept them at work for several evenings like that, pouring out our miseries and demanding their sympathy and embraces. It never occurred to me that they would be hurting with guilt, not until much later. I got used to school, obviously, and when my father eventually got a job, we moved to Ealing and I went to a comprehensive, which was much better.

'I don't think I ever got over those early days, though. Even after all these years I can't get over the feeling of being alien in England, of being a foreigner. Sometimes I think that what I feel for England is disappointed love.'

She smiled again, apologetically, as if she had let slip something intimate and shaming. She looked so despondent that I suppressed the scoffing words which rose to my lips. Disappointed love for that self-regarding old bitch, mangy and clueless after a lifetime of sin! Then suddenly it came to me that I understood what she really meant. 'Were you married to an Englishman?' I asked.

She stared at me, her eyes large with surprise. An instant later they moistened with pain. It was only momentary, then she looked away and looked back with a disbelieving grin. 'How clever you are,' she said. 'How could you tell?'

'It was something about the way you spoke of England as disappointed love. It sounded as if you meant more than just the place.'

'I suppose he had come to mean England to me in the years we were together, though I didn't think that at the time,' she said, leaning back and tilting her head as if she was looking back into the distance, trying out my suggestion on the life she had lived. 'I don't seem to think very much about things when they're happening to me, do I?'

'What happened?' I asked, and wondered if I had asked for too much. She wondered too, but after a moment she spoke.

'He left. About a year ago. He met someone else.'

She gave me what was meant to be a brave smile, but I saw her lip trembling and her eyes turning moist again. 'I'm sorry,' I said. And then she could not prevent the tears running out of her eyes.

She reached into her handbag and dabbed at her face, and after a moment she regained enough control to stop the tears.

'I'm sorry,' she said. 'It's so long ago, but sometimes it comes back and hurts so much. I'd better not talk otherwise I'll start again.'

The airline staff bustled around us again, retrieving trays and offering us more tea and coffee. I could feel the tempo of the plane's engines changing and guessed we were beginning the descent. I thought I should say something to her about Emma, give her something back for the confidence she had given me, tell her that I felt an echo of that disappointed love in my own buggered heart, but I didn't know where to begin.

'My father was so opposed to the marriage . . .' she said. 'I told him that I was twenty-seven and could make decisions like that for myself. That what I felt for this man was something valuable and I had no intention of letting it go. He didn't come to the wedding, and forbade my mother from coming, and then he refused to see me afterwards. I knew from my mother that he became so depressed that he just wasted away, and five months later he had another heart attack. I saw him in hospital a few days before he died. In those few months he had turned into a frail and feeble old man. Nobody said it, but it was I who had done that to him.'

'He did it to himself,' I said, softly, fearing to intrude into her grief, dreading to sound critical in matters that were too intimate for me to offer an opinion. But I don't think she heard me.

'Then after ten years he left,' she said. She turned away, her chin cupped in her palm, and gazed out of the window.

Don't think that my fat neighbour was inactive throughout all this. I haven't reported his brave deeds because I thought it would diminish the impact of Ira's words, and to be honest I was becoming hardened to the smells, while still admiring the range, variety and potency of his production. When Ira fell silent, he released a heavy sigh that hung over our heads in a dense cloud for a few moments and then began to descend. He reached across me and touched Ira on the arm. 'Armenian,' he said to her, tapping himself on the chest. 'I go round the world. Business. South Africa, Saudi Arabia, Brazil, Switzerland. Everywhere I travel on the plane but not eat meat. Not on the plane. Headache, stomach, no sleep. No meat, not on the plane. My daughter live in Canada. I go there now. Pray to God, He will help. Not pray to cow or monkey, but God Our Father, He will help.'

Ira smiled her thanks and looked away again. So the geyser had been there all along, sitting in his swamp miasma, listening in, making notes and preparing his little homily about Our Father. As he retreated into his haze of fumes, he gave me another snarling stare, his bulging face working with muttered words. I smiled my thanks too.

'I'm sorry about the melodrama,' Ira said, leaning nearer and speaking in a lowered voice. 'I don't know what made me speak like that . . . to . . . well, a complete stranger. I hate it when people do that to me. It must have been your clever guess. It just caught me completely by surprise.'

I shook my head. 'It was my frank, sincere and sympathetic face that did it. Don't be sorry about that.'

She composed her face for an instant, her eyes sharp with knowledge. The plane was coming in to land, and I leaned back in my seat, staring ahead and bracing myself. 'Were you married to an English woman?' she asked.

'I still am,' I said. I couldn't be bothered to explain. 'And while I was away I began to understand that that is how I think of England. My life with her. And I began to be afraid that we have allowed things to go too far between us, and when I came back she would no longer be there and she would have taken what I know of my life here away with her. It's more complicated than that, but what you said about disappointed love sounded familiar.'

There was no more time to talk as I had to concentrate on

preventing my soul from parting company with my body as the plane screeched and whined towards the hurtling ground. We exchanged telephone numbers in the chaos of descending cabin lockers and jostling passengers, all of whom were ignoring the repeated requests to remain seated until the plane came to a complete stop. We parted company as we approached passport control. I reached into my flight bag and could not locate the wallet in which I kept my passport and travel documents. I put my bag on the floor and knelt down beside it for a thorough search, only looking up to see Ira striding away unawares, unconcerned, across the huge Arrivals hall.

'I've lost my passport,' I said to a young Indian-looking woman in uniform who was standing nearby, instructing passengers on which queue to join.

She was calm and sensible, uninterested in sharing or sympathizing with my terror. They could put me back on the plane, lock me up, throw me into the North Sea. *Persona non grata*. Illegal immigrant. Asylum seeker. Refugee. She passed me on to a security guard, who also looked Indian, and he marched me to the last counter in passport control. This was obviously where the dodgy cases were brought. As we waited for the immigration officer to finish with the passenger ahead of me (who looked Filipino), the security guard gave me a smile and said everything would be all right. How could he tell? My face was brown, I was on a flight from below the Equator, and I wanted to enter England without a passport. How could he tell that everything would be all right?

Emma had promised to come and pick me up at the airport, and I thought maybe I should have her called in so she could tell them I was one of the good natives, not a drug-pusher or an arms-dealer or a white slaver. The immigration officer was a man of about thirty, clean-shaven, wearing metal-rimmed spectacles and a light-blue shirt. His full, oval-shaped face was composed and his eyes were unrevealing as he listened to me. 'I've lost my passport,'

I said, expecting him to smirk. Yet another poor rat attempting to squirm into our sceptred isle. 'I had it on the plane, because they checked it as I boarded the aircraft, but now it's disappeared.'

It was as if I had not spoken. 'Were you travelling with a passport?' he asked, speaking softly and directly, a man in no hurry, with nothing to hide, comfortable with himself.

'Yes.'

'What flight were you on?' he asked, leaning on his elbows and inclining his head slightly, as if this could be crucial information.

'The Kenya Airways flight.'

'What passport were you travelling on?' he asked.

'A British passport.'

'A British passport?' he asked. I nodded, and he raised his eyebrows in an ambiguous gesture. Did he disbelieve me or was he just saying *oh dear* to himself? 'What happened to it?'

'I lost it, or somebody stole it. I don't know. Listen, my wife is outside waiting for me. Is there a way of getting word to her so she doesn't worry?'

'Do you have any identification?' A library card, a Visa card, my photocopying card for school; everything else was with the passport. 'Please take a seat, Sir. We'll have to see if the Passport Office have any record of a passport issued to you.'

'How long will it take?' I asked.

He shrugged and went into the office behind him. So I sat, anticipating humiliations and delay, tormented by thoughts of expulsion or worse, worrying about Emma waiting outside, wondering what would happen to my luggage, to my life. I picked up a newspaper, and it was full of news of the murderous fatwa Ayatollah Khomeini had just issued against the novelist Salman Rushdie. He was another admirer of silence, the Imam.

The young woman I had spoken to first of all came to speak to me. She took my name and went downstairs to make sure my luggage was kept to one side. She found a way to ring the aircraft, and found out that they had found a passport which they had handed in to the security office. She rushed to the office and came back with my wallet. Safe, not an illegal immigrant, not a refugee, not a homeless vagrant.

I came out an hour after everyone else on the flight had been through, but Emma was still there. By this time she was so worried that I had missed my flight that she rushed towards me and embraced me deeply and long. It was wonderful. In the car I couldn't stop talking, and touching her, stroking her arm, patting her thigh, feeling her hair. I couldn't wait for the day to end so we could make love. When we got back to the flat, Amelia and I sat with her in the kitchen as she prepared a celebration dinner, drinking and talking about all the things that had happened to all of us in the last three weeks.

We were a bit drunk when we went to bed, just nice for a jolly romp, but Emma said she was too tired to make love. After a moment I asked her if there was someone else, and she said yes, there was. Then as we lay there in the dark, she began to talk about him and about all the things that had been happening to her over the last several months. She told me her life was a narrative which had refused closure, that she was now at the beginning of another story, one which she was choosing for herself, not a tale she had stumbled into and then could not find a way out of. Clever Emma. I wish I could unhear what she said, so that my silences are not filled with her words and her voice. She told me how her feeling for me in recent times had changed from a fanged love that made her want to diminish and silence me, into something much worse, so that now she found the thought of being near me or being touched by me unbearable, and had spent weeks of misery dreading my return. She talked for hours, and I lay beside her, disbelieving, afraid to move. When I tried to persuade her, to explain, to defend myself, she stopped me with a torrent of abuse in an idiom unaccustomed to her, and went on pouring poisoned words in my protesting ear.

At the end of the week she left. May God block her anus with clotted blood.

I plan to join an evening course on plumbing. I want to get to the bottom of the blocked toilets. I want to know what clogs up the works.

The course I'm after is at the City Institute of Interior Design, a prestigious institution on plumbing, where they go into this matter in proper style. I say that so you don't think it's one of those two-month YTS-type things, or one of the probation-service programmes that are run for ex-convicts, redundant teachers and social workers who need to be retrained to do something useful for society after a lifetime of self-indulgence and false consciousness. On this course I'm after, they go into the technical and social history of plumbing, and study developments in design techniques using computers and up-to-date software, with simulation chambers and video reconstructions of seminal moments in the plumbing process. You don't go anywhere near water or lead pipes or U-bends or ventilation shafts or any of that sort of sleaze and unpleasantness. It's a proper intellectual engagement with the subject. Apparently the demand for the course is outstandingly, staggeringly high, so the secretary to the course convener told me on the phone, and there is no certainty that I'll be impressive enough to be among the lucky ones to be chosen. I guess the one thing in my favour is that I have no practical experience of plumbing.

Despite this uncertainty about my future, I have been doing some reading. You'd have thought you would be able to go into any library and look up plumbing and find a whole row of well-thumbed books on this vital subject, so intimately necessary to a quiet and contented life, essential, you might say, to civilized life as we know it. Not so, far from it. However, I found bits and pieces here and there to start me off on my studies.

It was no surprise to discover that the first water-closet with a trap was proposed by an Englishman in the sixteenth century. Sometimes it seems that any idea of any value first occurred to an Englishman, especially (though not exclusively) in the era of Good Queen Bess: cricket, ale pie, the slave trade, table-tennis, colonialism, kedgeree, gravity, sociology, and, not least, the flush toilet. The name of the Englishman in question was Sir John Harington (sometimes spelt with two rs), and he wrote a whole book on the topic, *The Metamorphosis of Ajax*, subtitled *A Discourse on a Stale Subject* (ha ha ha), a philosophical disquisition on moral dimensions in the production and disposal of what we in the plumbing interest call water-borne waste. It is a hilariously unfunny piece of wit, but you still can't take away from him credit for the fact that he was the first person since the Romans to give the matter systematic thought and to come up with what turned out to be the solution. It had been an ongoing concern for centuries, of course, what to do with it all, but it took an Englishman to come up with the goods. He had plenty of time on his hands, it's true, but so do orangutans, and you wouldn't expect them to come up with a plan for a water-closet with a trap. Give the man some credit.

Like Pocahontas, then, Sir John was around at the time of Good Queen Bess and Jimbo Stuart. Unlike Pocahontas, who was only a pretty, savage princess whose destiny crossed with England's and who died evilly in one of its many swamps, Sir John was a proper English gentleman. The Queen was his godmother, he went to Eton and Cambridge, and he fooled around at Court for a while before returning to his lands in the West Country. These lands, by the way, were given to Sir John's father by Good Queen Bess's dad, who had simply taken them away from a troublesome corruptor of souls, a Catholic or something. There Sir John wrote poems and translated Virgil, Plutarch and Ovid, descending on the city for an occasional binge. He went to Ireland as one of the undertakers for the repeopling of Munster after a bit of ethnic cleansing, and returned a dozen years later to fight in a full-scale colonial war. Like I said, a proper English gentleman. He knew Sir John Hawkins, Sir Walter Raleigh and one or two of the other lovers of roasted shoulder of mutton of that time.

While he was in Ireland Sir John was knighted, along with every other Old Etonian in sight, by the English commander the Earl of Essex, who by this act of arrogation pissed off Good Queen Bess good and proper. So Sir John was banished to the West Country again, where in due course he wrote his ingeniously boring book about toilets. He thought it would cheer everyone up and make the Queen think him smart, but it didn't. And no one thought much about his plan for the flush with a trap either, or gave any thought to the U-bend or the S-parallel for generations. So that was that for another 200 years, back to buckets and chamber-pots and squatting in the nettle-bed, until another Englishman came along with an improved plan. Is it not a relief that it was an Englishman? He was a watchmaker called Jenkins and he lived in Stepney, which as it happens was a salubrious suburb in those days. Thus was the dawn of civilization. Of course, this was only the beginning, and a great many problems and improvements lay ahead before plumbing became what it is today. And it wasn't all pipes and lead poisoning, which is another subject altogether, but how to transport water, keep the clean from the dirty, keep the water tables from mingling, etc.

Why this interest in plumbing? It should be obvious really, but I'll say it anyway. Because I don't want to talk about Emma, and I'm not going to. When I've done my course on plumbing I'm going to offer my services to my homeland, strictly on an expatriate salary, so we can sort out those blocked toilets. I had thought I would go and see the Prime Minister again and say, *OK, I'm ready, let's get rid of the stuff*, and he would rise and embrace me and we would go off to the renovated colonial hotel and celebrate my return to the fold, and put our umbrellas in the elephant-foot stand which Akbar would have found hidden in a disused store, or which would be a tasteful replica he had had made in London. But unfortunately the Prime Minister has gone after all. They locked him up for insulting the flag. One of his security guards saw him standing on his veranda wearing a flag as a loin cloth, and so, despite his wiliness and his ranting displays, off to the jakes with him.

Ajax. Age akes. Age breeds aches. I could have told her ages ago – that my father was Abbas and he left my mother before I was born, that he probably came to England, that Uncle Hashim was really my stepfather, my benefactor, that my father's sister was really Bi Nuru, and that I made up the whole pack of lies which was my life with her because I could. I don't even know if that is true, or if there are more complicated reasons for what I did which I do not have the wit or energy to analyse. Emma would have known how to put everything more clearly. If that sounds evasive then it will have to stay that way until I can raise the calories to return to it. I don't care.

I try to think of her as dead, gone, extinct, but I am defeated by everything I see. The simplest show of affection between two people makes me want to cry out with bitterness at my loveless life, at the way she has taken almost everything away, so cruelly. I find myself constantly replaying our recent lives together, to see if that will deliver me to where I am now. I don't know how I'm going to get through to the other side. I have to kill the person I know myself to be so as to find this other one I am going to become. She left and I so wish she hadn't. How could she do it? Did I really fail her that much? I think it was her intelligence that made her impatient with me. As she became more sure of her powers, she became less tolerant, and all I could offer was a slow-witted, vegetable adoration. Now that she's gone, I find myself living in

England for reasons I no longer know. And sometimes I wonder whether this is what happened to my father Abbas, and whether I should make more effort to locate him. It shouldn't be that difficult. Then what would I say to him? *How has it been for you after all this time, Dad? Was it worth it?*

Water is a gift to the dead. The soul of the dead is parched with thirst for life and craves to drink the water of memory, but can only drink the water of oblivion. This is an Orphic conceit. Yet what matters is not being dead. This is another place where plumbing comes into things.

I want to stop now, but there are still one or two other small matters to relate. This is not a fairy story, or a confession, or a tract of redemption, resolution or sublimation, and I am happy to concede that what I think I understand is overcome with dispute as I soon as I put it into words. Words are like that. Pregnant, sly, slippery, undiminishing in their rereadings as they make their ritual voyage into memory.

I meditate on my father Abbas. I like saying his name to myself. I meditate on the callousness, or the panic, or the stupidity that could have made him act with such cruelty. Is he perhaps living two streets away from me? Have I passed him by in the street, in the supermarket? I imagine him, in his sixties, sitting alone with his silences.

Amelia left six weeks after Emma. I don't know what else I expected. I suppose it was predictable. At first she was as devastated as I was, and we sat weeping together evening after evening like lost souls. We stayed up until all hours, drinking and playing music, and talking tougher and tougher as the booze worked on us. Then she got a grip on her life, somehow. I think it was her friends who helped her do so. And she had things to do, people to see. Then after those first few weeks she watched me as I sat by the bottle every evening (I'm still sitting beside it) weeping at my loss and my buggered heart and my shattered life, and she could not disguise her exasperation and her derision. In the end she told me how contemptible I was, how much I disgusted her, and that she was going to move in with a friend who had a flat in Camberwell. It was the old Amelia, not the excited daughter who had wanted to be taken to the dark corners of the world because she belonged there through her father, not that romantic interlude in her life, but the hard, metropolitan creature who could take everything in her stride, and who despised my blunderings through life with genuine hatred. She rings me now and then, and one day she will come and see me, she says. It will be nice to see her.

Only one more thing. I did not want another twenty-year silence, so I wrote to my mother after Emma left. I wrote abjectly, expecting triumphant lectures, but instead I received a heart-broken reply from Akbar, dictated by my mother but with his commentary on her anguish and (as he put it) that of *your whole family* at the devastation that had befallen me. It was not what I thought any of them would say, after all the disapproval, though I don't imagine that the Wahhabi grandee allied himself with this general goodwill. He had the world to think about. *Come home,* Akbar said, as he closed his letter. But it wasn't home any more, and I had no way of retrieving that seductive idea except through more lies. Boom boom.

So now I sit here, with the phone in my lap, thinking I shall call Ira and ask her if she would like to see a movie. But I am so afraid of disturbing this fragile silence.